HOMICIDE: Life on the Street

"Despite all the attention given to *NYPD Blue*, *Homicide* is the much better show. It is, in fact, the best dramatic series on television. [Andre] Braugher is the best actor on TV, period."
—*New York Daily News*

"A cop show where the words fly as fast as the bullets . . . Jagged, jump-cut and pulsing with energy . . . The writing is as sharp as a switchblade."
—*Wall Street Journal*

"One of TV's best dramas . . . gritty, slice-of-life TV, a street-smart cop show that seems to be less fiction than cruel reality."
—*San Diego Union-Tribune*

"*Homicide* has a distinct, sharp tang and cool touch all its own. In its stutter-cut editing, its rich characters and subplots that unlike *NYPD Blue* are spread all around the precinct, and especially in its digressions on life and death and assorted idiosyncratic esoterica, this show is one of a kind in a crowded field."
—*USA Today*

"The reason God made a 10 P.M. on Fridays."
—*Atlanta Journal*

And don't miss . . .
HOMICIDE: THE NOVEL

Pembleton and Munch are uneasy partners assigned to the murder of two Gypsies. In a clash of cultures, stereotypes—and detective egos—they work the city's backstreets to bring the killer to justice . . .

HoMiCiDe:

VIOLENT DELIGHTS

JEROME PREISLER

BOULEVARD BOOKS, NEW YORK

HOMICIDE: VIOLENT DELIGHTS

A Boulevard Book / published by arrangement with
National Broadcasting Company, Inc.

PRINTING HISTORY
Boulevard edition / November 1997

The Putnam Berkley World Wide Web site address is
http://www.berkley.com

ISBN: 1-57297-340-4

BOULEVARD
Boulevard Books are published by The Berkley Publishing Group,
a member of Penguin Putnam Inc.,
200 Madison Avenue, New York, New York 10016.
BOULEVARD and its logo are trademarks
belonging to Berkley Publishing Corporation.

PRINTED IN THE UNITED STATES OF AMERICA

10 9 8 7 6 5 4 3 2 1

For Suzanne

HOMICIDE:
VIOLENT DELIGHTS

ONE

"AND WHY THE hell *shouldn't* I like holidays?"

Call it a vocal difference of opinion, call it a heated debate, call it an out-and-out argument, Tim Bayliss, Baltimore City Homicide, knew he was about to have one with his fellow detective John Munch, and didn't relish his prospects in the least. He saw his chances of winning as slim and could only wonder how he'd been dumb enough to snap at Munch's bait.

"You want all the reasons, or just my top ten list?" Munch said.

Bayliss sighed resignedly and looked out his window at the beckoning spring morning. Glorious sunshine, blameless blue sky—it was as if the promise of the long Memorial Day weekend had given the city a rare and delightful shimmer. Bayliss imagined that glow radiating into the air from the men and women leaving the downtown office towers during the early rush hour, all of them beaming like lightbulbs with the wattage of happiness as they rushed off toward wide-flung vacation spots.

"Maybe we should just forget the whole thing," he said, turning back to Munch. The squad room's drab green walls and steel-gray fixtures contrasted sharply with the scintillating brightness outside, making Bayliss wonder if he shouldn't maybe put a vase of flowers on his desk, add a nice, seasonable touch to his work environment.

Sunflowers would be nice, he thought. A dozen sunflowers. Each with a bonnet of yellow petals, and on the stem two leaves that looked like little waving arms.

"Never start what you can't finish, Timmy-boy," Munch said. Tall and rail-thin, with grayish hair and a narrow face that bore a perpetually dry expression, Munch sported a navy blue suit, a fastidiously pressed white shirt, a Windsor-knotted silk tie, and wire glasses that gave him the aura of a CPA or a lawyer rather than the seasoned cop that he was.

"All I did," Bayliss said, "was ask if you were going to Megan's barbecue tomorrow."

"And I said I don't celebrate holidays."

"And I didn't say *anything* after that."

"You raised your eyebrows, which is as good as making a negative comment, leaving me no choice but to explain the *reason* I don't do holidays," Munch said. "Maybe then you'll think twice about your own attitude."

"Hey, hold it right there!" Bayliss held up his hand like a school crossing guard. "I happen to feel my attitude's *normal—*"

"You better listen for your own good," Munch said.

Bayliss gave him a look of acquiescence, figuring the only way to keep Munch from having his say was to climb the stairs to the rooftop and jump off. And even then he'd need to cover his ears, since Munch probably wouldn't stop yammering until after he'd hit the pavement.

"How long's this gonna take?" he asked.

"As long as it takes me to say *E. coli*," Munch said.

"Huh?"

"*E. coli*," Munch repeated.

"I heard you the first time," Bayliss said. "I just don't understand how that has anything to do with what we're talking about."

Munch had the pained look of a teacher who'd encountered a grievously slow student.

"You have any idea how many people become critically ill from *E. coli* poisoning on Memorial Day?" he asked.

"I think you mean *Ebola*."

Munch glanced at Detective Mike Kellerman, who'd put in his two cents from the coffee room entrance, where he stood holding a steaming paper cup and a Clark bar.

"And I think you should stay out of this," Munch said testily.

He wasn't exactly wild about Kellerman, not because he found his personality disagreeable, nor because Kellerman had done anything to offend him, but because he was the most recent addition to the squad, and by Munch's own rules of initiation you had to give the new kid on the block a hard time. In sharp contrast to this was how he felt about his former partner Stanley Bolander, who'd gotten kicked off the squad because he couldn't keep his pants on at a police function where there had been a contingent of female officers, many of whom were justifiably outraged when he'd gone sliding down a hotel bannister in his boxer shorts. Whatever his problems relating to the opposite sex—aggravated that day by one too many vodka-and-tonics—Bolander had proven himself to be an honest, hardworking, stand-up partner many times over, and would always be aces in Munch's book. For him it was just putting things in their right perspective. When you were out on the street working a case, you had to trust your partner with your life, and how could you do that before you were sure what type of guy he was?

Right now Kellerman looked like a beekeeper who'd gotten used to the occasional sting.

"I was just saying . . . about what causes the food poisoning, that is—"

"*Ebola,* for your information, is an African virus that eats your flesh and turns your brain and vital organs into

3

jelly," Munch said. "Not to mention making your tongue peel away in layers, which in some cases might not be such a bad thing."

"You sure you aren't thinking of mad cow disease?" Bayliss said, trying to deflect some of the flack from Kellerman.

Munch's patience was stretching thin.

"Mad cow disease is the brain virus that makes you go into convulsive spasms and then die," Munch said. "Besides, *Ebola*'s carried by *monkeys*," he said.

"So?" Bayliss said.

"So why would they name something mad *cow* unless it *infects* cows?"

"Maybe it infects cows *and* monkeys."

"Listen," Munch said, "my point is that thousands, maybe *tens* of thousands, of people will wind up in hospitals this weekend from eating contaminated meat."

"Contaminated with what?"

"Bayliss, are you listening or am I talking to the *walls* here?"

"I just asked—"

"Contaminated with *E. coli*, salmonella, botulism, *and*, now that Kellerman brought it up, mad cow disease," Munch said. "You see what I'm saying? Every hamburger that gets slapped on a grill is a ticking bomb. And being that Memorial Day is the kickoff to the barbecue season, people all over America will be *eating bombs*."

"Sounds like a terrorist conspiracy," Kellerman said, seemingly amused. A blond, blue-eyed, handsome guy of about thirty, he was wearing black Levi's and a thin cotton shirt that accented every little flex and ripple of his well-developed muscles. Even his *breathing* brought about wavelets of sympathy in the fabric.

Munch frowned. Now that he thought about it, one thing he *did* find irritating about Kellerman—besides the fact that he was always hogging the weight bench in the downstairs gym—was that he didn't know how to act deferential to senior members of the squad.

"Laugh now, convulse tomorrow," Munch said. "When they carry you from Russert's backyard on a stretcher, remember that I warned you. *If* you're conscious."

Kellerman opened his mouth as if to respond, but then apparently changed his mind, and sipped his coffee, letting Munch's comments ride.

"Hey, Munchkin, forget the diseases, I want to hear when you're gonna quit slammin' my partner."

Munch rubbed a hand across his forehead. He didn't see why the whole world was getting involved in what had started as a one-to-one conversation—or argument, or debate, call it what you will—especially since everybody seemed to be lining up against *him*.

The guy who'd sprung to Kellerman's defense was Detective Meldrick Lewis. He had just entered from the Aquarium, which was what the detectives in the squad called the narrow waiting area where suspects about to be interrogated or booked for murder often elbowed up against witnesses to their crimes and the grieving families of their victims—an uncomfortable arrangement nobody hated more than the cops, who simply didn't have anyplace else to put them all.

A burly, light-skinned black man of thirty-two, Lewis knew the evils in his town better than most, namely because he'd spent his youth clawing his way up from the ghetto streets that bred them. Today he was wearing an electric-blue blazer over a pale pink shirt, a Garcia tie with a surrealistic pattern that seemed to depict self-devouring mutant amphibians, and rusty blue jeans. His quirky sartorial preferences were a constant source of bemusement at the station house, as was his similarly unconventional taste in music, which leaned toward rock bands whose atonal sonic experiments went light-years beyond the fringes of alternative.

"*Slamming* your partner?" Munch said. "I'm trying to explain something that might save his life. Yours too, if you plan on going to the barbecue"

"Oh yeah?" Lewis said. "An' what exactly is that? You

sayin' we all gonna be wiped out by beef patties this weekend?"

"Well, if they aren't cooked through . . ."

"Aw c'mon, we've served *hundreds* of burgers at the Waterfront," Bayliss said, referring to the landmark tavern owned by Munch, Lewis, and—occasionally to his regret—himself. "Maybe *thousands*. And not a single customer's croaked on us. Or even had stomach cramps."

"That," Munch said, "is because we've got conscientious help in the kitchen. People who know the internal temperature of cooking meat's gotta reach one-sixty degrees, one eighty if it's poultry—"

"You zoned or somethin', man?" Lewis said, swapping glances with Bayliss. "When it ain't me flippin' burgers back there, it's my *grandmother*."

"Leaving Grandma aside a second," Munch said, "in that situation you aren't the person *eating* the food, which means you're acting in a professional capacity, which gives you some remove. It's a different story when you're cooking for yourself on the backyard grill. Hungry people get impatient."

"*I'm* getting impatient to drop this subject," Bayliss said.

Kellerman laughed and turned toward his desk.

"Fine." Munch threw up his arms in frustration. "You guys want to die of some dreaded mega-bug, go ahead. My conscience is clear."

"Look, I just meant we got sidetracked from our original conversation," Bayliss said, wondering if he'd hurt Munch's feelings.

"That's because you started arguing with me—"

"We were having a difference of opinion," Bayliss corrected. "The point is, how this started out, you were telling me why you hate *all* holidays."

"And . . ."

"And what's your problem with Christmas? Or New Year's? People don't barbecue on *those* days."

"No, they don't." Munch exhaled wearily. "But they

do drink and drive. You ever see the stats on Yuletide highway fatalities?"

"All right, forget them," Bayliss said. "What about Thanksgiving?"

"Yeah," Lewis said. "*Everybody* likes Thanksgiving."

"Except the people that get heart attacks at the dinner table from family stress," Munch said contentiously. "Not to mention from overeating. If you don't believe me, ask my brother Fred the mortician. His place always gets busy on Turkey Day."

Bayliss regarded him for a long moment.

"Okay, super," he said finally. "I give up."

"An' I gotta go talk to the loot," Lewis said.

"And I only have one question."

This from Frank Pembleton, the unit's resident crusading supercop, who had until now been minding his business over at his desk. Although Pembleton was a hard guy to get close to—even Bayliss, who was both his partner and best friend, would concede that—he and Munch had developed a pretty good rapport when they'd teamed up to work the Bash murders last November. Still, that didn't stop them from occasionally getting on each other's nerves.

"Shoot," Munch said.

"Could your opinion of Memorial Day have anything to do with the fact that you're stuck on *duty* all weekend?"

Munch looked at him.

"Huh?" he said, gulping as if he'd swallowed an egg. "What do you mean?"

"I mean," Pembleton said, "that I saw your name on the roster for Monday. Which, since the rest of us will be off, makes me wonder if that's why you're suddenly anti-holiday."

"There's no connection," Munch said. "Absolutely none."

"Sure there ain't," Lewis told Bayliss in a stage whisper. "Trust m'man Frank to get *his* number."

They both chuckled.

7

"Either of you guys want to say what's so funny?" Munch said.

That cracked them up again. Bayliss covered his mouth with his hand, snorting laughter. A moment later Lewis slapped him on the back and turned toward Lieutenant Giardello's office, wiping tears of mirth from his eyes.

"Nice to know I'm so hilarious," he grumbled under his breath. Then he shook his head moodily. So he *was* the only member of the shift working Monday. Why should that cloud his objectivity? The truth was that he hadn't even gotten to tell Bayliss his all-time number one reason for dreading holidays both religious and secular. And he'd really needed to hear it. Tim was a glass-half-full sort of guy, positive to the end. It wasn't as if he didn't recognize that everyone had a dark side, but he had too much faith in the better part of human nature. Munch figured that was why life very often disappointed him. Why he got hurt so often.

The problem with holidays was that they gave people an excuse to throw out the rules and forget about consequences. And once their inhibitions deserted them, well, what were they but crazies? Crazies loose on the streets, running around everywhere, getting into trouble. Even cops were susceptible . . . maybe especially susceptible because their jobs wound them up so tight. Every Saint Patty's Day there were news reports about brothers in blue beating the crap out of each other, or getting shot in drunken brawls, whoop-dee-doo.

Holidays, Munch reflected, were when usually normal folks lost control. When they did stupid things. And when the ones who were already nuts got more dangerous and unpredictable. All in all it made the world a more complicated place to live in, especially if you were the person cleaning up the mess . . . which Munch sometimes viewed as his job in a nutshell.

Of course, maybe he'd be surprised this time around. Maybe the first big warm-weather weekend of the year would pass without incident. Nobody would eat any

8

spoiled food, or get into a head-on, or fuck up too badly. The lunatics would stay in their cages. Maybe it would be that way this year.

Maybe. And if that were the case he'd be glad and relieved. In the meantime, though, he would prepare for the worst. *Somebody* had to mind the keys to the asylum, and the schedule on the bulletin board said he was the one.

Memorial Day weekend—ready, set, go.

Russert's barbecue and Bayliss's optimism aside, Munch couldn't understand how the others could be so unconcerned. Cheerful, in fact.

Just thinking about it gave him the jitters.

TWO

DRIVING WEST OUT of Baltimore on I-70, you will reach the city of Frederick in slightly over an hour, and continuing past its outskirts, find yourself amid sweeping grain fields, livestock pastures, horse farms roamed by graceful Pimlico-bound thoroughbreds, and, here and there, tiny old towns whose homes gather respectfully around the jutting white spires of eighteenth-century churches. Turn left on State Route 340 toward the Potomac, hang a quick right onto a country lane that curves past a winery and some local produce stands, and after about three miles you come to an access road leading up a low, pine-shagged hill.

It is on the crest of this hill that the eight fieldstone structures of the Central Maryland Psychiatric Center for the Criminally Insane crouch behind a twenty-foot-high stone wall that is topped with coils of razor wire, and passable only through a heavy iron gate guarded round-the-clock by teams of armed sentries. Arranged in a U with the main building in the center, the eight barracks-style maximum security wards surround a wide, bucolic campus on which tree-shaded walking paths wind between duck ponds, flower gardens, and grassy exercise courts.

However peaceful things look on the exterior, it tends to be a different story *inside* the hospital, which confines over five hundred violent offenders—rapists, murderers, and the like—who have been judged incompetent to stand trial for felony raps, or found not guilty of their crimes by reason of insanity, or shuffled out of state prisons after being deemed too unstable to mix with the general inmate population. "Mad and bad" is the motto Central Maryland's dangerous residents voice with a pride usually reserved for members of a military outfit or college fraternity . . . and in their case the shoe definitely fits.

At six P.M. on Saturday, May 27, a staff guard named Eddie Dubick stood by a vending machine in D-ward, a building occupied by forty-five longtime inmates who were generally considered to be hopeless incurables, yet functioned well enough within the controlled institutional environment to gain certain privileges not afforded to their fellows. Among these was nearly unrestricted access to a common room where they could watch the latest videotaped movie releases and listen to popular and classical music CDs, or occupy themselves with a variety of magazines, books, and board games. Through a letter writing campaign, one inmate had convinced some well-placed benefactor at the Baltimore Symphony to sponsor a fine arts program offering piano, violin, and flute lessons. The cafeteria regularly served up porterhouse steaks and shrimp scampi, with turkey dinners on Thanksgiving, and roast ham for Christmas. Twice daily, patients who wanted to stay in shape were escorted to the indoor athletic room in the main building, where they could take advantage of a running track, Nautilus room, aerobic classes, and a regulation Olympic swimming pool.

As far as Eddie Dubick was concerned, all the inmates lacked were Turkish steam baths and a chesty female masseuse, but he figured some bleeding heart politician would eventually see to it that they got them too. In his three years at the hospital, not a day had gone by when he didn't resentfully wonder if the lunatics had it better than he did, what with everything they were given to help soften up their stays. Nobody had ever handed him a free gym or video club membership, or worried about his wife having to stretch her food budget by cutting coupons out of the Sunday paper. The kitchen at the hospital never skimped, though. There was even a bakery that served up fresh dessert pastries.

Now Dubick hunted some change out of his pocket and began feeding it into the snack machine. Four patients presently occupied the common room: Mutter Campbell, Ernesto Gonzalez, old Johnny McCulloch, and Quasim the Preacher. As usual Campbell was staring blankly into a magazine, looking as if nothing could disturb his private little world, although it must have been another story the day he'd raped a fourteen-year-old girl and then killed the girl and her mother by setting them both on fire—this was around 1991 or '92. He didn't waste a minute getting back to his old tricks after being paroled, and had wound up in some kind of standoff with cops when they wanted to question him about another rape. Threatened to set a whole block of row houses on fire before they talked him into surrendering.

Mutter had been locked away in Central Maryland ever since and, like most patients, was a perfect kitten as long as he took his meds. In the past few months they'd been increasing his dosages and he'd gotten very quiet, but before that he' had made a lot of small talk with Dubick. At first it had been the usual gab about sports, the weather, news events, that sort of thing. Then he'd told Dubick about the used car business he'd run on the outside. Guy had a ton of money put away—go figure. With some of these wackos, you could see them being able to behave normally on the outside, at least for a while. It was like they kept the craziness on tap for special occasions. But watching Mutter at the table with

13

his *People* magazine—looking at the pages between the covers, yet not looking at them—Dubick found it hard to imagine he could have ever passed himself off as sane, although his wife sure must have been fooled the day she'd married him. Dubick had seen pictures of her and she was a pretty one.

Dubick studied the selections behind the clear plastic panel of the snack machine, then pulled the lever for a Baby Ruth and waited as the machine jerked and hummed and dropped the candy bar into the receptacle. With any luck Quasim wouldn't raise one of his fusses tonight. He was the only D-warder that ever had serious outbursts these days—well, unless you counted McCulloch's nearly constant, compulsive licking—but he seemed pretty calm over there by the television. Of course you had to be extra careful with him at dawn, noon, late afternoon, sunset, and especially at bedtime . . . whenever he said his Moslem call to prayer. Last Tuesday he'd started out the way he usually did, chanting something like "I bear witness that there is no God but Allah," repeating it about fifty times—and then he'd exploded without warning. The familiar chant had transformed into "Where are all the *razors*?" and he had beat his head against the wall until it was bloody, then torn off all his clothing and messed himself and gone rolling around naked in his own filth.

Dubick peeled the wrapper off his candy bar and took a bite. He didn't envy the poor attendants who'd had to mop up after Quasim. In fact, he wouldn't trade headaches with those guys for any amount of money in the world. His job was bad enough. Life might have been different if only he hadn't been so careless a few years ago, hadn't blown it with the state police . . . but thinking about that made him depressed. What was done was done.

Well, come tomorrow there'd be some money in his bank account, and he and Sheila would be getting away for a while. Two weeks in the Cayman Islands, a room in a first-rate hotel—she'd been floored when he brought

14

home the reservations. And of course she had fretted about the cost of their trip. But he explained that he'd been quietly stashing away part of his paycheck so that he could take her on a surprise vacation, and that seemed to reassure her . . .

"Hey, Eddie, how about you share that chocolate?"

Dubick glanced over at McCulloch, who sat across from Gonzalez at one of the long rec room tables. There was a chessboard between them, but McCulloch's attention was focused on Dubick. The old coot never stopped trying to get his hands on freebies.

"Buy your own," Dubick said. "I ain't the one has my room and board paid by the government. And gets a Social Security check every month."

McCulloch looked pained. He brought his hands up to his mouth and licked all ten fingertips, running his tongue across them from right to left, thumb to thumb. Then he dragged them across his face, covering his cheeks with shiny skids of wetness. With his unkempt white hair and rough features he resembled a grizzled alley cat, one with spit whiskers.

"Now, look what you done," Gonzalez said to Dubick. "Gone and made Mac nervous."

"You're so concerned about your pal, why don't *you* buy him a candy bar?" Dubick said.

"Ain't nobody in this room a workin' man 'cept you," Gonzales said. "Lemme outta here so I can get a job, I pay for anythin' you want."

Dubick smiled a little. "You guys are just *so* god-damned generous."

Having sat quietly until now, the Preacher shifted in his chair by the television.

"Tell the man to eat tha' shit hisself, Ernesto," he chimed in. "Ain't nothin' but poison anyway."

"Poison?" Gonzalez asked.

"Fo' people of *color*," the Preacher said. "Whitey make them candy bars, soak 'em all fulla radiation in the laboratory, then be sellin' 'em to the black man. Wanna kill the black man. Burn the black man's sperm, stop him from makin' babies, wipe him *out*."

Dubick bit off another piece of his candy bar and chewed. The Preacher glared at him with undisguised hostility. At the table Mac was still smearing saliva all over his face.

"That right?" Dubick said. He'd heard Quasim's song a hundred times if he'd heard it once, and was wondering why he bothered getting into conversations with these warped bastards. In Quasim's case, he was talking to a guy who'd raped and beaten ten, twelve elderly women, several of whom had been in wheelchairs. Sooner or later he'd go crazy himself if he kept it up.

"You *know* it be," the Preacher said.

"This true about all chocolate bars or just Baby Ruths?" Dubick said, unable to resist provoking him.

"Baby Ruth, Kit-Kat, Nestles, fuckin' *M&M*'s," the Preacher said. "Don' make no difference."

"And how come all this radiation doesn't fry the *white* man's balls?"

"Yoah scientists the ones cookin' up the shit, go ahead 'n' ask *them*," the Preacher said. "An while you at it, ask 'em 'bout how they made AIDS to kill the black man."

"In case you ain't heard," Dubick said, "it happens AIDS affects white people *too*, so how you going to explain *that*?"

"Ain't hard." The Preacher looked as if he'd just descended from the Temple Mount with an answer from Allah himself. "They figure it be *worth* losin' a few hunnred thousand a' they own—"

"I know, I know," Dubick said. "To kill the black man."

"Got *that* straight," the Preacher said.

Dubick decided he'd had about enough of Quasim. He finished eating his candy bar, tossed the crumpled wrapper in the trash, and glanced impatiently at his watch. A quarter after six. Surprising he wasn't more nervous . . . but then, he was looking past tonight.

Looking ahead. Another day or so and he'd be out of this toilet bowl, cruising the Atlantic, smelling fresh sea air instead of sweat, medicine, craziness, and the odor of piss and shit barely disguised by disinfectant.

Whistling tunelessly, Dubick crossed his arms and paced toward the door to the outer corridor. Through the wire-reinforced glass panel in the door he saw Frank Stella walking from the cafeteria at the far end of the hall. He was carrying a paper coffee cup in violation of the rules, which barred inmates from taking any food from the area where it was served. In fact, he was breaking the rules just by being in the hall without supervision, but Dubick's superiors would hardly care about that. This was a comparatively easy ward, and sometimes regulations had to be overlooked to keep the loonies from getting wound too tight.

Dubick made eye contact with Stella through the pane of glass and the inmate acknowledged him with a grin. He bit his lip edgily. If any of the ward's residents belonged in jail rather than an institution, Stella was the man. A habitual offender, he'd been a soldier in the LoCicero family for twenty years prior to landing in Central Maryland, and during that earlier period had racked up half a dozen hits for his gangland bosses— the last three committed before a restaurant full of witnesses when he'd walked up behind his victims' table with a loaded piece and shot each one through the back of the head, *boom boom boom*, blowing their brains right into their pasta dishes. After his conviction on the triple murder indictment Stella's defense lawyer, a mob-connected slick named Harry Reamis, had gotten him examined by a team of prison shrinks, who'd decided he belonged in the tender care of mental health workers rather than death row turnkeys.

Dubick would never understand how they had made that evaluation, never in a million years, unless maybe Reamis had slipped them a little cash incentive under the table. Because when *he* looked into Stella's cold blue eyes he saw perfect sanity. That, and the predatory viciousness of a shark.

He took a step back from the door as Stella pushed through.

"Evenin', Dube," Stella said. A tall, bony man with bristle-short blond hair, his hollow eyes, sunken cheeks, and pale complexion gave him an almost cadaverous appearance. This up-from-the-grave look was exaggerated by the hospital denims that were always too loose for his spindly frame, hanging off him in baggy folds regardless of their size.

Dubick pointed to the steaming cup in his hand. "What's with the coffee?"

"Huh?" Stella looked down at the cup as if he'd been unaware he was holding it before that moment. "Oh, *that*."

"Walking around with it could get you in trouble," Dubick said.

"Ain't looking for none," Stella said. "Just felt like I needed a lift tonight. To keep me going strong, you know."

Dubick stared at him.

Stella stared back. The smile spreading across his colorless face looked like a crack in a sheet of ice.

"You seem kinda upset, Dube-cat," he said. "Didn't think you'd mind me bringing a hot drink in here."

"I'm not the only guard in D-ward," Dubick said, his eyes still locked on Stella's. "And the rest aren't as nice as me. One of them sees you with that coffee, he'll put you in early lockup tonight. Plus maybe suspend privileges for everybody in the ward."

"All that hassle over a cup of joe, huh?"

Dubick nodded.

"Goddamn it, Stella, why you gonna be a pain in the man's ass?" McCulloch said, turning in his chair. "I don't want no screws coming around to bust up my game."

"Butt out," Stella said without looking over at him. "What goes on between me and my pal Dube has nothing to do with you."

"Got *everything* to do with me if I have to leave off my game," McCulloch said.

Stella closed his eyes and remained very still for about thirty seconds. Then he opened them and turned his head slowly toward McCulloch.

"Push me any further, you decrepit old shit, and I'll shove those chess pieces down your throat till you choke," he said.

"Okay, that's enough," Dubick said. "If you guys don't settle down I'm closing the room and—"

"*And?*" Stella watched him with cold eyes. "And *what?* You gonna teach us to be good boys, Dube-cat? Or write us all up in your shift report and let the director take care of it?"

"You better think twice before you open your mouth again," Dubick said sharply.

"I done plenty of thinking already," Stella said, and smiled. "Decided that from now on I'm gonna say whatever the fuck I want."

"Then we got problems."

Stella kept smiling his rigid smile. His eyes narrowed to slits, giving him a sly, surreptitious look.

"Problems," he echoed.

Dubick nodded.

"Wouldn't want that, now would we?" Stella said, glancing around at his fellow inmates.

Nobody answered. Nobody moved. Tension throbbed like a heartbeat in the silent room.

Stella turned back to Dubick.

Still grinning.

"Well." He dropped his coffee into the trash and eased a hand behind his back. Dubick could see that the tail of his oversized shirt was hanging out. "Well, well, well."

"What do you think you're doing?" Dubick said, and lowered his own hand until it was hovering above the metal baton on his right hip.

Stella was reaching under his shirttail.

"I'm warning you—"

Dubick's sentence was interrupted as Stella suddenly whipped a gun from beneath the shirt, then brought it up in front of him with both hands.

"Forgive me, Dube," Stella said, aiming the gun barrel at his head. "But I don't want to hear any more of your bullshit."

His mouth gaping wide, his hand frozen above the cylindrical handle of his baton, Dubick stared at the gun. It was a big bore .357 Magnum, a small cannon—one shot from that thing could knock a grizzly bear off its feet.

"Jesus Christ," Dubick said. "You are making a hell of a dumb mistake."

"Shut up and put your hands over your head," Stella said. "Now."

Dubick slowly raised his arms. Like the rest of Central Maryland's guards, he was prohibited from carrying a firearm by administrative order, the concern being that an inmate would seize it during an escape attempt. Now, as Stella reached around his side and slipped the baton from its leather belt holster, Dubick wondered if the suits upstairs had ever considered what would happen to a basically weaponless guard confronted by a maniac who was *already* holding a gun.

Keeping the Magnum trained on Dubick, Stella thumbed back its hammer and glanced quickly over his shoulder at Mutter Campbell.

"I'm getting the hell out of here, Mutter," he said. "You want to join me?"

Campbell looked up from his magazine. Set deep under a heavy ridge of forehead, his piggish little eyes were glazed from his nightly med cocktail.

"Yeah," he said, lifting his ponderous three hundred-pound bulk off his chair. "I'm coming."

Stella grunted and tossed Dubick's baton to him. He caught it with one mittlike hand.

"Hold on a minute, what about my *chess* game?" McCulloch said agitatedly. "You two keep this up, you're gonna blow our privileges!"

Stella looked over his shoulder at him, his hard eyes completely divorced from his smile. He was still leveling the Magnum on Dubick with both hands.

"That so," he said.

"It's the truth, you idiot!" McCulloch said. He compulsively ran his tongue around his mouth, ringing it with moisture. "The chess is all I *got!*"

"Then here's something else," Stella said, abruptly pivoting on his heel, swinging the gun toward McCulloch, and pulling the trigger.

There was a loud blast and a spout of flame from the weapon's muzzle. McCulloch had just enough time to realize what was happening before he was knocked off his seat by the impact of the high-caliber slug, the roof of his head disintegrating in a spattery crimson mist. Stella squeezed off a second shot even before McCulloch hit the floor, the bullet catching him in the left side of the face and exiting out the right, blowing away a huge chunk of his jaw. Several of his teeth ticked off the wall like pebbles striking a windshield. Landing in a twisted heap near the overturned chair, his nearly headless body went into a grotesque series of spasms, legs kicking jerkily on the tiles, arms thrashing, fingers twitching and scratching at the air.

Stella swept his gaze over the stunned faces of the other inmates and turned the gun back onto Dubick, who registered his expression with horror and disbelief.

He was still smiling, but the smile had changed a little, loosened up at the corners, as though the sick amusement were leaching out of it. His gaze had also lost some of its glittering sharpness. In fact, Dubick thought uneasily, he almost looked bored. Like somebody who'd been on a roller coaster often enough to be familiar with every turn, bump, and plunge . . . often enough to start looking for new ways to get his adrenaline flowing.

"Let's go," he said, gesturing toward the door with his chin. "You first."

Dubick pushed through the door into the narrow outer corridor, Stella sticking close behind with the gun rammed into his spine, Mutter Campbell trailing both of them, his immense, elongated shadow gliding across the walls and ceiling. About fifteen yards ahead of them the corridor angled to the left, then led straight down to the main entrance. They could hear hospital personnel rushing from their stations near the entrance in response to the gunshots, the frantic rattle of their heels against the floor sounding like scattered snare drumrolls punctuated by the pounding bass-pedal thuds of Campbell's heavier footsteps.

They were within a few feet of the turn when two men in guard uniforms came rushing around the corner of the hallway. The guards caught sight of the advancing figures and stopped short in front of them, their faces excited and confused, batons gripped in their white-knuckled fists.

"Drop the sticks and get down on your damn bellies!" Stella shouted.

He brought his gun up from Dubick's back and jammed its snout into his right ear, forcing his head sideways.

The two men exchanged frightened glances but remained standing.

Stella cocked the Magnum.

"Do it now or he's dead!"

The guards hesitated another moment, looking at Dubick, who stood before them with his hands up high above his head. Then they nodded to indicate they were yielding.

They let their batons clatter to the floor, folded to their knees, then stretched full-length on the floor, their faces pressing against the scuffed linoleum.

Stella jostled Dubick forward, keeping the gun to his head, pausing briefly while Campbell snatched up the relinquished batons.

They left behind the two prostrate guards, rounded the corner, and hurried down the hall, pausing again in the waiting area just inside the building's entrance.

The desk security man in the reception booth was chattering into his hand radio as they appeared, his face tight with panic behind the booth's bulletproof glass partition. Dubick knew that by now he'd have heard about the break from the hall guards and was probably notifying the sentries at the gate. He also knew that, unlike the ward guards, both the desk man and sentries were armed.

"Put your hands up where I can see 'em!" Stella shouted at the desk man.

The guy yawped at him, the whites of his eyes enormous.

Stella screwed the nose of his gun into Dubick's ear. "*Do it now!*"

The desk man nodded shakily and complied.

Stella pushed Dubick through the double doors of the ward's main entrance. Outside a dark sprawl of lawn sloped off toward the perimeter fence. On one side of the building was the parking area reserved for D-ward's employees and infrequent visitors.

Searchlights along the fence pinned Dubick and Stella the moment they entered the courtyard, the high-intensity beams sweeping over them from three directions and turning night into noonday.

"Go on toward your car, Dube-cat," Stella said. "I'll be right with you."

Dubick nodded and started forward, upraised hands trembling, sweat staining the underarms of his uniform shirt.

"Lay down your weapon and step back against the wall!" The sentry's electronically amplified voice blared amid spikes of feedback from a speaker atop the guardhouse. "You are in serious breach of hospital ru—"

Stella whooped laughter. "*Your* ass is in breach of *my* rules, boy, and if you don't start obeyin' them, Dubick here's gonna lose whatever brains he's got!" He laughed again. "Now you and your pals are gonna let us head over to the parking lot for Dube-cat's car. Then you're gonna open the front gate and stand there twiddlin' your little peckers till we're long outta here. Got it?"

"There's nowhere for you to go," the voice from the

PA system called out. "Surrender immediately and it'll be easier for y—"

"I asked if you *got it!*" Stella shouted, pressing the gun against the side of Dubick's head. "Answer me yes or no, you dumb bastard!"

Silence.

Trembling, his heart pounding, Dubick squinted into the bright light, at the motionless shapes of the sentries.

"Yes," the voice said flatly after perhaps a minute. "Do nothing to harm your hostage. We're letting you pass."

The escapees progressed toward the parking lot with Dubick still at gunpoint, their dark outlines striped by the roving, grazing, crisscrossing lights from the guard stations. There were less than a dozen cars in the lot, all of them belonging to D-ward staffers. Dubick could see his own Ford Taurus in its regular space less than fifty feet ahead of him

"Get out your car keys, Dube-cat, we're all going for a ride," Stella said. The sly, cold-blooded smile was back on his face.

Dubick reached into a trouser pocket for his key chain and seconds later was pulling open the driver's door of the Ford. Drenched in sweat, he slid behind the wheel on Stella's barked command and waited for the two inmates to climb into the backseat. Then he heard the rear door slam forcefully shut and felt the Magnum nudge his temple.

"Let's roll," Stella said into his ear.

Dubick glanced into the rearview mirror, his eyes moving from Stella's excitedly grinning face to Campbell's bland, blockish one. After a moment he turned the key in the ignition, backed the car out of its slot, and staring straight ahead, pulled onto the drive curving to the front gate.

Looking on with helpless, wide-eyed frustration, the sentries saw the Ford move past them through the gate, saw it turn onto the road leading down to the interstate, saw its taillights shrink to tiny red pinpoints and then vanish into distance and darkness.

It was nearly five minutes before one of them managed to compose himself enough to reach for the phone and call the police.

THREE

"KILLED THE SUCKER five times," Lewis said. "Top that."

"I just did," Kellerman said, holstering his Glock.

"'Case you can't hear me with those things in your ears, I said *five*—"

"Heard you just fine." Kellerman opened his palm to show he'd already popped out his earplugs. "But *my* man took six to the heart."

"Bull*shit*, six."

"You don't believe it, see for yourself."

Kellerman pressed a button and their shooting range targets glided closer on overhead tracks. When they were within reach, he unclipped them and passed his target over to Lewis.

"Try not to weep," he said.

Lewis took his time examining the practice figure, which was shaped like the upper torso of an average-size male. What the hell, he had eyes, and maybe it was only postponing the inevitable, but he didn't like the idea of making Kellerman's self-satisfied grin any bigger than it already was.

"Well?" Kellerman said.

He waited, sniffling a little, his sinuses irritated from the smell of burned gunpowder. Beside him a shooter slammed a full load out of his automatic pistol with rhythmical pumps of the trigger, seventeen rounds in rapid succession; he either desperately needed to unwind or was getting ready for a minor war. One thing was certain, that was a pre–Crime Bill magazine in his piece, the 1994 legislation having outlawed the manufacture of clips with more than a ten-shot capacity, though it was still legal to use one providing it had come off the line before the bill's enactment. Kellerman had never quite understood the outcry from gun lobbyists over the restrictions, unless maybe walking around with a lethal firearm was all fun and games to those guys, in which case Kellerman thought they should be forced to visit a trauma center or the city morgue or the scene of a drive-by shooting before they could testify in front of Congress, take a firsthand look at the damage a *single* bullet could do to an infant whose stroller had been wheeled down the wrong street at the wrong time.

But then, Kellerman thought, what the hell did *he* know about politics.

"Well?" he repeated, growing impatient with Lewis.

"I don't know." Lewis ran his fingertips over a huge gouge in the target's chest. "Can't tell if this here was made by one or two rounds . . ."

"You *gotta* be kidding, anybody can see those are overlapping hits—"

"All right, quit moanin', you win," Lewis said. "I spring for coffee."

"*And* cheesecake?"

"And cheesecake."

"And that's still only *half* the bet."

Lewis slipped off his protective goggles.

"Some guys want everything," he grumbled.

Ten minutes later they were across the street from the shooting range, in a diner that had both the shape and porthole-style windows of a railroad car, and by no mere coincidence, since that was precisely what it had been in

28

bygone days, before some clever entrepreneur of the late 1960s had gotten the idea to purchase hundreds of trains from the defunct B&O at a steal, yank out their guts, refit them with booths, ovens, griddles, and counters, and sell them off as inexpensive prefab luncheonettes.

"So when you gonna tell me why your wife isn't coming to Meg's barbecue," Kellerman said.

He sliced off a piece of his lemon meringue pie with the edge of his fork and ate it, thinking it was pretty decent, if not nearly as tasty as the homemade cheesecake he'd looked forward to having with his coffee. But the place had been out of blueberry cheesecake and he wasn't wild about strawberry, the only other available choice, especially now that Munch had gotten him uptight about food diseases and the newspapers were running stories about a bug that was carried by strawberries and gave you a terminal case of the runs or something.

Lewis smacked his lips in disgust.

"Hey, *you* made the bet," Kellerman said.

"I know I made the bet, I was *there* when I made the bet, I heard the words comin' out my big, stupid *mouth* when I made the bet—"

"So what's the problem?"

"Who says I got a *problem*?"

"Well, you're making all kinds of noises instead of answering a simple question—"

"That's where you're way off base, man, because what I'm doin' is expressin' how much I like this cake. Which I wish I could eat in peace."

"Enjoy it while you can," Kellerman said, wondering what the damn strawberry virus was called anyway. "Now, getting back to our bet, you were supposed to tell me why you and Barbara weren't going to the barbecue together . . ."

"Look, who says we got to be joined at the hip, hang out with the same people, like the same stuff?"

"It's just that I thought you guys were trying to work things out—"

"Who says we *ain't*?"

Kellerman looked at him. The hardest damn thing about getting to know Meldrick Lewis was getting to know Meldrick Lewis, and Kellerman sometimes wondered why he bothered trying. The guy was sealed tight, a strongbox that had been padlocked, bolted shut, and wrapped in chains for good measure. Of course, he was also his partner, and your partner was family, and Kellerman had been raised in a family in which *everybody* said what was on their minds, both at home around the dinner table and at his father's bottling plant, where he'd worked every day after school, and every summer when school was out, and where there had been no way for him and his dad to escape the daily tedium *except* by talking to each other about anything and everything, over the repetitive clank of machinery and the drone of conveyor belts. After growing up with such a gabby bunch, Kellerman had felt confident of being able to talk to anybody. Until he met Meldrake, that was. He was a unique case—the most contained, secretive person Kellerman had ever met.

Take tonight, for example. The homicide they were working was a cut-and-dried affair in which the perp was an old woman named Violet Holmes, who'd gone after some punk kid because he killed her cat with a BB gun, good reason *to* go after him in Kellerman's mind, except Violet had cracked open his skull with a baseball bat, sending him to his premature demise and making Kellerman's sympathies irrelevant. Murder was murder, as Frank Pembleton might say; the only issue not yet determined was whether it was first or second degree— premeditated or a crime of passion—and there was conflicting eyewitness testimony pointing both ways. They had been discussing this at the range without reaching a conclusion, getting bogged down in details, when, hoping to clear his head, Kellerman had tried changing the subject for a few minutes and asked Lewis a personal question, God forbid. At that point he had clammed up, prompting Kellerman to make his little wager, using the lure of coffee and cake to get Lewis to bite at the *second* part of the bet . . . for all the good winning it had done, because here they were at the coffee shop and Lewis *still* wasn't talking.

No doubt about it, he was a rare bird.

"Okay," Kellerman said. "If you're gonna keep insisting there's nothing wrong, I quit."

Lewis peered at him over his coffee cup.

"You happy now?" Kellerman said to break the silence. "I said you won't be getting any more questions about your home life. Not from me, anyway."

Lewis regarded him a moment longer. Then he cocked his head sideways, screwed up his face as if some invisible third party had whispered sound but unpleasant words of advice into his ear, and sighed.

"I didn't tell you nothin' was wrong, Mike," he said finally. "I just ain't sure you'd understand."

"Me?" Kellerman touched his fingers to his chest. "Mister Understanding *himself*?"

Lewis sighed again, slowly lowered his coffee cup into his saucer, and leaned forward, motioning for Kellerman to do the same.

Kellerman slid to the edge of his seat and waited.

"Okay, here it is," Lewis said in a hushed, confidential voice. "You ever give a woman your opinion about the clothes she wears, the way she does her hair, that kinda thing?"

"You mean compliment her?"

Lewis shook his head. "More like offerin' advice. A male perspective on her *look*, you know."

Kellerman rubbed his chin. "I'm not sure what you mean."

"Then let's start over," Lewis said. "Say your ol' lady wears these foxy outfits . . . short skirts, tight blouses, nothin' indecent, but the kind that show off what she's got, which happens to be *fine*. You with me this time?"

"Uh-huh."

"All right," Lewis said. "Now, say you like these outfits on this woman, *really* dig 'em, an' say so all the time while the two of you are datin'. But once things get serious—"

"You saying once you *marry* her?"

"I'm sayin' after there's a solid commitment." Lewis gave Kellerman a sharp look. "You gonna let me make my point, or what?"

"Sorry," Kellerman said. "Go ahead."

Lewis waited a minute, then continued. "Anyway, one day you start thinkin' about how *other* guys are reactin' to her outfits, and it kinda makes you a little concerned, and you mention it to her. For her sake, that is."

"For *her* sake?" Kellerman said.

"Right."

"So it's not because you're jealous, or insecure, or anything."

"Right."

"Just wanted to be clear on that," Kellerman said chidingly.

Lewis frowned.

"I knew you wouldn't get it," he said. "Maybe if you'd grown up on *my* block—"

"Whoa, time out," Kellerman said. "Please tell me you aren't starting in with that 'it's a black thing' crapola."

"Ain't about me *startin' in* with it," Lewis said. "Things are what they are."

Now it was Kellerman who sighed heavily. "The idea that I can't understand something just as well as you can because I'm Caucasian is *racist*."

"Way I see it," Lewis said, "what's racist is *denyin'* the differences between ethnic groups. Thinkin' everybody got to see things the same when they ain't had the same cultural experiences."

"Right, right," Kellerman said. "And even if you think I'm just a dumb white boy—"

"Those're *your* words," Lewis said.

"—how's that got anything to do with Barbara and her slinky wardrobe?"

"'Cause in the real world, when a dude sees a black woman in one'a them outfits, right away he thinks *hooker*," Lewis said. "A white woman struttin' her stuff around some upscale neighborhood, she's *liberated*. Cinderella in tights, thong panties an' a T-shirt with no bra under it. You catchin' me?"

Kellerman looked at him with his innocent blue eyes. "Well, I suppose . . ."

"No," Lewis said, cutting him off. "Like I been sayin', that's the way it *is*."

Kellerman kept looking at him.

"I don't give a *shit* about my woman turnin' heads," Lewis went on, "but I also don't want nobody on the street makin' suckin' noises at her, or grabbin' her behind when she's packed into some train goin' to work."

There was an awkward silence. Kellerman reached for his coffee cup, looking almost comically abashed.

"Well," he said.

"Well," Lewis said.

They sat and drank their coffee.

"So I guess Barbara didn't appreciate your, uh, advice," Kellerman said.

"Matter of fact, she did," Lewis said. "Went out an' bought a whole *closet* full of new clothes. Changed her hairdo while she was at it, since I also told her she'd look good in cornbraids instead'a processin' her hair. Switchin' to a more natural look, you know."

"Well . . ." Kellerman cleared his throat hesitantly. "Excuse me if I sound dumb, but then what's the problem between you two?"

"I didn't like the new clothes on her," Lewis said.

Kellerman looked at him.

"Oh," he said.

"Or the braids."

"Oh."

"Truth is, I liked her old look better," Lewis said. "*Much* better."

"Uh-oh," Kellerman said. "Did you actually *tell* her this?"

Lewis nodded.

"Words just slipped out," he said. "When she was kinda modelin' for me."

"And what happened to you being worried about all those big, bad, slobbering wolves on the street?"

"I don't know what to tell you, man," Lewis said. "Ain't no logic behind these things."

Kellerman rolled his eyes up at the ceiling.

"So what you think?" Lewis asked.

"I think," Kellerman said, "you're going to the barbecue alone."

Lewis frowned.

"Sure glad I told *you* my personal shit," he said. "Seein' you turned out to be such a big help."

Kellerman shrugged and took a bite of his pie.

"Hey, it could be worse," he said.

"Yeah?"

"That's right," Kellerman said. "*I* could be the one who isn't showing up at Russert's shindig."

"How's that *worse*?"

"Two reasons," he said, swallowing what was in his mouth. "For one thing, as long as I'm there, you'll have somebody to hang out with, since I don't have a date either."

"Great," Lewis said. "An' what's the other reason?"

Kellerman looked at him and smiled impishly.

"Nobody loves you better than me," he said.

". . . HAVIN' A PARTY, everybody's singin', listenin' to the *muuusic* on the ra-di-*ooo-ooh* . . ."

Dubick tried to phase Stella out but it was no good, he couldn't do it, the more he ignored the crazy fuck the louder he kept singing, if that was what you wanted to call it . . . repeating the same line or two from that old Sam Cook number in an off-key holler, going on and on for hours now, aware he was getting on Dubick's nerves, scraping them *raw*, enjoying the fact that Dubick couldn't do anything about it. Probably thought that bit about the radio was funny . . . yeah, Dubick bet he did. They'd had the dashboard multiband on all night—or since the signal from the hospital had dissolved into popcorn-crackle static on Dubick's handheld radio, anyway—and been listening to police communications about the escape, scanning the frequencies used by the staties, county sheriffs' departments, and local-yokel cops. Dubick knew exactly where to look for these broadcasts on the dial, and figured he should be grateful his fleeting career as a law officer had given him *some* kind of edge in life.

". . . everybody's singin', listenin' to the *muuu*—"

A frown creased Dubick's brow. Stella had abruptly stopped crooning in back, and in a queer way the silence was only increasing Dubick's unease.

He glanced in the rearview and felt the skin prickle between his shoulders.

Stella was grinning at him.

Grinning at him in the mirror, almost as if he'd been reading his thoughts.

"Something troubling your heart, Dube-cat?" he said. "You *know* you can tell me about it. I mean, that's what friends are for."

Dubick said nothing.

He flicked his eyes back to the road, a looping pitch-black two-laner about fifteen minutes outside Antietam on the West Virginia side of the state line. The dashboard clock read eleven-thirty. He'd been driving for almost five hours straight now, having first passed over the wooded mountains of western Maryland, then hop-scotched across the Potomac maybe three, four times, stitching a twisty route through two states, swinging southward in a wide curve that took them as far down as Charlestown, then backtracking along the Shenandoah River on a course that would eventually lead into Baltimore, keeping to these godforsaken back roads to avoid the police barricades. Another benefit he could claim from his days in a Smoky the Bear hat was knowing where the troopers would set up their road-blocks; in that way they were like the mice that some-times crept into his apartment, always picking the same spots in the walls to build their nests, their little mouse-brains unable to imagine anybody would figure out where they were hiding and do something about it.

Stella had leaned forward, folded his arms over the seat rest, and propped his chin up on his wrists.

"If you're gonna be keepin' your lips zipped, I'll just have to try and *guess* what's wrong," he said, his breath hissing dryly against Dubick's ear.

Dubick didn't answer him.

"Could be you don't like keeping company with mental patients," Stella said.

Dubick didn't answer.

"Hmmm, seems like I'm runnin' cold." Stella tapped himself on the forehead. "Hey, I got it! Maybe you're peeved at the way I held the gun on you back at the nut house. Pokin' you in the ear with it, and all. Is that it?"

Dubick stared into the night.

Stella leaned farther over the seat rest.

"Now listen, Dube-cat, I have a feeling I'm gettin' warmer. That I'm right on top of what's burnin' you, matter of fact," Stella said. "But I really don't think you should ruin this here friendship of ours just because I did a good job of acting to impress your buddies. I mean, we had to look *convincing,* didn't we?" He ruffled the hair on the back of Dubick's neck. "As if I'd really harm one'a these li'l buggers!" he said.

"That's enough," Dubick said, tilting his head away from him. "I don't have to take this horseshit from you."

Stella clucked his tongue and moved his hand onto Dubick's shoulder.

"Boy, you *are* pissed," he said. "And what's worse, I do believe you're kinda afraid of me."

"Nobody was supposed to get hurt back there," Dubick said. "What the fuck was that all about, you shooting McCulloch?"

"Mac shot off his mouth, I shot off my gun." Stella shrugged. "Figured that made us even-Stephen."

"You blew the old man away for no sa—" Dubick caught himself and shifted uncomfortably.

Stella's hand tightened on his shoulder.

"What was that you were gonna say, man?" he said.

Dubick was quiet. The Ford hummed over the narrow macadam, its headlights struggling to push back the gluey darkness. He felt pressed, hemmed-in by the relentless pine woods on either side of the road.

"Tell you what I think was gonna come out your mouth," Stella said. Squeezing his shoulder. Breathing down his neck. "I think you was gonna say I shot Mac for no *sane* reason."

Dubick kept his hands steady on the wheel and shook his head.

"What's the difference what I think," he said.

"It's just that I wouldn't want any misunderstandings sproutin' up between us," Stella said. "I mean, if we three buddies can't get along in this li'l car of yours, then what chance is there for *world* peace an' harmony, huh?"

Dubick tried to shrug off Stella's bony fingers but they kept digging into him.

"Y'see, there was nothin' crazy about why I killed Mac," Stella said. "The broken-down old sonuvabitch was all worked up, jumpin' out his chair, yellin' about his chess game bein' interrupted and whatnot. If I'd let him go on like he was, he might've trotted right out of the dayroom, caused a whole commotion in the halls. And *that* might've put a crimp in our plans." Stella's grin was malevolent as a knife blade. "Hope that makes you feel better about the extreme measures I had to take."

Tomorrow, Dubick thought. Tomorrow I'll be in the islands.

He shook his head again. "Like I said, how I feel doesn't matter. What counts is that Campbell has the money for me when I drop you two off. Fifty large."

Humped in the backseat, Campbell was still, his drugged, liquidy eyes half there with them, half in some faraway place.

"Hell," Stella said, indignant. "First you're in a huff over Mac, then you're afraid Mutter's gonna welsh on your payoff. Bet it's all the drivin' tonight that's making you so tired an' irritable."

"How about you do me a favor, quit trying to analyze me," Dubick said. His foot fluttered over the brake as he rounded a sharp curve. "We got about an hour to go before we get to Baltimore and I don't feel like talking."

Stella clucked again. "Believe I'd be doin' you a greater kindness by relievin' you of your chauffeur duties."

"Right," Dubick said dismissively.

"I'm serious, Dube. What you should do right now is pull over to the shoulder of the road an' climb out from behind the wheel. So we can switch places."

Dubick tensed. He'd thought Stella was just needling him, but this was sounding like he really *did* mean it, and he wanted to quash the idea before it went any further.

"Look, there's absolutely no way I'm gonna——"

He broke off in midsentence, going rigid with shock as Stella's Magnum came up to his ear.

"Stop the car," Stella said. "Now."

His hands suddenly trembling on the wheel, his heart squeezed into his throat, Dubick veered over to the gravel shoulder of the road and slowed to a halt.

Keeping the Magnum to his head, Stella reached across Dubick's chest with his free hand, grabbed his door handle, pushed open his door, and prodded him to get out with the gun muzzle. Once he was outside, Stella exited through his own door on the left side of the car. Campbell appeared on the right seconds later, his giant form seeming to *swell* from inside like a slowly expanding parade float.

Dubick stood at the fringe of the woods, not quite understanding what was happening, or maybe not wanting to understand. Stella held the gun on him. The moonlight filtering through the trees hurled mottles of shadow into the bony hollows of his cheeks, giving the eerie illusion that he'd daubed them with war paint.

"Well," he said, cocking his gun. "Looks like it's quittin' time, Señor Dube-*gato*."

Dubick licked his lips. Out of the corner of his eye he saw something with wings bounce from a branch and go churning off into the darkness. The rusty nightsong of insects seemed deafening.

"Please," he said. Were the crickets really that loud? He could hardly hear himself over their chittering. "I never did you guys wrong. Did everything like we planned."

Stella's grin was a bloodless cut across his features.

"I want to let you in on a little secret," he said. "You payin' attention?"

Dubick looked at him.

"I asked if you were payin' attention," Stella demanded. "Mustn't go all quiet on me now."

"I-I'm listening," Dubick said.

"Good, real good." The shadows on Stella's face shifted in the sudden breeze. "See, kittycat, the truth is you never knew me. Not once in all the years you seen me walkin' around the loony bin did you have any idea who I really am. And now, at last, I'm gonna tell you."

Stella paused and stepped closer to Dubick, bringing the out-thrust revolver within an inch of his face.

"You know the bogeyman folks are afraid of when they're babes lyin' in their cribs?" he said. "The bogeyman that makes 'em shiver in bed when they're old, and know every night that falls could be the last night of the world for 'em?"

He came closer.

Touched the tip of his gun to Dubick's nose.

"Well, Dube, I bet you already guessed it, but I'm gonna say it aloud to be sure you got it right," he said. "I'm the bogeyman. Everybody's worst nightmare. And you know what? *In spite* a' bein who I am, I ain't gonna kill you."

Dubick wasn't sure he'd heard him right until he lowered the gun, and even then a part of him was disbelieving. It took a concentrated effort of will to breathe, but when he finally did he could feel some of his terror running out of him.

"Thank you," he said with numb relief, and realized he was sobbing. "Thank—"

"Now, don't get too happy," Stella said. "What I meant was that Mutter's gonna do it *for* me."

Dubick felt the words hit him like physical blows. His emotions tilting wildly back toward panic, he looked over at Campbell, who had been standing perhaps a foot or two behind Stella, unmoving, hands at his sides, standing there like a slab of granite. Dubick jerked his glance upward from Campbell's muscular body to his face, and in the thin moonlight could see that Campbell was staring at him, his features fixed and inexpressive . . .

Except for his eyes.

Something was changing in his eyes, coming alive below their look of glassy sedation like some kind of finned monster awakening at the bottom of a deep, still lake. Something that was all thrusting rage.

Dubick heard a sharp *click-clack* and saw one of the spring-loaded batons Campbell had taken from the hospital snap out to its full length in his hand—maybe his *own* baton, he thought with a surge of horror. Campbell started toward him, moving past Stella with giant steps, gripping the baton, his hand lifting it from his side, moonlight flashing off its steel tubing.

Dubick turned toward the forest, thinking he could make a run for it, hide in the forest—oh sweet Jesus, if he could only make it into the forest, they'd never find him. The breath rasping out between his teeth, he stumbled toward the bristling fringe of trees, heard Campbell's feet crunching heavily down on gravel behind him, and had just enough time to see Campbell's shadow overtake him before he felt an incredible strike of pain across the back of his legs and collapsed to the ground. He threw his hands out to break his fall but landed hard on his face anyway, felt skin tearing open on his lips, his chin, his forehead. He moaned, thrashed around onto his back, saw Mutter Campbell standing over him, reaching down with one thick hand, still holding the upraised baton in the other. And then Campbell leaned forward and the hand closed around

40

Dubick's shirt collar and yanked him to his feet as if he weighed absolutely nothing.

The baton swung down at him and smashed into his forehead, causing another terrible explosion of pain, filling his brain with white lightning. Something hot and wet ran into his eyes, blinding him. Far away he could still hear the insects chirping, and now there was laughter too, nightmarish laughter, and of course he knew who it belonged to, knew it was the kind that would frighten babes in their cribs and make you shiver in bed when you got old . . . the kind he would hear on the last night of the world.

The baton swung up and down, up and down, and through it all the laughter never stopped.

FOUR

FOR BALTIMORE MURDER detectives, hearing a higher-up mouth the word "redball" elicits a reaction that might be reasonably likened to the one given Paul Revere by the colonists as he galloped past their homes shouting that the British were coming . . . not that anyone need look back as far as the American Revolution to find the origin of the phrase, which comes from the days when cops speeding toward a crime scene had flashing red *balls* of light on the roofs of their patrol cars rather than electronically synchronized, multicolored *racks*. As to what "redball" means to homicide cops—well, it is *supposed* to signal that a murder has occurred that is either so horrendous, complicated, politically sensitive, or indicative of a threat to the public safety that the whole police department will be lending a helpful hand in the investigation. What it *actually* tells them, however, is that a lot of people are about to stick their noses where they don't belong.

Meldrick Lewis knew there was a redball in the making even before he saw the crowd of officers and emergency personnel gathered at the spot where the body had been found. In truth, he had suspected it since five

A.M., when Lieutenant Giardello had gotten him out of bed with a phone call, his voice urgent as he told him to skip the usual 8:40 muster at headquarters, and instead get hold of Kellerman and head straight for the Franklin Avenue exit on U.S.-70, where a passing motorist had reported seeing a dead man lying on the roadside. The only other detail Gee had shared before hanging up was that the stiff was wearing a uniform.

As Kellerman eased their unmarked Plymouth up to the police sawhorses closing off the exit ramp from the highway, Lewis stuck his arm out the passenger's window and flashed his tin at the officer posted to turn away traffic. The cop nodded, pulled aside one of the barricades to let them pass, and Kellerman drove on up to where the rest of the official vehicles were parked more or less in a semicircle.

"*Look* at all these guys," Lewis said. By his rough count there were nearly a dozen officers flocking over the vic—local blues, state troopers, even a pair of deputies from the Howard County Sheriff's Department. In addition to the catalog of uniforms, he noticed several lab techs, Scheiner from the M.E.'s office, and a square-jawed, buzz-cut plainclothes investigator sitting with his legs stretched out the open driver's door of the highway patrol cruiser, the radio mike in his hand, watching Lewis and Kellerman arrive with an expression that was anything but comradely.

"Think Dudley Do-Right there's gonna be trouble?" Kellerman tipped his chin toward the state investigator.

"I can handle him," Lewis said, trying to understand how the state cops had been alerted to the body's discovery in the first place. Since the Baltimore police had caught the squeal, somebody in the department had to have tipped them. But who would have done that? And why? "C'mon, man, let's see what the commotion's about."

He pushed open his door and started toward the crowd of cops and techies without waiting for Kellerman, walking the way he always did, walking the *walk*, chest thrust out, hips and shoulders rolling, moving with a loose, easy shuffle and a straight-up attitude that was no bluff, that told you his roots were on the street, that he knew the street better than anybody else on it, that he got his *edge* from it, man, and you better not have something to say.

"Watch out, watch out, let us through," Lewis said, announcing his presence to everyone within earshot. He glanced back at Kellerman, motioned for him to stick tight, and plunged into the crowd of uniforms, holding his badge over his head. "Detectives Lewis and Kellerman, *takin' charge*!"

He jostled up close to the corpse and found Scheiner squatting over it, studying a gash on the dead man's head through a pencil-thin magnifying scope, the toe of his left foot inches away from a spill of blood.

"Yo, Scheiner, what are *you* doin' outta bed early on a Saturday morning?" Lewis said.

"Same thing you are, Meldrick." A hunched, bespectacled, frazzle-haired man in his mid-sixties, Scheiner preferred having his subordinates do the field work these days, and was almost never seen out of the gore-splattered surgical smock that he wore around the forensics lab. This morning he had on a rumpled navy-blue sport coat and gray cotton slacks, which made him look, if not quite dapper, then at least less ghoulish than usual. "Got a call from on high warning me to stay hands on with this one."

Lewis squatted beside him. The victim was sprawled on his back, his skull crushed, his features bloodied and distorted by what must have been a savage beating. There would be no problem identifying him, though, not even if it turned out somebody had lifted his wallet — the tan guard's uniform he was wearing had a shoulder patch that read "Central Maryland Security" and a plastic name tag on the breast pocket that read "E. DUBICK."

"Central Maryland," Lewis said. "Ain't that a psych hospital?"

"High security," Scheiner said. "For violent screwballs."

Lewis made a low sound in his throat, extracted a pair of latex gloves from his jacket pocket, crouched lower over the corpse, and lightly touched its arms and jaw.

"Got some rigor," he said.

"And he's still warm," Scheiner said. "And there are fly eggs on his mouth and eyelids."

"Maggots?"

"Just the undeveloped eggs," Scheiner said.

Lewis nodded. "Figure he been dead, what, six, eight hours?"

"You're in the ballpark," Scheiner said.

"Can you give me a cause of death?" Lewis asked.

"Well, tentatively."

"Yeah, right," Lewis said.

"Pending my autopsy, that is."

"Right, right, right." Lewis wound his hand in the air.

"Somebody cracked him in the head."

Lewis looked at him. "That the best you can do?"

"Cracked him one *good*," Scheiner said. "And then hit him about two dozen more times just for the fun of it."

Lewis scratched under his chin.

"Whoever wailed on him was either pissed off or nuts," he said.

"Maybe both."

"Anything else?"

"A couple of things," Scheiner said. "Here, let me show you."

Still on his haunches, he shuffled around the body until he was straddling its feet, then tugged down a sock to expose a knob of bare ankle.

"Number one," he said, "the ankle's white, no discoloration from the blood sinking to the lower extremities."

"Ought to be black-and-blue after all this time," Lewis said.

"The word is *livid*." Scheiner scowled. "Don't make me get back on your case about using correct medical terminology."

"You mean like 'cracked him in the head'?"

"I believe the words I used were 'blunt force trauma'," Scheiner said. "And don't confuse the issue."

"Awright, chill out," Lewis said. "There any black-and-blues higher up on the body?"

Scheiner sighed testily. "There are marks on his arms, and, as you can see for yourself, his cheeks. Most of them look like bruises, but a few are definitely hypostatic. The blood shifted to those areas after he died."

"Body's been moved," Lewis said.

Scheiner nodded. "Could be I've got an idea from where."

"*Could* be?"

"A tentative idea," Scheiner said. "Pending lab analysis."

Lewis wondered if the M.E. had a replay button that somebody kept pushing.

"Tell me about it," he said.

Scheiner pulled a clear Ziplock bag out of his medical satchel and displayed it for Lewis.

"Exhibit number two," he said.

Lewis took the bag from his hand, held it up to the sunlight, and examined its contents.

"Pine needles," he said.

"And some bits of pine*cone*," Scheiner said.

Lewis looked around at the sprawl of warehouses and industrial smokestacks on either side of the highway ramp.

"Ain't no trees in sight," he said.

"But there are solid belts of pines in the woods between here and Central Maryland," Scheiner said. "I won't swear to it, but my guess is these needles come from a Longleaf, or maybe a Loblolly."

"A *what*?"

"Don't look at me, I didn't make up the name," Scheiner said. "My point, if you'd please stop with the distractions, is that the *size* of the needles and cones is a good clue to the size of the tree."

"Ones in the bag look pretty big."

"I'd say they're from a mature tree, and these things will grow anywhere from eighty to a hundred feet tall."

"You in the Boy Scouts when you were a kid?"

"Always hated the Scouts," Scheiner said. "But somehow I got to be a troop leader while I was raising my sons. Again, don't ask."

Lewis smiled a little. "What part a' the body you take the needles off?"

"They were clinging to our friend Mr. Dubick's head and shirt collar," Scheiner said. "Either he liked wearing garlands in his hair, or they were on the ground where he fell when he was clobbered."

Lewis quietly observed the vehicles whooshing along the highway as he considered what Scheiner had told him. Traffic was heavy for a Saturday morning, particularly in the westbound lanes, where motorists in campers and cars with luggage cupcakes on their roofs were heading out to the lakes and hiking trails for the holiday weekend.

A couple miles farther west, he thought, and the corpse would have been outside the city limits, and the headache of finding his killer would belong to the deputies from Howard County, and he'd just be getting ready for his morning shower.

"Why would whoever aced this guy haul his body all the way here . . . instead of just leaving him back in the woods, I mean?"

This from Kellerman, who had until now stood listening to Lewis and the ME in silence.

"I'm askin' myself the same question," Lewis said. "You gotta wonder if maybe . . ."

Lewis let the sentence trail, his eyes suddenly focusing on a point behind Kellerman's right shoulder. Kellerman turned to see what had snagged his partner's attention, then realized it wasn't a what but a *who*—specifically, the state investigator who had been peering at them from the radio car when they arrived at the scene.

"Don't let me interrupt," the investigator said. He wore dark clip-on lenses over his metal frames and looked every inch the lawman in his beige suit, white shirt, rep tie, and tasseled loafers. "Although I'd ask that you stop handling my evidence."

Lewis stared at him.

"*Your* evidence," he said.

"Yes." The investigator smiled icily and pointed to the badge clipped to his lapel. "I'm Special Investigator Lambert, Major Crimes, Maryland State Police. One of the blues told me you're from Baltimore Homicide."

"Detective Meldrick Lewis," Lewis said, rising to his feet. "My partner's Detective Mike Kellerman."

Lambert acknowledged Kellerman with a stiff little jerk of his chin.

"A few ground rules," he said to Lewis. "My section will be responsible for coordinating all investigative operations in this case. Naturally we'll welcome any input your department chooses to provide, but—"

"Hold it," Lewis said. "You *serious*?"

Lambert stared at him.

"Yes," he said.

On the highway the sound of a driver blaring his horn grew loud and then faded with distance. Lewis moved closer to Lambert and rubbed the back of his neck. Here we go, he thought.

"Maybe you better take a look around," he said. "So you're straight about where you are, see what I'm sayin'?"

Lambert kept staring at him. "I know where I am."

Lewis shook his head.

"You sure?" he said. "'Cause if you did, you'd realize you're in the city of Baltimore. Same place as me. And the dead body I been lookin' at."

"I told you," Lambert said. "I know where I am."

"Well, seein' as that's the case, then maybe you're confused about some other things," Lewis said. "Like the fact that the BPD has jurisdiction over any murder committed in the city limits."

"This isn't just any murder," Lambert said. "There are other factors to be concerned with."

"Other factors, huh?" Lewis said. "Like what?"

Lambert ignored his question and glanced over at Scheiner, who was still down on one knee examining the body.

"Excuse me!" Lambert shouted, and started past Lewis. "No further evidence collection will be done until my own—"

"Hey, just a minute." Kellerman stepped in front of him. "My partner asked you a *question*."

Lambert took a long breath, and expelled it sharply through his nostrils. The muscles of his prominent jaw were working.

"Okay, here it is," he said finally, pivoting back toward Lewis. "As ought to be obvious, the victim was on the security force at Central Maryland, which, as you also may be aware, is a hospital for the criminally insane about a hundred miles west of here. Early last night he was taken hostage at gunpoint by a couple of escapees and forced to drive them off the hospital grounds. My office was contacted by the Howard County sheriff, who asked for assistance and later agreed that we were best qualified to assume primary responsibility for the manhunt."

"You catch the guys who escaped yet?" Lewis asked.

"No."

"Guess I don't have to ask if you got the hostage back alive," Lewis said, and nodded toward the corpse.

Lambert's jaw tensed again.

"Yeah," Lewis said. "Bet the sheriff's glad he called you for help."

Lambert remained silent, his lean neck set, his teeth clamping down on his anger. Lewis hoped he hadn't gone too far antagonizing him, but what could you do? Give a guy like him an inch and he'd be stepping all over you the first chance he got.

"These two fruitcakes got names?" Lewis asked, letting a conciliatory note slip into his voice.

Lambert stood there gritting his teeth another moment, as if deciding whether to let his antagonism boil over into an open confrontation. Then he nodded, seemingly more to himself than Lewis.

"One we believe instigated the break is Frank Stella," he said. "He's a mob button man who squirmed out of a life sentence in prison by bamboozling the shrinks."

"Doesn't ring any bells," Lewis said. "Who's his chum?"

"Big ape name of Mutter Campbell. He—"

"I know who he is," Kellerman cut in. He glanced at Lewis. "He was a suspect in a half dozen cases I was working when I was in Arson. A textbook pyro. His file must've been an inch thick."

"Sounds like the same man, all right," Lambert said. "Creep's into fire and prepubescent girls, not necessarily in that order."

"Got any idea where they might be plannin' to hole up?" Lewis asked.

Lambert shrugged. "They're Baltimore boys. And they left Dubick in the inbound lane of the Baltimore highway. Seems a safe bet they're visiting the hometown."

"You figure that out by yourself, or somebody help you?"

"Go ahead and mouth off," Lambert said. "I can guarantee it's *your* ass that'll end up busted."

Lewis looked at him. "Yeah? How's that? You come steppin' on *my* turf, woofin' about takin' *my* evidence, holdin' back information—"

"What information?"

"Aw, save it," Lewis said. "You been after these birds all night, and I'm supposed to believe you don't have any leads to where they're headin'?"

"That's right," Lambert said. "However, I *am* going to give you some free advice."

"Huh?" Lewis said. "Go ahead, man, let's *hear* it."

"Keep a lid on this," Lambert said. "Don't talk about it to the press, or anyone else not directly involved in the investigation."

"I can't believe we're back to you tellin' me how to run my—"

"I'm *suggesting*—"

"That I keep my mouth shut about those wackos scratchin' their hostage?"

"About everything you know regarding the case," Lambert said. "Including the escape *itself*."

Lewis shook his head while that sank in.

Kellerman was staring at Lambert incredulously. "Let's see if I'm straight about this," he said. "We have a couple headcases who already killed one guy and might be getting into more trouble right this minute. Might be planning *anything*. And you want to keep it under wraps."

"Yes."

"Memorial Day weekend starts *today*, man," Lewis said. "We got people in the parks, people out catchin' holiday sales, kids off from school, a whole big *city* fulla warm bodies. Don't that mean anything to you?"

"Yes," Lambert said. "It means we'd better be careful not to start a panic."

"Hey, let's get *real*," Kellerman said. "You ask me, we better make *sure* the papers slap pictures of those two nuts on their front pages. If people aren't warned—"

"There's been nothing to indicate they're an immediate threat to the public—"

"Come *on*," Lewis said, and gestured angrily at the corpse on the ground. "He's all the damn indication I *need*."

Lambert sighed impatiently. "Look, we aren't getting anything settled here—"

"Right about *that*—"

"So maybe it would be better to let your bosses do it," Lambert said, suddenly looking past Lewis.

Lewis started to reply, then simultaneously noticed Lambert shifting his attention and heard the sound of a car pulling onto the exit ramp behind him. He turned, watched a black sedan with tinted windows and official City Hall plates stop near the other parked vehicles, and waited to see who got out.

The first passenger to exit the rear of the limo was a

formal-looking woman with angle-cut blond hair and a large pad and clipboard under her arm. Lewis didn't know her name, but recognized her as the assistant to the mayor's liaison to the police department, whose name he *did* know, and who followed her from the car a moment later. Ross Stanton was a short, balding guy of about forty who always wore pin-striped suits, likewise always had a strained expression on his face, and never stopped making a show of checking his wristwatch, as if to indicate he was being detained from some far more pressing event in his busy schedule.

Third and last out the door was someone else Lewis knew, Captain George Barnfather, who ranked directly above Lieutenant Al Giardello in the department's chain of command and was the sort of button-down blue whose chief role in the department, as far as Lewis could tell, was to make every detective's job more difficult than it needed to be.

He took a deep breath. The arrival of the Three Musketeers at the scene was a pretty rotten omen.

"What's happening?" Barnfather said, hurrying over ahead of the others. A slender black man in his mid-thirties, he held himself very erect and had a shiny crust of service medals on the shoulders and breast pockets of his uniform jacket. To Lewis he looked like a pen on some high-level bureaucrat's desk, one made of brass or gold and studded with jewels, and used exclusively to sign important documents.

"Well . . . ," Lewis said.

"Who's the primary here?"

"Uh, I am, Captain," Lewis said. "Detective Kellerman's my—"

Barnfather had already turned to Lambert.

"Bruce," he said, "good to see you."

"You look great, George," Lambert said. He smiled and gripped Barnfather's hand. "How's the family?"

"Fine, fine," Barnfather said. "And yours . . . ?"

Lewis shot Kellerman a quick glance, controlling himself, figuring it was best not to open his mouth. So the state boys had gotten tipped to the murder because Lambert had juice with Barnfather—*how's the family*—wasn't that peachy, wasn't that just fucking wonderful.

He watched from the sidelines, only half paying attention as Lambert was introduced to Stanton and his assistant.

"We were having a professional disagreement about whether there ought to be a press blackout," Lambert was saying. "Detective Lewis here feels . . ."

". . . absolutely concur with your assessment of the situation. How about you, Ross?"

". . . the mayor's office also believes it ought to be kept quiet for the time being . . . avoid throwing a scare . . ."

Lewis tuned them out completely now, moving off to stand in a wide swatch of sunlight that kept the early morning chill off his shoulders. Looking up at the sky, he could see some upper-altitude cirrostratus clouds to the southwest, thin and fibrous, resembling scattered strands of webbing. He liked studying the sky, observing its colors and clouds and their patterns, putting it all together and interpreting what it meant. Often he would watch the nightly weather roundups on TV so he could compare his own reading with that of the professional forecasters, and occasionally he'd disagree with them, predicting rain or snow when they said the sky would be clear and sunny, or warm weather when they said a cold front was blowing in. Never mind their satellite maps and radar, he did it the old-fashioned way, and when he got it right he would go out and buy a new CD, or a part for the Cobra he was restoring, whatever, just to reward himself—although his greatest satisfaction came from beating the hotshots at their own game.

He felt a slight tug at his sleeve, lowered his eyes from the sky, and saw that it was Kellerman, tugging at him and frowning as the bosses waved them over, their superior, resolute expressions leaving no doubt that thousands upon thousands of defenseless citizens would be kept from knowing that two homicidal fugitives from an insane asylum were roaming like wolves in their midst. Lambert stood there rubbing elbows with the BPD officials in fraternal solidarity, looking smugly pleased.

"Guess we're outnumbered," Kellerman said unhappily.

Lewis flung an arm across his shoulders.

"But not outclassed," he said.

FIVE

"WHAT SCARES ME about these bugs is that they're in a state of constant mutation," Munch said.

"You talking viruses again?" Bayliss said.

"*And* bacteria."

"Which reminds me," Kellerman said. "What the hell's the one grows on strawberries?"

"That'd be cyclospora," Munch said.

"I prefer raspberries anyway," Bayliss said.

"Hate to tell you, Timmy, but it's not particular about the kind of berry it uses as a host," Munch said.

Bayliss frowned, already getting itchy. How did Munch manage to reel him into these conversations? Maybe he'd fallen victim to the same morbid fascination that made people gawk at car wrecks or mail away for those glorified snuff videos he'd seen marketed on television, like the one where you got ninety minutes' worth of animals tearing the guts out of smaller animals, or the one they'd been advertising lately that showed fighter pilots being blown out of the air and crashing to their fiery deaths.

". . . really ought to consider it a minute," Munch was saying.

Bayliss glanced at his watch. They were in the corridor outside the sixth-floor briefing room at the station house, awaiting the arrival of the brass and somebody or other from the mayor's office for a departmental huddle about the Stella-Campbell escape.

"Consider what?" he asked.

"The fact that these microbes were around millions of years before human beings. They've proven their adaptability. We haven't."

"Maybe we oughtta talk about something else," Bayliss said, scratching his arm.

"You *always* want to talk about something else when a subject makes you uncomfortable."

"That's not true."

"I'm telling you it is, Timmy," Munch said. "You're as predictable as they come, a creature of habit. Most people are. Which just illustrates my point."

"What point was that again?" Kellerman said.

"That human beings hate change," Munch said. "Germs, on the other hand, are *into* it."

"Germs are into change," Bayliss echoed. "Where'd you hear that? From a germ psychology expert on Oprah?"

"Go ahead and act cute," Munch said. "But you better pray you never get an antibiotic resistant infection."

"*What* infection?" Bayliss said.

"Take your pick," Munch said

"*Which* antibiotics?" Kellerman said.

"Well, for openers," Munch said, "the ones in the wholesome all-beef patties you'll be wolfing down at Russert's barbecue."

"Maybe I'll just stick to the chicken wings," Kellerman said, the skin prickling between his shoulders.

"Won't help," Munch said. "The cluckers are also loaded with antibiotics."

"Hold on," Bayliss said, wishing the meeting would get under way so he could move onto a more cheerful subject, such as the brutal murder of a hospital guard by two rabid maniacs—oh, what a beautiful morning it was. "Now you're saying it's cows *and* chickens?"

"That's right," Munch said. "Farmers put the stuff in their feed to make them grow bigger, never mind that it's causing the bacteria in their bodies to develop resistant genes, and that the genes get passed along to humans who eat the livestock."

"Russert better make sure she's got plenty of corn on the cob, now that everything else is out," Bayliss cracked.

Kellerman laughed feebly.

"Very funny, boys," Munch said. "But I'll give you one guess as to what's used to fertilize vegetable crops."

"Yo, Mike, your homey from Arson bring us that Campbell file?" Lewis yelled from down the hall. He was carrying two coffee cups.

"Got it right here," Kellerman said, showing him a manilla folder. "Also have printouts of the rap sheets for both nuts."

"All *right*." Lewis approached and gave one of the coffees to Kellerman.

"How come you didn't bring me and Bayliss any coffee?" Munch said.

Lewis looked at him.

"Well, for one thing, you an' Bayliss are already *holdin'* coffees in your hands."

"But you didn't *know* that until just now." Munch frowned at him disapprovingly and turned back to Bayliss and Kellerman. "I'm still waiting for you guys to answer me."

Bayliss rolled his eyes. "Can we *please* drop it?"

"Drop what?" Lewis said.

"Munch was just asking if we know how our produce gets fertilized," Kellerman said.

"Shit," Lewis said.

"What's wrong?" Kellerman said.

"Nothin'."

"So why'd you say 'shit'?"

"'Cause that's what farmers *use*," Lewis said.

59

"Oh yeah," Kellerman said. "Right."

"Actually it's mostly *cow* shit," Munch said. "Cows being—"

"Full of shit," Bayliss said.

Kellerman chuckled. "Shit machines."

"I'd prefer the term *fecally bountiful,* but if you guys insist on making clowns of yourselves, go ahead," Munch said. "Main thing's that you understand your average cow excretes over a hundred times the amount of shit as a person every single day of its life. And that each deposit, so to speak, is crawling with hundreds of thousands of bacteria, which gets into the fertilizer, which is mixed into agricultural soil, which is what those ears of corn Kellerman was talking about grow in—"

"Okay, we get the drift," Kellerman said, once again feeling like he had fleas in his shirt. He scratched under his collar and peered down the hall at the closed door to Giardello's office. "What the hell's goin' on in there? The meeting was supposed to start ten minutes ago."

"Heard Gee pumpin' up the volume when I sashayed past," Lewis said. "It sounded to me like he was givin' Stanton an' Barnfather his opinion of their press black-out, an' it wasn't good." He nodded at the file folder under Kellerman's arm. "Lemme take a peek at that while we're hangin'."

"Do any of you know," Munch said, "that some strains of disease-causing bacteria have mutated so they can metabolize antibiotics? They're *eating* whatever we throw at 'em. Also . . ."

"Dear God, let it end." Bayliss looked heavenward and wrung his hands under his chin.

"Hard to believe Campbell was hitched so long," Lewis thought aloud, scanning the contents of Kellerman's file. "Woman lives with a headcase like him, she's either gotta have a few screws loose herself, or be keepin' her eyes shut *tight.*"

"The marriage was common law," Kellerman said. "I interviewed the wife a couple times. Name was something like Latoya Madden, right?"

"Jolanda," Lewis said.

"Nice woman, believe it or not," Kellerman said. "It probably isn't in the case file, but I think she finally walked on Campbell after the last time he got busted."

". . . tuberculosis and staph infections are becoming untreatable, which means we're looking at a species-threatening plague that could kill off nine out of ten people on *earth*," Munch was saying. "And I hope you're all doused with mosquito repellant when you're pulling out the chaise lounges Monday, because a bite from the wrong bug could give you *Dengue*—"

"Oh, come on, Munchkin, we all know you're just covering up."

He looked at Sergeant Kay Howard, who had paused beside him on her way into the briefing room.

She looked back at him, a half smile on her lips. Tough, pretty, with a flowing mane of hair the color of an Irish sunset, she was most outstandingly distinguished from the other detectives at the door by her sergeant's rank, her eye-catching femininity, and the fact that she was the only one of them having herbal tea instead of coffee this morning—not because she actually liked drinking anything with a name like Glorious Meadow Bouquet or Zesty Lemon Festival, but because her doctors had ordered her off caffeine after she was nearly killed by a bullet to the heart, put there courtesy of a crazed shooter named Gordon Pratt.

"Covering up *what*?" Munch said.

"The real reason you're on the schedule Monday instead of taking the day off," Howard said.

He kept looking at her

She likewise kept watching him, her green eyes twinkling with mysterious amusement.

"You going to share your insight about my true motivations or just tantalize us with that crooked little grin?" he said at last.

She shrugged. "I can spell it out in two words. If you're positive you want me to. In front of the guys, I mean."

"Look, we're all friends here," he said.

"I just figure you might be embarrassed. When it comes to showing they're vulnerable, sometimes *men* . . ." She shrugged again. "Well, you know."

"No, I'm sorry, I don't," he said. "I'm the guy who posed buck naked for a photographer, remember? You haven't learned the *meaning* of the word vulnerability till you've had skin shots taken of yourself, so let's hear it, Miss Know-it-all."

"Vera Bash," she said.

He blinked. "Huh?"

"*Veeeeerrra,*" she started to repeat slowly, stretching out the name.

"I heard you the first time," he said. "But I don't see what she has to do with anything."

Bayliss simultaneously winked at Lewis and nudged him with his elbow. Munch had met Vera Bash maybe five, six months back, right around Christmas, while he and Pembleton had been working a double murder in a Gypsy fortune-telling joint run by her father. As Bayliss recalled, the affair had been complicated by some kind of feud among Gypsy clans, one of them being Vera's, and there had been a related kidnaping, and Vera's father had gotten killed, and she'd wound up with custody of her fifteen-year-old niece and gone back home to D.C., where she was a college teacher, although that obviously hadn't prevented Munch from giving her plenty of solace—and not over the phone, either, because the buzz was that things had been hot and heavy between them ever since.

Right now, though, Kay's face had the word *gotcha* written all over it, making Bayliss positive she knew something the rest of the detectives in the squad room didn't.

"You and Vera having problems?" he asked.

"No," Munch said.

Kay was poking the inside of her cheek with her tongue.

"No problems, huh?" she said.

"None," Munch said. "And if we were having any, it'd be nobody else's business."

"Absolutely," Kay said. "That's why I hustled away from your desk the second I realized you were arguing with her on the phone last week."

"We weren't *arguing*, we were *disagreeing*; everybody here always gets those terms confused —"

"Well, whatever, I must've heard you inviting her to the barbecue half a dozen times."

"So what?"

"So it was pretty obvious she couldn't make it, 'cause the second you hung up, you marched into Gee's office and volunteered to work Monday."

"*Volunteered?*" Kellerman said. "I thought it was your turn in the rotation."

"Munch, Munch, Munch," Bayliss said. "You mean you were gonna risk catching all those mutant bugs and *join* the rest of us?"

"Till the *love*bug bit an' he decided he didn't want to go without his baby," Lewis said. "Snagged twice in as many days."

"Oh, oh, Gypsy woman . . ." Kellerman crooned.

Bayliss was laughing hard.

"*Twice* in two days," he gasped, clutching his middle. "I can't handle it."

"Glad you all find me so entertaining," Munch said, thinking that if the yucks kept coming the way they had been lately, he'd have to try his hand at stand-up comedy. "But I can do without the comments, especially from our Boy Wonder."

"Hey, Frank!" Bayliss waved to Frank Pembleton, who had been standing down the hall having a conversation with somebody from Auto Theft while he waited for the meeting to kick off. "Come on over, you gotta hear this."

"What's up?" Pembleton said, joining him.

"Thanks a lot, Howard," Munch said. "I'm truly blessed having a friend like you."

"Look, don't blame me, I *told* you I didn't want to say anything . . ."

"How come Vera isn't coming to the party anyway?" Kellerman asked. He'd been suddenly struck by the fact that both Munch and Lewis had significant others who'd taken a pass, and was wondering if it was mere coincidence.

"Yeah, how come?" Bayliss asked.

"She told me . . ." Munch let the sentence dangle and motioned toward the door to Giardello's office. "Sorry to leave you all hanging, but here comes the marching band."

They all abruptly fell silent, their eyes turning toward the door. It had swung open and Barnfather and Stanton had stepped out into the hallway, with Gee bringing up the rear, looking anything but pleased by whatever had transpired between the three of them. A tall, bulky black man—actually, half his bloodline was Italian, though, without knowing his name, you wouldn't have guessed it unless you'd tasted his homemade *stracotto,* or heard him talk about his grandfather's exploits in the Sicilian underground during World War Two—Giardello came stalking up to the briefing room with an enormous frown on his ordinarily calm face.

"Let's get started," he grunted, and shepherded the detectives into the room with a sweeping gesture of both hands. "We have a lot to talk about."

Munch quickly ducked inside, very glad they did, and even gladder that none of it would be about him.

THE TWO MEN sat on a bench in the children's playground, their backs to the low metal rail dividing it from the softball field, landscaped meadows, cobblestone walks, and paved jogging paths that made the park a tree-lined oasis for Baltimore residents. It was a lovely spring morning, soft breeze rustling through the foliage, tang of budding azaleas in the air, dogs chasing Frisbees, young couples spreading picnic blankets on the gently sloping lawns. On the next bench over a white-haired old woman was scooping bird seed from her shopping bag and tossing it to the blackbirds, sparrows, and squirrels congregating around her like a happy hour crowd at a table of hors d'oeuvres

A little girl in a flowered shift came running up to the benches in pursuit of a ball she'd been thrown. The ball was large and had pictures of cartoon characters on it: Bugs Bunny, Elmer Fudd, Daffy Duck. Before her pumping legs could gain enough ground, it started to roll under the bench where the two men were sitting, and she came to a short stop in front of them, her lips pouted in frustration.

One of the men bent down and intercepted the ball, then held it out to her with his large hands.

"Here," he said.

Her pouted lips reshaped themselves into a smile and she took it from him.

"What's your name?" he asked.

"Rachel," she said. "What's yours?"

"Mutter," he said.

"That's a *funny* name," she said, and giggled, and then went trotting off with her ball.

He straightened up and watched as the girl and her playmate, a slightly taller girl in candy-striped Oshkosh biballs, resumed their game of catch.

"Kids," Stella said to him, shaking his head. "Sayin' all kinds of stupid shit."

Mutter said nothing and kept staring at the two children. They both had fawnlike brown eyes, wavy brown hair, and dark complexions, a resemblance that unmistakably showed them to be sisters.

Stella frowned. He felt slighted by Campbell's utter lack of acknowledgment; at least Dubick had been good for some friendly chitchat. And besides, they had important things to talk about and no time to waste. It was risky to stay in one spot too long. Even in the street clothes Dubick had packed away for them it was risky. They had to keep moving.

"Exactly what's so interestin' about them young whippersnappers?" he asked, hoping to ease Campbell out of his silent absorption.

Campbell said nothing and watched the girls toss the ball back and forth. The area was filled with the sounds of children at play, seesaws bouncing off rubber base mats, feet skipping on the hopscotch squares, shovels thunking against the sides of buckets in the sandbox, squeals of excited laughter from the jungle gym and crawl tunnel. At the far side of the playground yet another girl, this one perhaps ten or eleven years old, sat on a swing and described a broad, perfect arc in the air, her legs kicking out rhythmically, her hair flapping off her neck in a reddish-blond swirl.

"They're pretty," Campbell said at last, keeping his eyes on the girls with the ball.

His answer caught Stella by surprise. Not because of what he'd said—Stella had heard stories about Campbell and suspected he already knew the particulars of his fancy for little girls—but because he had been prepared to give up on coaxing *any* kind of response from him.

"We got to make some plans," he said. "Decide what we're gonna do next."

Campbell fell back into silence again, although now Stella sensed he was still with him, considering his words.

He waited for Campbell to say something else. The seesaws thumped. Swings rattled on their chains. The birds around the old lady on the nearby bench swished and fluttered as she tossed them another handful of sunflower seeds.

"Jolanda," Campbell said.

This time when he spoke an odd spasm made the entire left side of his face tremble and pull violently upward. Stella had occasionally noticed a similar tic back at the hospital, but seemed to remember it as having been milder—a *lot* milder, in fact. Now it looked as if somebody had sunk a fishing hook into his cheek and then jerked back hard on the line.

"Who's that?" he said.

"My wife."

"You thinkin' about payin' her a visit?"

"Yeah," Campbell said. "After a while."

Stella thought about that, and also wondered whether the facial tremor, or whatever the hell it was, ought to concern him at all. Probably it should, if only because people might notice it. The last thing he wanted was for either of them to attract attention.

"Y'know," he said. "I really have to make some personal calls of my own. Say hello to some friends. Visit my mother."

"How much money we got?" Campbell said.

"Well there, Mutter, you just put your finger on one of our biggest problems. Seems Dube-cat didn't exactly pack a full load in his wallet. And his credit cards are too hot to handle."

"I asked about the money."

"Thirty bucks, by my count, and cuttin' that down the middle don't leave either of us with hardly nothing."

"I want to bring Jolanda a present," Campbell said. "When I see her."

Stella gave him a doleful glance. "That's a nice sentiment, to be sure. 'Cept out here in the real world we gonna have expenses. I bet a hefty fella like yourself can go through fifteen bucks wortha *chow* in just a day or two."

Campbell made a low sound in his throat but was otherwise silent. He hunched forward with his elbows on his knees and watched the girls run and toss their ball.

"What we gotta do is get us *buyin' power*," Stella said quickly. Campbell's eyes were getting slushy; he wanted to make his point before he slipped back into the Twilight Zone.

Campbell's thick face slowly turned toward him.

"How?" he asked.

Stella grinned. If he had to keep his wagon hitched to Campbell awhile—and he didn't figure he could shake him loose just yet, for a variety of reasons—then he might as well make the most of it.

"A spree of armed robberies," he said, his grin spreading across his face. "As they'd say in the headlines."

Campbell looked at Stella another moment, then nodded and turned his gaze back to the game of catch.

They sat on the playground bench in the morning sunshine.

From behind the bird woman a squirrel suddenly bound toward the sprinkling of seeds and the sparrows and blackbirds exploded into the air, abandoning their meal, aflutter with panic as they scattered toward the safety of the trees.

THE BRIEFING ROOM was a cramped rectangle with cinderblock walls, a long green chalkboard opposite the door, and as many chairs as could be packed inside without having to stack them one atop the other to the ceiling.

". . . so if there are any questions I'll be glad to answer them," Lambert was saying from where he stood next to the chalkboard.

A few of the detectives glanced up from their notepads, but Lewis was barely paying attention. He had the Campbell file open on his lap and wanted to finish poring through the reports it contained. And besides, Lambert didn't exactly match his image of an open and sharing kind of guy.

The meeting had started out with an obviously chagrined—some might have said *fuming*—Giardello advising the detectives on his shift to maintain the press blackout until further notice, his attitude suggesting that he did not want to be personally associated with the decision, and that Barnfather had not only pulled rank to overrule his objections, but also pulled political strings that reached all the way up to the police commissioner, and, through Stanton, His Honor the Mayor himself.

Giardello had gone on to offer some ground rules for working the case, explaining that each participating law enforcement agency would retain authority within its local jurisdiction, take responsibility for handling its own evidence, and conduct an open exchange of information with other agencies, emphasizing that all investigators operating outside their jurisdictions would do so only with the consent of those in charge, and in accordance with any decisions and restrictions they set forth.

After the lieutenant finished, Barnfather had given his standard cadet school pep talk, slipping in a reminder that not a word was to be uttered about the escape to anyone outside the department, along with several couched warnings that anyone who violated his directive would be walking a foot patrol in Western, and concluding with an announcement that the case was twenty-four hours from going redball—acting as if he thought the offer of additional manpower would be welcomed, but knowing full well that every member of the squad would view the possibility of departmental interference as a threat hanging over his or her head like a noose.

Next up had been Stanton with a brief sermon about the mayor's confidence in his police force and their ability to work hand-in-hand with the state patrol, county cops, and any other organizations that might become involved in the search. He had underscored the need for mutual assistance and cooperation, endorsed the lieutenant's guidelines, and then quickly turned the floor over to Lambert, who assumed the haughty posture of a visiting Middle Eastern caliph, leaving on his sunglasses and keeping his beak nose up in the air, giving the Baltimore detectives what he claimed was a to-the-best-of-his-knowledge account of how the escape went down, though Lewis had felt it was conspicuously lacking in details, and suspected Lambert had, for whatever reasons, not even come close to leveling with them.

He noticed that Pembleton had stopped taking notes long enough to ask Statie something, and perked an ear in his direction.

"First, on behalf of every detective in this room, I want to thank you for all your help . . . ," Pembleton said.

Lewis bit his bottom lip to suppress a grin. Here it comes, he thought.

". . . but what confuses me, and I'm sure you can clear this up, is how the fugitives managed to drive two hundred miles without running into state and county roadblocks."

Lambert looked at him. "I don't know," he said flatly.

Pembleton raised his eyebrows. "It seems to me they must have had information which allowed them to anticipate where you would set up your checkpoints," he said.

Lambert was still looking at him. "Obviously they did," he said.

"Do you agree that it's critical for us to find out how they came by that knowledge?"

"Important, yes," Lambert said. "I don't know if I'd use the word *critical*."

Pembleton uh-huhed.

"As long as we don't write it off as a crazy stroke of luck," he said. "Pardon my language."

Chuckles around the room.

"It's being looked into," Lambert said, unsmiling.

Lewis raised his hand. Pembleton had hit upon a question that had been nagging at him all morning.

"Yes?" Lambert said, turning his head toward him.

"About the gun Stella and Campbell were using," he said. "It was a .357 Magnum, right? Real big sucker."

Lambert nodded curtly.

"So how you suppose it got inside the hospital?" Lewis asked.

Lambert was staring at him through his dark lenses.

"I have no idea," he said. "It's something else we're investigating."

Although he figured that was about as much as he was going to get, Lewis couldn't resist pushing him a little further.

"Seems like it'd be tough," he said. "We're talkin' about a maximum security institution, meanin' any visitors would have to be searched on entry."

He could see Lambert's body stiffen, though the statie deserved credit for keeping most of his anger bottled inside.

"Every security system has loopholes," Lambert said. "If you've read the workup on Stella, you know he'd have the brains to recognize and exploit them."

Lewis didn't say anything.

"Any further questions?" Lambert said.

Nobody raised a hand.

"Then I'll let your own primary investigator take over," he said, trying to sound humble.

The room was quiet while Lewis stepped up to the chalkboard and the state cop returned to his chair, everyone watching the two men, feeling the tension between them.

Lewis stood without speaking a moment, then pulled the rap sheets on Stella and Campbell out of his file folder and, without preface, began slowly reading off their combined priors: murder, murder, rape, arson, murder, murder, murder, kidnaping—the list went on and on, including some of the most sordid criminal offenses on the books.

"Guess it's safe to say they're a couple of bad dudes," Munch said when he was finished.

Grim smiles from everybody in the room, Lewis being no exception, though he did not care for the limelight, and felt peculiar addressing a large group of people, drawing their full attention, having their eyes on him as they waited for his directions. But, thanks to Giardello rushing him out to the crime scene, this was his case, bingo, like it or not.

"Best thing goin' for us right now is that we already know who done it," he said, looking up from the folder. "Worst thing's that the longer these two stay loose, the better the chance they'll do it again."

"Which means we oughtta get busy," Bayliss said.

Lewis nodded.

"Maybe these guys are wackos, but they had lives before they got sent up," he said. "Question I been askin'

71

myself is, if I was in their shoes, what would I do? They're gonna need cash. Somebody who can give 'em a place to hole up, or get them out of town. It's gonna be hard for them to make it without help. Hard to stay away from old friends."

"Friends who might not want to have anything to do with them," Howard said.

"Or us," Kellerman said.

Lewis shrugged. "Or maybe they will, depends who they are. I'm still waitin' for Records to dig up Stella's case file, but what I got on Campbell is that he lived with a woman for a bunch'a years, an' that her last known whereabouts were here in the city. Could be he'll try an' contact her."

"So let's discuss who you want to check out whom," Pembleton said.

"Yeah," Lewis said. "Let's."

He had been thinking about how to divide the initial casework before the meeting, and now he told the other detectives what he'd decided, keeping his plan simple: he and Kellerman would pursue the existing leads on Campbell, while Pembleton and Bayliss tried to uncover information on Stella and run down his underworld contacts. At the same time, Howard, Munch, and Russert would start knocking on doors in the vicinity of the highway exit where Dubick's body was found, and also attempt to locate the car in which he'd been forced to drive the killers from Central Maryland, and which by now presumably had been ditched. This would involve checking traffic summonses and abandoned vehicle reports, as well as the somewhat delicate task of putting uniformed patrolmen throughout the city on the lookout for any vehicle fitting its description without cluing them in on the specific reason for the search.

That was pretty much it, except for hashing out some procedural details, and less than ten minutes later Lewis and Kellerman were standing out in the hallway watching Giardello disappear into his office, while Barnfather, Stanton, and Lambert tramped over to the elevators, and the rest of the detectives went drifting toward their desks in the squad room.

"Where you think we should start working our end of things?" Kellerman said, leaning back against the wall.

"Central Maryland," Lewis said.

Kellerman looked at him. "What the hell are you talking about?"

"The hospital those nuts escaped from," Lewis said.

"No *shit*," Kellerman said. "What I mean is, weren't you the guy making different plans a minute ago? The guy who told everybody we were going after Campbell's—"

"Look, man, I know what I told them," Lewis said. "But I wanna know how that gun got smuggled into the place. *And* I'd like to talk to the hospital staff, maybe some of Stella and Campbell's pals there. See what we can find out."

Kellerman was still looking at him as if he were speaking Swahili.

"Are you for *real*?" he said. "You heard Giardello in there: we have no authority to work this investigation outside the city—"

"I ain't arguin' that," Lewis said dismissively. "But we got the same right to take a drive upstate as any other citizens."

"Right," Kellerman said. "Just two day-trippers on an excursion to a local funny farm."

"Hey, I ain't twistin' nobody's arm," Lewis said. "You down with me on this or not?"

Kellerman took a deep breath and pushed himself off the wall, thinking it wouldn't be the least bit pleasant when they had to face the music on this one.

"Yeah," he said. "I'm down."

Lewis clapped him on the shoulders with both hands and gave him a playful little shake.

"One thing's for sure," he said.

"What's that?"

Lewis grinned.

"Be cheaper than the zoo," he said.

SIX

THEY WERE DRIVING out toward Central Maryland, the sky a clear, shimmering blue, sunshine and fresh air flowing through the car's open windows. Behind the steering wheel, Lewis was tapping his fingers to a song on the radio while Kellerman alternated between checking his map and admiring the budding, pollen-swollen greenery on either side of the road. Occasionally they would pass a cultivated field and the strong smell of organic fertilizer would come pouring in with the breeze.

"Weather's sure nice," Kellerman said, leaning back and turning his face into the sun.

Lewis glanced up at a thready strip of clouds.

"So far," he said.

"What do you mean?" Kellerman said. "The guy on the radio says we're gonna have blue skies all weekend."

"Guy on the radio been wrong before." Lewis shrugged. "Anyway, like you said, today's a piece of candy. You gotta admit takin' this ride wasn't such a bad idea."

"It isn't the ride I was worried about," Kellerman said.

"You worry too much," Lewis said. He bobbed his head to a percussive chop of rhythm guitar coming from the radio's speaker. "Ought to learn how to hang back and relax."

"I dunno," Kellerman said. "You get out in the country, it's easy to forget the whole world's going to hell."

Lewis gave him a quick sidelong glance.

"What's *wrong* with you?" he said.

"What I just said." Kellerman frowned. "Here's all this nature around us, and I'm not saying it ain't beautiful, but think about why we're here."

"*You* think about it," Lewis said, and turned the volume up high on the radio. "I'm too busy enjoyin' myself at the moment."

Kellerman made a face. "I hate when you do that."

"Do what?" Lewis said.

"Ask a question and then phase me out before I can answer," Kellerman said.

"Ain't phasin' out *anybody*. I was just groovin' on the sounds—"

"Listen, you asked what's bothering me, now gimme a chance to explain, will ya?" Kellerman said, and lowered the volume. "I mean, we're on our way to a nuthouse, looking for info on a psycho Mutt-and-Jeff act who've already killed *twice* since they escaped."

"Tell me something I don't know," Lewis said.

"What you *do* know oughtta be scary enough," Kellerman said. "You read Campbell's file. His idea of a good time is molesting kids and starting fires, and the creep's loose in a city of almost a million people. Right this *minute* he could be planning a holiday cookout we'll never forget."

"You want me to step on the gas, say the word," Lewis said.

Kellerman sighed. "It isn't just Stella and Campbell. You been listening to Munch the past couple days?"

"Hard to avoid it," Lewis said.

"All that stuff about germs and plagues and ninety percent of the human race dying off . . . Jesus, it makes my skin crawl," Kellerman said with a little shiver.

Lewis steered the Dodge along a gentle curve in the road. "What got me thinkin' was the part about that *Ebola* virus turnin' people's guts to grape jelly."

"Fucking horrible, isn't it?"

"I guess," Lewis said. "Tell you the truth, it gave me a moneymakin' idea."

"Hey, I'm *serious*."

"So am I," Lewis said.

"Really?"

"*Really*," Lewis said.

"How can you think of turning a profit from the end of mankind?" Kellerman said, wondering if this entrepreneurial brainstorm was going to be anything like Lewis's last one, which was to flood Memorial Park and turn it into a giant water sports arena.

"Space suits," Lewis said.

The signal on the radio started fading and he tried vainly to adjust the tuner, then gave up and switched to another station.

"You gonna send people into *space*?"

Lewis shook his head. "No, man. Ain't you ever seen *The Andromeda Strain*? Or that movie *Outbreak*, where Dustin Hoffman and Rene Russo play doctors—"

"Who *wouldn't* want to play doctor with her?" Kellerman said.

"That aside," Lewis said. "I'm talkin' about the orange plastic space suits government people wear when they're around some kinda biological threat . . ."

"Wait a minute." Kellerman said. "You mean like the ones they put on when ET got sick?"

"You *got* it," Lewis said, and snapped his fingers. "Now imagine if we put out an infomercial spellin' out the danger these germs present to the human race, and offerin' the space suits at a fair price. They'd come in all different sizes . . . y'know, newborn, toddlers, kiddie, adult, an' so on. We could even make 'em in custom colors." He paused a moment and looked over at Kellerman. "Do the arithmetic, man. Figurin' on your average family, that'd be five suits for every home in America."

Kellerman thought about it.

"I dunno," he said. "Those space suits must be pretty expensive."

"We can mass produce 'em so they're affordable," Lewis said. "Maybe one, two hundred bucks a pop."

"That's a whole lot more than a fire extinguisher or smoke alarm or something."

"An' a lot cheaper'n health insurance," Lewis said. "Don't sound like too much to me, not when you're buyin' safety for your loved ones. We ain't sellin' bathing suits, man. This is *plague* wear. Armageddon attire."

"Still can't see people shelling out that kind of dough," Kellerman said. "It'd be a hard sell."

"You kiddin'? With Munch as our company spokesman? Goin' on the tube plus maybe givin', like, seminars? These ads would run for months, an' just look at what he did to *your* head in *two days*."

"Well, I guess . . . ," Kellerman said.

"This product would catch on big," Lewis said. "Guaranteed."

Kellerman heard the rusty squawk of crows from somewhere off to the right, looked out his window, and saw a dark constellation of the birds spiral up from a grainfield and flap toward a distant silo.

"Armageddon attire," he thought aloud.

"Some concept, huh?"

Kellerman wasn't certain, although he *did* know he wanted to change the subject.

"Maybe you could start by getting one of those suits for Barbara," he remarked.

Lewis suddenly pulled a face. "What's *that* supposed to mean?"

Kellerman shrugged again. "Just that it'd solve your problem about the style of clothes she wears. Kind of hard to look provocative in a space suit."

Lewis was glowering at him.

"In fact, I'd say they're pretty neutral," Kellerman said. "*Unisex*."

Lewis said nothing.

"What d'you think?" Kellerman said, trying to conceal his amusement.

"I think this is what I get for openin' up to you," Lewis said. "I'da had any sense, would've kept my mouth *shut* . . ."

"Meldrick—"

". . . makin' a joke outta my marital difficulties . . ."

"Mel—"

". . . serves me right, musta been outta my *skull* to say anythin' . . ."

"*Mel*." Kellerman was waving his map between them with one hand and pointing out the left side of the windshield with the other. "The turnoff to the hospital's coming up."

"I see it," Lewis said. "Now, do me a favor, an' don't talk to me anymore till we get there."

Kellerman smiled faintly. "What happened to the guy who was telling me to hang back and relax?"

"Got sick an' died," Lewis said, and drove on in a silent huff.

SET FAR BACK from the gate at the bottom of the hill, Central Maryland's administration building was nested within clusters of birch and hickory trees that separated it from the outlying patient wards and rendered it almost invisible from the roadway leading up to it. One minute you were searching for it through the foliage, the next you were practically crashing your vehicle through its glass entry doors.

The security man at the gate had called ahead to announce the Baltimore detectives and then directed them to the building, where, after leaving their car in its semicircular drive, they were met in the front hall by a delegation of uniformed guards and dark-suited hospital officials, then escorted past the reception booth and down a long first-floor corridor to a door with an engraved brass plaque that said "Robert Blair, Ph.D." on the top line and "Director" beneath.

At her desk in the carpeted waiting room the receptionist sat typing on a computer. She was a young black woman wearing a simple gray dress and a purplish silk scarf around her neck. As Lewis and Kellerman approached, she stopped working and eyed them with starch impassivity over the top of the video display screen.

"The doctor is expecting you," she said, speaking with a faint West Indian accent.

She rose from her seat, opened the door to the inner office, and motioned them through.

As they entered the room, Blair stood behind his desk with his back toward his visitors, gazing out the wide bay window at the hospital grounds.

"I wish I could say it was a good morning," he said softly, turning toward the detectives. His hands were clasped over his middle. "But I don't suppose either of you gentlemen would be here if it were."

"I'm afraid that's true, sir," Lewis said, introducing Kellerman and himself.

Blair went over to the desk, motioning them toward a pair of leather chairs across from him. A tall, thin man with an undershot chin and thinning gray hair, he had on a tweed blazer over a check shirt, an olive necktie, and tan slacks. The puffiness under his eyes seemed a good indication he'd been losing sleep.

Lewis sat and glanced around the office, thinking that, top dog's office or not, it was pretty damn showy for an institution funded almost entirely with taxpayer dollars. Large and high-ceilinged, the room had a marble fireplace to the left of the door and a bookcase lined with leather-bound medical volumes to the right. The desk was made of some kind of antique wood, mahogany maybe, and there was an authentic-looking Frederic Remington bronze on top of it. The maroon Turkish rug in the center of the room had a stylized, angular floral-spray design. The walls were hung with equestrian prints: there were pictures of the fox hunt with riders in colorful garb, and of muscular thoroughbreds galloping along a nineteenth-century course, or being walked by their handlers, or roaming a meadow in placid solitude.

"So," Blair said, running his fingers along the edge of a brown folder on his desk, "has there been any progress toward finding the escapees, or am I being too optimistic at this early stage?"

"No such thing as an early stage when people been murdered," Lewis said. "The faster we can bag Stella and Campbell, the better."

Blair drew a breath.

"Of course," he said. "It's been a difficult time for me, and perhaps I'm not as clearheaded as I ought to be. What can I do for you?"

"Sir, we just have a few questions about what happened last night," Lewis said. He was rubbing his goatee. "Accordin' to the state police, Stella was usin' a .357 Magnum when he shot that other patient—"

"John McCulloch," Blair said. "The poor man was a model inmate. He'd been with us for twenty years and never once caused any trouble. A tragedy."

Kellerman let out a "Well . . ." before he could catch himself.

Blair glanced at him, his eyebrows raised. "Yes?"

Kellerman looked awkward.

"Maybe this has nothing to do with anything," he said hesitantly, "but I have to wonder how nice a guy he could've been. This is a hospital for the criminally insane."

"The key word being 'hospital,'" Blair said with a hint of indignation. "This is not a correctional institution. The men who are sent to us are given treatment, as opposed to the punishment they would receive in prison, and for valid reasons—they either have been judged to be without responsibility for their offenses, or diagnosed as being in need of specialized care by trained psychologists. In Mr. McCulloch's case the former applied, and his mental health had improved tremendously over the long course of his therapy."

"Uh, gettin' back to the gun," Lewis said. "One thing

I been wonderin' is how it slipped past hospital security."

Blair sighed heavily.

"That's one of the more troublesome questions hanging over this incident," he said. "I've been trying to learn what I can, but right now it's still a mystery."

"Maybe it'd help if you tell us what your security procedures are," Lewis said.

Blair sighed again, as if he felt reviewing the subject would be a needless and distressful chore.

"Our chief of security would have to give you the finer details," he said. "However, I can tell you that all visitors to our wards are subjected to bodily searches and must pass through a metal screening system. Any bags or containers they carry with them—including packages of food and the like—are also examined by guards."

"Do you have video surveillance equipment? Motion sensors?" Kellerman asked.

"Unfortunately the answer is no to both," Blair said. "We've been planning to install cameras for some time, but cutbacks in government funding have forced several postponements on us. It's a familiar story, I'm afraid."

"Anything else?" Lewis said, thinking that from the looks of things in his office, Blair hadn't had to deal with his salary being adversely affected by any budget cuts— surprise, surprise. He figured he'd probably have bags under his eyes too if he had to worry about losing such a cushy setup.

". . . can't stress often enough that this isn't a correctional facility," Blair was saying. "The days when mental patients were restrained in iron cages ended with the last century, thank heaven."

"We ain't here to criticize," Lewis said. "Just tryin' to get a clear picture of how the escape could have happened."

Blair released dismayed sigh number three.

"I understand," he said after a moment. "And you'll have to forgive my defensiveness. Granted, our security procedures aren't all that high-tech, and there's no doubt room for improvement, but up until last night they always worked."

Lewis nodded and jotted something down in his pad.

"Dr. Blair, before we change the subject, does your staff have to go through the security checks?" he asked.

Blair looked at him. "Well . . ."

"Yes, sir?"

"There are rules against hospital personnel bringing anything that could be remotely defined as a weapon to work with them, and I assure you they are strictly enforced. A female attendant caught with a knitting needle would be in serious trouble. Even the guards carry collapsible batons instead of guns."

"Sir," Lewis said, clearing his throat, "is that a yes or a no to my question?"

Blair straightened his shoulders.

"At Central Maryland we try to create an atmosphere of trust between administrators and workers," he said. "As such staff members are only randomly screened."

Lewis's gaze brushed Kellerman's, signaling that he wanted him to carry the interview for a while; he knew from experience that even people who'd never committed an offense more serious than a parking violation withheld information when being questioned by cops, and that the tag-team routine kept them from getting too comfortable with their evasions.

"In other words a weapon could have been smuggled in," Kellerman said, taking Lewis's pass and running with it.

"I suppose it's theoretically possible," Blair said.

"Well, the gun had to have gotten into this place somehow," Kellerman said. He paused a second, thinking. "How about background checks on employees? What's your routine for that sort of thing?"

"In that regard I don't believe we're different from any other professional organization . . . if anything our standards are higher than many. Our physicians and therapists all have impeccable academic credentials and come largely through referral."

"How about orderlies, maintenance crews, and so on?"

"We require applicants to give us their work histories extending back over a five-year period. Then we contact their previous employers for an evaluation."

"And the security personnel?"

A pause.

"Well . . ." Blair frowned. "To be honest, we don't examine their backgrounds as carefully."

Kellerman looked at him.

"Just to make sure I'm not misunderstanding you," he said, "we *are* talking about your guards now, right?"

Blair nodded.

"The people who watch over your inmates," Kellerman said. "Who stand between them and the public."

Blair nodded.

"Can you explain *why* they're the exception?" Kellerman said.

"Quite easily," Blair said. "You see, they're contracted from an outside service . . . and again, this is standard operating procedure for the majority of state hospitals. We have over six hundred full-time health care workers at Central Maryland. Our personnel office has its hands full keeping track of them without having to be concerned with an additional group of perhaps a hundred security guards, so we leave that to a licensed security firm. How they conduct their checks is up to them, but they presumably do a thorough job."

"Can you give me the name of the outfit you deal with?"

"I believe it's called Safeway Protection," Blair said. "My receptionist can get you their address and phone number, if you'd like."

"I'd appreciate it," Kellerman said.

Another short pause.

"Uh, Dr. Blair, while we're here together, I'm wondering if there's anything you could tell us about Stella and Campbell?" Lewis said.

"Such as?"

"I don't know." Lewis shrugged a little. "Like how

they got along with other patients, or if there mighta been certain staffers they talked to more than others . . . whatever you feel's important."

Blair tapped the file folders on his desk.

"I can assure you there were no red flags that could have shown they were planning an escape," he said. "As it happens, though, I was reviewing their case histories just before you arrived and did note some . . . uh . . . interesting particulars."

The detectives waited.

"Both men have been close to ideal patients," Blair said. "Stella had a somewhat longer than average period of adjustment, which is to say there were some behavioral problems associated with his transition from a prison environment, but these leveled off within six months. Campbell, on the other hand, was very responsive to our program from day one." A sorrowful expression lowered over his face. "He came to us in a state of deep psychosis, and had seemed to be making tremendous progress."

"That it?" Lewis asked.

Blair nodded.

Kellerman had been absently eyeing the Remington statuette on the desk.

"No offense intended, Doctor, but the situation being what it is, maybe it'd be helpful if you could focus on information that's more relevant to our search."

"I see," Blair said. He reared back in his chair. "Might I presume the type of medication the patients were taking to be of interest?"

Lewis looked sideways at Kellerman. *My turn to run with the ball.* "Seems like the kinda thing we oughtta know," he said.

"My greatest concern in this area would be with Mr. Campbell, as Mr. Stella required minimal drug treatment—irregular doses of Valium or Xanax to relieve nervousness or tension, and for occasional insomnia. That's about it."

"An' Campbell?"

Blair opened the file on his desk and leafed through the papers inside it.

"Our records indicate Mr. Campbell was being given maintenance dosages of haloperidol and lithium. The latter to treat his depression, the former to control symptoms of his psychotic condition."

Lewis stared at him.

"Not what you'd call an over-the-counter remedy."

Blair smiled frostily.

"No," he said. "Not at all."

"How's it gonna be when Campbell ain't gettin' these drugs?"

"I'll try to put it as plainly as I can," Blair said, sounding as if he thought he was talking to a couple of none too bright children. "The term we use for neurological side-effects associated with the use of antipsychotic compounds is *dyskinesia*. A distinction is made between tardive dyskinesia, which develops in patients *during* a prolonged period of treatment, and withdrawal-emergent dyskinesia, which patients may experience *after* use of the drug is discontinued."

"So you're sayin' Campbell's lookin' at cold turkey," Lewis said.

"Yes," Blair went on. "And it may be significant that he was already showing moderate signs of TD before the escape. Typically, patients who experience negative symptoms while taking the drug are prone toward more severe, uh, abnormalities if usage is interrupted."

"What you mean by 'abnormalities?'"

"The early symptoms would be similar to those he displayed during treatment with the drug—uncontrolled twitching movements of the face and body, rapid heartbeat, increased sweating. A tendency toward a shuffling walk. In recent months Mr. Campbell also had been having some difficulty with his speech, which is fairly typical."

Lewis was thinking this sounded like a perfect example of the cure being worse than the disease, and a glance at Kellerman's face indicated he shared his reaction.

"How bad's it gonna get?" Lewis asked.

"Most troubling to me is the potential for increased anxiety and paranoia," Blair said. "On rare instances patients experience what might be delicately called inappropriate physical arousal . . . an obvious concern given Mr. Campbell's past sexual offenses."

Nobody spoke for a long moment.

"Seems to me," Lewis said finally, running a hand over his chin, "we could be in for a real shitstorm."

"Yes," Blair said in a low, hesitant voice. "We could be."

More silence.

"Dr. Blair," Kellerman said, "we'd like to take a look around Stella and Campbell's ward, maybe talk to some of the other patients. Especially the ones who witnessed the break."

Blair shook his head. "I don't know, we've already had the state authorities in there. Your presence in D-ward could be highly stressful to the patients . . ."

"We'll be quick," Lewis said. "An' I promise that if you do us this favor, we won't be the ones to send reporters in your direction."

"I expect they'll find me in any event," Blair said heavily, then took a deep breath and gave Lewis a relenting nod. "All right, I can let you into the ward for half an hour. Not an instant longer."

"Then I guess that'll have to be long enough " Lewis said, motioning to Kellerman.

The detectives rose from their chairs, eager to get on their way.

FROM WHERE HE stood beside the corner pay phone, Stella could see the long row of stores across the street and watch the traffic moving beneath the stoplights at the intersection—not a bad lookout, not bad at all, the only problem with it being that it simultaneously left *him* in plain view of the people walking past those stores and sitting inside those cars, trucks, and buses.

Which was the main reason he wished Mutter would get the hell away from the phone.

"Another quarter," Campbell said to him, reaching his open hand out of the booth.

"You musta thrown two bucks down the slot already," Stella protested. "We're running' low on change, Mutter."

Campbell looked at him, his eyes staring and expressionless. Then suddenly the left side of his face twitched and his mouth puckered up and his tongue slid in and out between his lips, pink and twisting and wormlike.

"Another quarter," he grunted.

The tongue darting between his lips.

In and out.

Stella looked at him with growing concern, thinking it was damn spooky the way his face would be like a zombie mask one second and then start quivering like a fish on a hot grill the next. Maybe he'd made a mistake sticking himself with Campbell. Maybe it was high time for him to seriously consider going it on his own.

First, though, he wanted the two of them to make a pit stop in the spic grocery across the street . . . which was the second reason he was itchy for Campbell to quit screwing around with the telephone. So far he'd seen very few customers walk through the door, but it was still early in the day, and he figured business would be picking up as it got closer to noon. He did not want to wait until the place was crowded with people.

He reached into his pants pocket, took a quarter from the small handful of coins he pulled out, and dropped it into Campbell's waiting palm.

"One last time, Mutter, an' I mean it," he said. "We got things to do. Goin' shopping, remember?"

For a moment Campbell just stared foggily at him from inside the telephone booth. Then he nodded, turned back to the phone, deposited his quarter, and began punching a number into the keypad.

It was the same number he had already tried half a dozen times, the only number in the world he knew or cared to know.

In all the world . . .

All of it . . .

The only one.

". . . KILLED MY FUCKIN' chess partner is what they did, shot Mac dead right here in this room, you can still see his blood on the fuckin' floor, my *chess* partner, those fuckin' *maricónes* . . ."

Lewis pulled at his beard, listening to Ernesto Gonzalez go on and on about something Lewis already knew, and thinking he had maybe twenty minutes to dig up something he *didn't* know before Blair had him kicked out of D-ward.

Well, he thought, maybe Kellerman was doing better at his end. Because they'd been crunched for time, the detectives had opted to split up the interviews rather than conduct them as a team, with Lewis questioning the inmates who'd been in the rec room at the time of the shooting, and Kellerman talking to those who hadn't.

Gonzalez gesticulated at a smeary pink stain extending across the floor from the legs of the table where he was sitting to the wall several feet away.

"That's Mac's blood, see, right there, his blood—he didn't do nothin' to those two pricks, just wanted 'em to be cool so we could finish our game, my fuckin' chess partner, they put him down for *nothin* . . ."

"Uh, Mr. Gonzalez—"

"It's Ernesto, man. Ain't gotta be formal."

"Ernesto," Lewis said. "I was hoping you an' your friend might be able to help me with a couple things—"

"Just 'cause the devils got us both in shackles don't mean we friends," the other patient at the table said. "An unbeliever is he, guilty of sin."

Uh-huh, right on, whatever you say, Lewis thought, looking over at him. A black man in a knitted white skullcap named Quasim, he was the only living witness besides Gonzalez to the McCulloch shooting, as well as the events leading up to Ed Dubick's abduction. That he was also a raving lunatic hardly came as a stunner.

"If we could just talk about last night . . ."

"That's when they killed Mac, fucking blew him away," Gonzalez said. "We was sittin' right here, playin' chess—"

"Think I got that part straight," Lewis said. "What I was wonderin', though, is if either of you remember anything Campbell or Stella said to the guard. Or anything he mighta said to *them*."

"Dubick was talkin' some shit about candy bars," Gonzalez said. "I remember it got Mac buggin' out—"

"That was *before* Stella come in," Quasim said. "After was when they had words 'bout Stella bringin' coffee from the cafeteria."

"There a problem with that?" Lewis asked.

"Be 'gainst whitey's rules to carry hot drinks in the halls," Quasim said. "Cursed be the makers of the pit, an' you who follow them shall share in their doom."

Lewis sighed. "So Dubick told him to get rid of the coffee, that it?"

Gonzales snorted laughter, and Lewis thought he even saw a trace of amusement on Quasim's clenched, hostile features.

"Dubick never tell Stella to do *shit*," Quasim said.

"Stella *or* Mutter," Gonzalez said. "Dubick didn't say 'boo' to them, man."

"Not since Mutter tell him 'bout his car lot," Quasim said.

"*Used* car lot," Gonzales said.

"Hold on a second," Lewis said. "Campbell *owned* this business?"

"He *say* he did anyway," Quasim said.

"On the outside, before he got sent here," Gonzales said. "He was always talkin' about it."

"'Fore the meds got t'him," Quasim said.

"You take the meds, after a while you can't hardly talk 'bout *nothin'* no more," Gonzales said.

"Meds be poison," Quasim said. "White devils put the blood of swine in it, make your tongue rot in your mouth—"

"What would Mutter tell Dubick about the car lot?"

"Mostly he'd be flappin' about how much money he made," Gonzales said.

"Temptin' Dubick with the coin of deception."

Lewis looked at them.

"You tellin' me Campbell offered him bribes?"

"Plenty times," Gonzalez said.

"More'n I can count," Quasim said.

"Him an' the rest'a the screws," Gonzales said.

"Every day," Quasim said. "Dubick the only one who believe Campbell got what he say he have."

"Either of you know what the money was for?"

Gonzalez shrugged. "Smokes, liquor, herb . . ."

"Few extra minutes in the exercise yard . . ."

"Extra desserts from the cafeteria . . ."

"Anythin' they wanted."

"Anythin' and everythin' "

"For Stella an' Campbell, Dubick bc the *Everythin' Man*."

"Sounds like he also had to be pretty dumb if Campbell couldn't pay up."

"Who tell you he couldn't?" Quasim said.

"I thought you just did," Lewis said.

"Said he didn't have all he claim," Quasim said. "That don't mean he had *nothin'*."

"Got cash from his woman," Gonzalez said.

"Black woman," Quasim said, frowning with disapproval.

"Sweet-looking babe," Gonzalez said. "Used to visit him here, stopped comin' maybe a year or two back. But he'd still get mail from her, you know. He told us they was married."

"Wasn't no *wife*," Quasim said.

"Well, that's what he called her."

"Don't care what that white man say, sister live with

91

him in sin and indecency, sister his *whore in chains*," Quasim said.

"This woman's name Jolanda?" Lewis asked.

"You got it," Gonzalez said.

"Sister love a thing that evil for her, hell be her resting place," Quasim said.

Lewis supposed that if Jolanda Martin had been sending Campbell money, and Campbell had been using that money to buy special privileges from Dubick, then the question of how the Magnum had gotten into D-ward became easy enough to answer.

"If Stella and Campbell were so tight with Dubick, why'd they pull a gun on him?" he asked, figuring a little confirmation couldn't hurt.

Gonzalez and Quasim swapped guarded looks.

"What we told you 'bout Dubick keepin' his hand out ain't no big secret," Gonzales said. "Could've come from anybody's mouth."

"No way he gonna find out we been talkin' 'less you spread the news," Quasim said.

"That happen, we gonna swear it ain't true."

Lewis all at once realized they had no idea the guard had been murdered, and were figuring he might eventually show up at the hospital and make trouble for them. He weighed the benefits of telling them they didn't have to worry about it, and decided it was probably best not to divulge anything they didn't need to know—as long as they kept talking.

"I hear you," he said. "I mean, there's friendly and there's friendly, huh? Dubick has a sideline sellin' Twinkies and cigarettes, the white coats figure this is a quiet ward an' look the other way. Even if somebody catches on and he's busted, what's the worst that can happen? Maybe he loses his job, maybe not, it's worth takin' a chance. But helpin' to boost a couple guys outta here, that'd give him a ton of worries."

Gonzalez nodded.

"Guess he'd want to make sure he wouldn't go down if *they* did," Lewis said.

"Maybe put on a show for the rest of us," Gonzales said. "Pretend he doin' something he don't wanna do."

"Think we fools," Quasim said.

"Biggest fool round *this* place'd be somebody who believe Campbell got enough green stashed away to score a ticket out," Gonzalez said.

"Somebody like Dubick," Lewis said.

"We ain't gonna say you wrong," Gonzalez said.

"Used car shop my *ass*," Quasim said.

Lewis was thinking it was no wonder Campbell and Stella iced the security guard; they had made him a bargain they never intended to keep, and could have had only one thing in mind for him all along.

He glanced at his watch. Ten minutes and counting to Blair's deadline, and he still wanted to talk to some of Dubick's former coworkers.

"You guys been a real help," he said, moving toward the door. "Thanks."

"Them sons of bitches kill Mac, my fucking chess partner," Gonzalez said. "You wanna thank me, burn 'em for it."

"These are the inmates of the fire, and in it they shall abide," Quasim said.

"Be okay with me," Lewis said.

AT ELEVEN-THIRTY THAT morning, Pembleton and Bayliss arrived at the remodeled Federal Hill rowhouse that was home to Harold R. Reamis, a criminal defense attorney whom Baltimore cops and prosecutors called Harry the Reamer mainly because the nickname had a certain comical and sleazy ring, like it might belong to the master of ceremonies at a nude beauty pageant or porn industry convention . . . and because it was hard to resist the temptation to heap scorn and ridicule upon a man whose legal shenanigans had resulted in an almost continuous string of acquittals and successful plea bargains for his clients, most of whom were notorious racketeers considered by law enforcement people and solid citizens alike to be among the scum of the earth.

Now the detectives climbed the building's front stoop, pushed Reamis's buzzer, and waited. This was not a social visit. An employee of the BPD did not pay Reamis a social call unless maybe he was on the take and wanted to personally thank him for paying off his kid's college tuition or buying the wife a new Lexus. No, the reason they were here was that court files showed Harry the Reamer to have represented Frank Stella through his entire career as a hired assassin for the LoCicero mob, dealing down several first-degree murder indictments to lesser manslaughter raps, getting others dismissed on technicalities, and, after having his most recent defense of the button trashed by prosecutors—a rare occurrence to say the least—rebounding with the claim of insanity which got Stella transferred from the Death House to the far more lenient auspices of the mental health care system.

Pembleton shuffled impatiently by the door, wondering if he'd luck out and catch Reamis at home, looking down at the gleaming white marble under his shoes. In poor minority neighborhoods like Greenmount and Franklin the rowhouse stoops were blackened with age and neglect, and sometimes huge chunks of the stairs crumbled away, making them hazardous to climb. What tenants usually did was cover the cracks and gouges with pieces of wood or flattened cardboard boxes, marking the spots to be avoided as they stepped up to the entrance. Calls to their landlords for repairs were generally ignored. Complaints to the housing authority were more often than not swallowed by bureaucratic quicksand. Once in a while somebody would set foot on one of these disintegrating steps and stumble despite the makeshift wood and cardboard coverings. On average the injuries they sustained were minor, although there were many instances of people winding up in the emergency room with concussions or sprains or fractured bones, and occasional deaths resulting from a fall off the steps were not unknown—mostly in cases where the accident victims were either very old or very young. But stories about people falling off broken stoops hardly made for sensational headlines. In neighborhoods plagued by gangs and drugs and prostitution these incidents were just bitter drops in the bucket. There were worse problems to think about.

Still, Pembleton was often struck by odd thoughts and observations. He noticed things. Big things, small things, all sorts of stuff, and very often he found that the smallest details could give the deepest insights. Right now, for instance, he found himself thinking that here in this fashionable neighborhood he could look up and down the block at rowhouse after rowhouse after rowhouse without seeing a single dirty or crumbled stoop. Which led him to the wider observation that here in this fashionable neighborhood a venal shyster like Harry the Reamer could live like a modern aristocrat, or perhaps a lordly vampire feeding on the blood of the common folk, elevated above the urban despair he helped perpetuate by making sure the criminals who flooded the streets with crack and heroin remained free to prosper.

That was how Pembleton's mind worked, taking in random bits of information, churning them around until they were processed, and then connecting them with broad intuitive and mental leaps. It was one of the traits that gave him the most impressive record of closed cases in the department. It was also the reason for the insomnia that kept him tossing in bed most nights. But he'd learned to live with that, and there was always coffee to keep him going during the day. Lots and lots of black coffee . . .

He was about to ring the bell a second time when a man's voice blared from the intercom above the nameplate.

"Yes?"

"Mr. Reamis?"

"Yes, who is it?"

"Baltimore City Homicide," Pembleton said. "We—"

"I'll be in my office Tuesday morning," Reamis said. And if we'd wanted to wait until then, we wouldn't have gone to the trouble of looking up your home address, Pembleton thought. They'd been surprised to find it in the telephone directory right above his professional listing, figuring a guy with his money and notoriety would want to keep his name out of the book—but you never knew with people.

"As I was about to say, we're sorry to bother you at home on the weekend, but this is an urgent matter—"

"All right," Reamis said. "Come up one flight, I'll be with you in a minute."

The buzzer sounded.

The detectives opened the door, went through the entry hall to a carpeted stairwell, climbed to the second-floor landing, and waited there in front of a heavy inner door with arching carved-wood panels. After a short while the door swung halfway inward and Reamis's face appeared in the opening.

"Let's see some identification," he said.

Pembleton flashed his tin and introduced himself.

Reamis nodded, but didn't budge from the doorway. A thin man of about fifty with brown eyes and a full, neatly trimmed salt-and-pepper beard, he was wearing a wine-colored bathrobe of some silky material and leather slippers.

"What's so important it couldn't wait? If this is about one of my cases—"

"Mr. Reamis, we're investigating a murder."

His eyes suddenly showed intense concern. Pembleton had seen that look hundreds of times before, and recognized it for what it was—he was running down a mental list of the people who were closest to him, rapidly checking off the names of those whose whereabouts he knew or thought he knew, narrowing in on the ones he hadn't heard from lately, or the ones whose lifestyles placed them among the likely candidates for violent death. Even slime like Reamis had family and friends.

"What? My god, who—"

"We don't believe the victim's anyone you know," Pembleton said, and watched relief settle over Reamis's features. "Look, if you'd care to let us in, we'll gladly explain."

Reamis stood looking out at them another moment, then sighed resignedly, opened the door the rest of the way, and motioned them inside.

He ushered the detectives through a mirrored foyer that smelled faintly of cigars and cologne and into a living room enveloped in green from top to bottom. There was an enormous green sofa breaching the surface of a league-deep sea of green carpeting, a flanking arrangement of green wing recliners and ottomans covered with green seat cushions, lavish green window draperies, some kind of green heavy-pile fabric covering the walls and ceiling. Recessed somewhere in the swaddling greenness overhead, the diffuse lighting fell upon the few adornments in the room to depart from the abiding color scheme: a round chrome coffee table, an ornately framed portrait of some aristocratic lady from a bygone era, and a wall-mounted collection of gleaming exotic daggers.

Bayliss looked around with fascination, thinking the surroundings made him feel like he'd entered an underwater cove, or maybe Captain Nemo's lair. But what the hell, who was he to judge anybody else's decorative taste, especially after his unforgettable fling with Emma Zoole, the coroner's sketch artist who had slept in a coffin—albeit a very spacious and softly upholstered coffin, as Bayliss had discovered while enjoying the hottest sex of his life under its upraised lid.

"It's mohair," Reamis said.

"Huh?"

"The wall covering," Reamis said with showy pride. "One hundred percent mohair."

"Oh."

Bayliss hoped he hadn't appeared overimpressed.

"That's, um, a natural fur, isn't it?" he asked, fumbling for a response.

"*Wool*," Reamis said. "Well, actually, that's what the

fabric used to be made of. The wool of mountain goats. I think they use cotton nowadays."

"Oh," Bayliss said. "If you don't mind my asking, do you use the Big Green Machine to clean it?"

"You'd have to ask my maid," Reamis said, unamused. He snapped his head around to Pembleton. "I've heard of you, Detective. You've got quite a spectacular reputation."

Pembleton shrugged, his expression flat.

"You don't have a very positive view of defense attorneys, do you?"

Pembleton shrugged again. "I've got other things to worry about."

"Yes, I'm sure you do," Reamis said tightly. "So how about telling me why you're here."

"There was a breakout at the Central Maryland Psychiatric Hospital," Pembleton said. "A patient and a guard were killed. One of the escapees was Frank Stella."

Reamis's eyes widened.

"When did this happen?" he asked.

"About seven o'clock last night," Pembleton said.

"My God," Reamis said,

"We're trying to get some background information on Stella, besides what's in the case files," Pembleton said, coming straight to the point. "Find out who he might try to contact, where he'd go to hide out, that sort of thing."

Reamis shook his head, picking at his beard.

"I can't believe I didn't hear anything about it on the news . . ."

"Mr. Reamis, whatever you can tell us would be appreciated," Pembleton said.

Reamis sighed heavily. "Detective, this comes as quite a shock. But much as I'd like to help, I'm bound by attorney-client privilege—"

"I know all that," Pembleton said. "And I don't expect you to break any legal confidences."

"Well, then, I don't see how I can—"

"I'll try to be very specific," Pembleton said, and took

out his pad. "Do you know whether Stella has any family members who live in the Baltimore area?"

"I've no idea," Reamis said.

"Any friends or acquaintances?"

Reamis shook his head.

"Are you certain you can't think of anyone?"

Pembleton stared at him over his pad.

"Sir, being that you represented him in a number of murder trials, I'm assuming you *do* know your client was a paid gun for the LoCicero family."

"Is that comment meant to be sarcastic, Detective?"

"Take it any way you want," Pembleton said. "Just don't play games with me."

Reamis's features darkened with resentment and indignation.

"Detective Pembleton, I was Stella's lawyer. I didn't make his personal affairs my business. "

"Just like you don't give a damn that he's a cold-blooded killer," Bayliss said.

Reamis looked at him. "He's been through the court system, and been punished for the offenses of which he's been convicted," he said. "How would you prefer to have it? Should we eliminate due process and the right to a defense?"

"Spare me," Bayliss said. "I heard it all during the Trial of the Century."

Silence.

Pembleton was about to ask another question when he heard a door click open at the end of a short hallway leading off to his right. The detectives both looked down the hall, saw a breathtakingly gorgeous young woman standing there in the door frame, her blond hair sweeping over her shoulders in a loose tussle, no makeup on her face, wearing nothing except a clingy white robe that bunched around her waist under an indifferently tied sash, and fell maybe an acre short of mid-thigh.

She came a little way out into the hall, bare feet whispering on the carpet, the hem of the robe gliding over the upper reaches of her long, slender legs.

"Is anything wrong?" she asked Reamis.

"No, no, it's okay," he said.

She seemed unconvinced.

"You sure there isn't—"

"Please, Teheran," he said insistently. "I'll be finished talking with these gentlemen in a minute."

She studied the visitors another moment, then shrugged, turned back into the room from which she'd appeared, and shut the door behind her.

"Teheran?" Bayliss said.

"Like the capital city of Iran," Reamis said, grinning devilishly. "Claims her mother heard it on the news when she was expecting—this was during the hostage crisis— and thought it would make a pretty name. It does have a fascinating ring, don't you think?"

Bayliss shrugged. "I suppose . . ."

"Being with her always makes me feel vaguely traitorous," Reamis said with a wink. "And as an Orthodox Jew, I can only *imagine* what the members of my synagogue would think if I introduced her to them. Probably expect her to plant a bomb among the Torahs."

Pembleton was watching Reamis's face. In spite of all his smiling and winking he seemed ill at ease. Jumpy. Of course having a couple of murder cops knock on the door would unsettle almost anybody, even someone who was used to dealing with them in courtroom showdowns . . . and furthermore they *had* apparently intruded on his holiday festivities.

On the other hand, though, he might have something to hide.

"Mr. Reamis, let's try and wrap this up," Pembleton said. "You know without my telling you that Stella's a dangerous man. You know what he's done in the past and is capable of doing if he remains free." He paused. "We want to stop him from harming innocent people. If you can think of where he might be headed, then calling us about it would be in everyone's best interest."

"Yes, absolutely," Reamis nodded. "Anything else?"

Pembleton looked at him, not really expecting him to

contact the police under any circumstances. All Reamis's expression said was *Go away*.

He decided to add a bit more persuasiveness to his approach before leaving.

"Actually, there *is* one thing," he said. "Can you remember when the Iranian hostage crisis took place?"

Reamis looked at him.

"Not exactly," he said, catching the question out of left field. "Must've been the mid-seventies."

Pembleton shook his head.

"Wrong," he said. "It's what cost Carter his reelection, remember? And the hostages were freed about when Reagan took office, which was 1981. Figuring it out's easy if you count how many presidential elections we've had since."

Reamis wet his lips but didn't say anything. He didn't have to; it was clear the point had registered with him. Pembleton wondered if he really hadn't done the math himself, or had thought a couple of detectives on the city payroll too stupid to do it, or had just made a careless slip of the tongue.

"Either your friend has been cooking up stories about how she got her name, or she's a very mature-looking sixteen-year-old," Pembleton said, nodding toward the door at the end of the little hall. "Could mean trouble for you if it's the second possibility."

Reamis licked his lips again.

"We've talked long enough," he said. No winks or smiles this time, he had dropped even the facade of agreeability. "I'd like you to leave."

"Somehow that doesn't surprise me," Pembleton said. "Please let us know if anything comes to you about Stella, though. As I mentioned a second ago, it'd be best for everybody's sake."

He looked at Reamis a moment longer, then closed his pad and nodded to Bayliss.

The detectives turned back into the foyer and let themselves out the door.

IT WAS THE same every spring; after the long lull that began with the first of the year—well, you did have Valentine's Day in February, thank heaven for *that* midwinter boost—Cupid must've been a florist before he passed through the pearly gates and got his wings— business suddenly cranked into high gear and kept going that way for the rest of the season. There were Easter and Passover in April, Mother's Day in May, weddings, engagement parties, and graduations galore through the end of June. By the time the summer doldrums hit, she was ready for a break. Of course boredom would set in after about a month, with the usual August belt-tightening and September's back-to-school shopping expenses add- ing immeasurably to her seasonal discontent. By the time the kids were back at school, she could hardly wait for Thanksgiving and the rest of the holidays to roll around again.

And so it goes, Jolanda Martin thought, carefully lifting a dried rose off the pile on her dining room table.

She had closed the shop today because her baby-sitter had been heading out of town for the holiday weekend, going hiking near Catoctin Mountain with her boy- friend . . . or was it canoeing? Well, Debbie had planned some sort of outdoor activity besides making out under the starry sky, that was for sure, and she'd asked for the day off, and Jolanda had figured she deserved it. Any- way, she liked being able to spend some extra time with Andrew and Vibeca. About an hour ago she'd brought them to visit their friends down the block so they all could watch Saturday morning cartoons together, and a little later on she'd be playing den mother to the whole gang and taking them to the National Aquarium.

Meanwhile, though, she had the apartment to herself, which gave her a chance to work on her dried arrange- ments. She desperately needed to have a few completed by Monday, and it was sometimes easier to put them together at home, where she wasn't constantly being distracted by customers and delivery people. This Mother's

Day had been her best since she opened the shop three years ago; she'd sold a ton of fresh flowers, made a handsome profit on the Mylar balloon bouquets she had recently started carrying, and gotten cleaned out of the dried stuff, which was proving to be a hot item thanks to the word-of-mouth reputation she'd gained around the city—an amazing thing, considering she'd only started doing the arrangements so she wouldn't have to waste her unsold flowers by tossing them once they got a little limp.

Jolanda looked at the empty basket in front of her now, still holding the stem she'd taken off the pile, visualizing the finished arrangement even before she set the first flower into place. This one would be mainly composed of yellow and orange roses, since she had plenty of them on hand, and since their colors would be nicely complemented by the tiny yellow sunflowers she'd brought last night from the shop.

Having already cut a Styrofoam base to fit inside the basket and concealed it with a layer of Spanish moss, Jolanda carefully pushed the bottom of the rose stem into the basket. The roses were the most fragile flowers she was using and she would nest them at the center, where they were less apt to be broken, interspersing them with the sunflowers, bits of eucalyptus leaves, and small clusters of yarrow that had been sprayed apple-green. She would add lavender sprays of statice closer to the outside of the basket.

She worked quickly but carefully, her long, slender fingers straightening, adjusting, taking more stems from the loose bunches on the table, sorting out the ones that didn't seem right because of their size, shape, or color. Though you had to be especially delicate handling the dried flowers, composing arrangements with them was perhaps the most satisfying part of her work, strongly reflecting her personal taste, allowing her much greater freedom to experiment than was possible with fresh flowers. When customers came into the shop for the latter, they often knew exactly what they wanted—or thought they did—and Jolanda always figured it was better to go with their preferences than have some disappointed bride complain that Jolanda had ruined her wedding by not throwing in enough pink, or going too light on this or that favorite flower. But she didn't have to worry about dried flowers rotting off the stem if they didn't sell right away; they could sit on the shelf indefinitely, prettying up the store until they caught some browser's eye. Lately they'd been catching quite a *few* eyes, something she found both financially and creatively rewarding—so much so, in fact, that she was contemplating hiring an assistant. She'd had her accountant go over her books to see whether she could afford an employee and he'd told her there didn't seem to be any problem, especially if she waited another thirty days, which was when the small business loan she'd taken out to finance her purchase of the shop would finally be payed off in full.

She reached for her scissors, trimmed a spindly cluster of statice, decided she still didn't like the looks of it, and tossed it into the trash can at her feet. With an assistant, someone who could take care of the fresh stuff and allow her to concentrate exclusively on the dried merchandise, she might even be able to venture into mail order . . . A printed catalogue was like having thousands of display windows nationwide, yet you risked less capital than if you opened just one new location, because you could base your expansion on orders that had already been received.

Big ambitions, she thought with a meditative little smile. Very big for a girl from Lafayette Avenue. Sometimes it was hard to think of herself as the owner of a thriving business, a prospective *employer* . . . hard to believe that six years ago, when old Mr. Greenfield had hired her as a part-time cashier in his flower shop—the shop she would buy from him upon his eventual retirement—she had been without any work skills, moving from one public women's shelter to another, in danger of losing her children to the state.

Hard to believe how few bright spots there had been in her life before that, how little respect she'd had for herself, and how bleak her outlook on the future had been.

There were still many nights when she'd lie awake for hours, her mind wandering back through the dark corridors of her past; nights tinged with memories of the projects and the friends she'd grown up with, slum children who'd been badly prepared for dealing with a world that was less generous with its successes, and more unsparing in its disappointments, than the comfortable white men who made contracts with America and gave their ultraconservative opinions on TV could ever imagine. Sometimes their faces would seem to flash through the darkness of her bedroom—girlfriends, guys she'd dated or hung out with, even some kids who'd been outside her circle of close friends, kids whose names she'd forgotten or never known—and she would wonder whatever happened to the great many who'd dropped out of sight over the years, wonder if they were in prison, or had died of drug overdoses, or in street fights that got out of hand, or in the drive-by shootings that struck down people in the old neighborhood like random lightning.

And sometimes when she thought about those kids, and about the steep price people often paid for their shortcomings, Jolanda would also recall something she'd heard from yet another television personality who'd had all the answers, a famous New Age guru who was doing publicity for a book she had written, making appearances on the talk shows and telling viewers that their ancestors were angels who had been cast from the stars after rebelling against the Almighty. Sitting there with Oprah and Ricki and their appreciative studio audiences, the New Age guru had explained that if everyone got together and wore white and prayed for world peace and maybe did some kind of dance at a certain time on a certain day it would be a sign to those on high that we were ready to have the gates of heaven open to us again, it would be like walking up to heaven's door and shouting, *Please, we've done our penance, forgive us, restore us to grace.*

Jolanda would remember the woman saying this, and would think that maybe she was right, and they *had* been angels of sorts, lost angels who might have made it to paradise if somebody had just told them which way was up, but who'd instead gone tumbling down to hell like rockets with faulty guidance systems. And lying there in bed, her blankets pulled up to her chin, she would pray, not for world peace but for those kids, pray for every one of them, even those whose names she couldn't recall; lying sleepless in the night, she would pray God had protected them from a world that so regularly turned dreams into crash wreckage, pray they weren't all buried in cemeteries, where the only angels were grave markers with wings of crumbling plaster, wings that would never raise them above the cast-iron gates that separated the living from the dead . . .

Okay, enough of that, she thought. Enough. No sense throwing shadows over a perfectly beautiful morning.

Jolanda studied her arrangement and decided it was just about finished, then considered tying a bow around the basket handle for some extra pizzazz. She'd brought a shopping bag full of colored ribbon home from the shop just the other day and left it in her bedroom closet.

Rising from the table, she went across the living room, and was walking past the kitchen entry when she noticed the message light blinking on her answering machine. She paused, unable to understand how the phone could have rung without her hearing it. Then it struck her that somebody might've called in when she'd brought the kids over to visit Robin and Jamal. She'd been talking to their mother awhile and been gone maybe fifteen, twenty minutes. And she hadn't been in the kitchen since she'd gotten back.

She went over to the kitchen counter where she kept her telephone/answering machine, pushed the playback button, and waited. The tape took surprisingly long to rewind; she'd either had a very chattery caller or there were several phone messages waiting for her.

The machine made a clicking noise as the tape wound back to its beginning and then began spooling forward.

Jolanda stood listening to silence. No, not exactly silence. Background noise. Or what would have been background noise if someone had been speaking in the *fore*ground. She could hear what she recognized as the sound of activity on the street: traffic; chirping birds; faint, floating snatches of conversation. The refrain of a hit song, swiftly getting louder, and then just as quickly fading on what she presumed was a boom box. Much closer to the mouthpiece she heard the sound of breathing— someone listening to the silence of the tape running at *her* end of the line.

It went on like that for a full minute. Then the clear automated voice of the operator cut through the mix of sounds, telling the caller to deposit five cents for the next thirty seconds or be disconnected. Seconds afterward there was a series of clicks and the line went dead. Then a beep on the answering machine to indicate the end of the message. Obviously whoever had called had been at an outdoor pay telephone.

The second call was the same. The tape had captured another minute's worth of comings and goings on the street, the breathing, the operator's canned announcement, and finally the sound of the connection being terminated. *Beep*.

The third and fourth calls were also the same.

So were the fifth, and the sixth.

There were ten calls in all before the tape reached its end.

Jolanda could not understand why someone would have stood out at a sidewalk phone booth placing one after another call to her number, dropping over two dollars in change into the phone, saying nothing . . . not unless they were trying to frighten her. In that respect, the shallow breathing had been more effective than the childish heavy panting she usually associated with prank phone calls. Somehow it seemed seriously weird.

She was gripped by a sudden, illogical concern for the safety of her children . . . illogical because she had left them at a friend's house not an hour ago, and couldn't see what some jerk calling her from a pay phone had to do with them anyway.

Still . . .

On impulse she lifted the receiver and hit the speed dial button for Robin and Jamal's house, thinking it was better to set herself at ease than to stand around worrying.

The phone rang once, twice—

"Hello, Cartoon Central," the kids' mother said, sounding very chipper as she picked up on the third ring.

"Hi, Carol, it's Jolanda . . ." She felt a little ridiculous. "Are the kids being good?"

"Perfect honeys. You know how they get hypnotized by those 'toons. What time you taking them to see the fishies?"

Jolanda hoped Carol hadn't picked up on her anxiety.

"Would another hour or so be okay? I'd like to get some more work done . . ."

"Take as long as you want; I haven't even bagged their lunches yet," Carol said.

"Thanks," Jolanda said. "See you in a while."

She hung up, feeling her nerves settle down, but still wondering who could have been calling her from the pay phone. Standing out there in the street, not saying a word, dropping quarter after quarter into the slot . . .

Well, she thought, there are a lot of weirdos in the world, and a lot of jerks, and plenty of weirdo jerks. Probably her number had been dialed at random and it wouldn't happen again. How much of a thrill could it have been just listening to a tape run on the answering machine? These nuisance callers were after *reactions*, and when they didn't get any, they moved on to the next poor victim.

Jolanda glanced at the clock, told herself that time was a-wasting, and returned to the dining room to start another basket. Within minutes she was deeply engrossed in her work, the peculiar phone calls pushed to the back of her mind.

It wasn't until the next day that she realized who the caller had been, and by then it was much too late.

"WE'RE TOO LATE," Kellerman said. "Look who's here."

He nudged Lewis with his elbow, then pointed toward the state police cruiser that had turned into the drive leading up to the hospital.

Lewis visored his hand over his eyes and peered through the glare of the cruiser's windshield.

"Lambert," he said.

"In the obnoxious flesh," Kellerman said. "Told you we should've got going."

"Hey, man, you're the one wanted to compare notes."

"I meant while we were walking to the car."

"Well, bein' I ain't no mind reader, you shoulda *said* that."

They were standing outside D-ward after having completed their interviews in the nick of time; Blair had called to notify the guard in the reception booth that their half hour was up even as they were questioning him. Like the other security guards, he'd told them next to nothing about Dubick, which hadn't really surprised Lewis—for better or worse, a code of silence seemed to go with wearing a uniform, and since he'd always assumed this was as true of doormen and janitors as it was of cops, he'd had no reason to expect these hired watchdogs would be any different. According to them, Dubick had been hardworking, honest, a great buddy and better husband, all in all maybe a notch below official sainthood. The only thing they'd let slip that was of any interest to the detectives was the news that Dubick was supposed to have started his vacation that very morning, and had booked reservations aboard a Caribbean cruise for himself and his wife.

If Lewis had believed in coincidences, the timing of the vacation and the break would have seemed like an interesting one. But since he didn't believe in them, all it seemed like was confirmation that Dubick had plotted the escape with Stella and Campbell from the beginning, and had been killed as the result of a double cross.

Before he could think too much more about it, Lambert's car eased to a halt about a yard in front of him, where the driveway curved past D-ward.

"Golly gee," Lambert said, shifting the car into park and leaning his head out his open window. "Who'd have thought I'd run into you fellas here."

"Something, isn't it?" Kellerman said.

"To be frank, it *does* seem a little odd, since it was just a couple hours ago that we heard your bosses explaining that you city boys were supposed to stick to your own turf," Lambert said.

"Way I remember, they were sayin' we had no *authority* here," Lewis said. "Nobody told us we couldn't ask a few questions."

Lambert's frigid grin appeared under his dark lenses.

"If that's the case," he said, "I'm sure you won't mind if I mention you were poking around outside your jurisdiction to Captain Barnfather."

Lewis shrugged.

"Go ahead," he said. "Bet you an' Barnfather tell each other all kinds of things."

Lambert stared at him balefully a minute. Then he nodded and put the cruiser back in drive, keeping his foot on the brake.

"Well, I've got my own investigation to conduct," he said. "Sorry I interrupted the conversation you two were having; it looked like you were going over something important."

"Just talkin' about the weather," Lewis said.

"It *is* a nice day, isn't it?" Lambert briefly tilted his

face up to the sky, then looked back at Lewis. "Enjoy it while you can."

He gave the detectives a clipped little wave, then pulled his head back inside the car and drove slowly past them toward the administration building.

"Barnfather ain't gonna like this," Lewis said, watching the cruiser curve along the driveway and vanish behind the trees in front of the building's main entrance.

Kellerman nodded, and silently followed him across the lawn to the parking lot.

SEVEN

ON THE WAY back into the city, Kellerman called Safeway Security Systems from his cell phone, using the number provided by Blair's secretary. The person that came on the line identified himself as Mr. Ryan, listened silently as Kellerman explained he was a homicide detective with a few questions about the employee who'd been killed during the escape at Central Baltimore, and then, sounding unmistakably belligerent, told Kellerman that his firm did not as a rule give out personal information about their guards, and that any exceptions to this policy would have to be okayed by the company's general supervisor, who would be gone until after Memorial Day.

"Maybe if we came by your office—"

"Sure," Ryan said. "Like I said, my boss'll be back next week."

"I'm afraid we can't wait that long."

Ryan exhaled into the phone. "Hey, what is this?"

"I told you, it's a murder investigation," Kellerman said. "Now, may I have your exact location?"

"I don't know," Ryan said. "I mean, I'm only the

weekend shift manager. I shouldn't even be talking to y—"

"Mr. Ryan, please," Kellerman said, cutting him off again. "If I have to hang up and dial the operator to get it, I'm going to be very irritable when we finally meet. So how about we make life easy?"

The shift manager released another sigh and gave in.

Safeway's main office turned out to be directly on the way to headquarters, and twenty minutes later Lewis and Kellerman were sitting across a scuffed steel desk from Ryan, hearing more about the boss being away and his unwillingness to risk his job by going into the personnel files without authorization.

"If you'd come Friday morning instead of today, my supervisor wouldn't be off, and we wouldn't be having this problem," he said.

"Dubick wasn't dead Friday morning," Kellerman said.

"I know that," Ryan said. "I was just saying if he *had been* . . ."

Kellerman hung his left ankle over his right knee and wobbled it impatiently. A round, hairless, neckless man with pinkish skin and beady brown eyes, Ryan reminded him a little of an armadillo. Probably he'd have liked nothing more than to curl himself into a ball and roll somewhere to hide.

"Look," he said, "I really wish you'd cooperate—"

"You'll get Dubick's file, don't worry," Ryan said. "I just don't see why it can't wait a couple days, is all."

Lewis leaned forward in his seat. He had managed to stay quiet until now but was tired of screwing around.

"I'm gonna tell you something, Ryan," he said. "Me an' my partner can leave here right now an' be back in an hour with a search warrant. You make us go through that hassle, I promise we're gonna haul out every personnel folder in this place, and probably take the file cabinets with them."

"On the other hand," Kellerman said, "you can save us a lot of time and let us take a peek at Dubick's file."

114

"Or better yet, make us a copy," Lewis said.

"So how we going to do this?" Kellerman said.

Ryan looked at them. "What makes you guys think I know where to find it, huh? I mean, all I'm supposed to do is take care of emergencies, like making sure a client's covered if one of the guards calls in sick and needs a replacement. That sorta thing."

"Consider this an emergency." Kellerman was still wobbling his foot on his knee. "You—"

"Yo, Mike, don't waste your breath tryin' to convince this hotshot," Lewis said. "He wants us to call a judge, fine."

"Hate to think of his boss's reaction when he finds this place turned inside out," Kellerman said, shrugging his shoulders.

Both detectives got up to leave.

"Hey!" Ryan shouted at their backs as they walked across the office toward the door. "Hey, hold on a second!"

Kellerman half turned. "What is it?"

"I never told you I *absolutely* couldn't help you guys, did I?"

Kellerman and Lewis exchanged weary glances.

"I'll make you a deal," Ryan said. "You get a Xerox of Dubick's file, nobody finds out who put it in your hands, okay?"

The detectives looked at each other some more.

"Okay," Kellerman said finally. "Just make it quick."

Ryan bounced off his chair, almost tipping it over in his haste to reach the file cabinets.

A LITTLE SHY of noon, Hector Flores took a break from mopping the floor of his Hamilton Avenue bodega, slipped a Ruben Blades cassette into the boom box behind his front counter, then lit a Newport and gazed out the plate glass window at the corner, where the morning sunlight had chased away the dope dealers, junkies, and strung-out prostitutes who cluttered the sidewalk all night, doing their business, their very nearness making him feel diminished, reminding him what a wicked, devouring place the city could be. Maybe it was a holiday elsewhere in Baltimore, but outside his door things like holidays didn't matter; outside his door it was the same story every day, the same painful routine playing itself out again and again: the robbing and hooking and drug peddling at night, the near desolation when the sun came out and the street people disappeared like roaches scurrying from a broom . . .

He breathed in a stream of mentholated smoke and let it curl out his nostrils. Right now the only people on Hamilton were a couple of out-of-place-looking white guys at the pay phone across the street, and a teenage boy skating past the curb on Rollerblades, but the lowlifes who'd spoken to him the night before would return with the next setting of the sun, and they would want to know if he'd chosen to accept their offer. Maybe he had been a fool not to jump at it, but it wasn't too late, they would be back a second and third and fourth time if he didn't have his answer by tonight, and *keep* coming back until he gave it to them, and probably let the offer stand even if he turned them down. He had time to make his decision, plenty of time. So why not at least consider their proposal?

Why not?

Sometimes, if you met her price, the city gave you what you needed, and far more rarely what you wanted, but too often she made you suffer every imaginable indignity, used you up, left you without a shred of hope or human feeling. Too often those who labored at honest jobs had nothing, and the worst kinds of scum seemed to get every reward the world could offer . . . scum like the drug dealers who had come into Hector's place last night, suggesting he consider laundering their profits through his store, offering to show their appreciation for this favor with several cash payments, say a first install-ment of $175,000, with more such gifts to come if everyone involved was satisfied with the arrangement and wanted it to continue over the long haul.

A hundred and seventy-five thousand dollars.

More money than he had ever imagined holding in his hands. Enough to get the landlord and suppliers off his back and keep them off, with a good-sized chunk left over for a new car, and expensive presents for his wife and kids. Enough for him to sock some away in one of those high-interest accounts the banks advertised in the paper.

A hundred and seventy-five thousand.

With more to come.

A small gesture, the pushers had said. A token. But one from their hearts.

Madre de dios.

A hundred and seventy-five thousand.

Hector took another long drag off his smoke. He knew of other shopkeepers in the area who had accepted similar offers . . . call it desperation, call it greed— these days he wasn't sure the reasons made any difference. The owners of the newsstand down the block were selling packets of heroin with brand names like Grave- yard and Wicked and Red Death from under the same counter where they kept their baseball cards and chewing gum. Dave's Hardware over on Boullard was doing numbers and had a one-armed bandit in back. Nobody talked about it, of course, but he'd heard the noise from the street, and saw them making improvements to their places while his ceiling collapsed and his stock shrank and his unpaid bills piled higher all the time.

Hector didn't think he was any genius, but he'd always figured he was smart enough to get along in this city. When he'd immigrated from the Dominican Republic ten years before, his eyes had been wide open. He had known that in America these days, the golden door the poet talked about in the inscription on the Statue of Liberty was closing to people with dark skin, and that the lamp of freedom had become a torch being angrily waved in their faces. He had not thought he would receive an open welcome. He had not expected to find the streets paved with gold, or believed there would be

117

milk and honey running from the taps. He had not wanted a free ride, only a chance to earn more than the equivalent of a thousand American dollars a year toiling in the eastern sugar plantations of his home country, a chance to take his family from a place where disease and starvation killed almost half the newborn babies before they reached their first birthday.

A *chance*.

While awaiting his green card, he had gotten a below-minimum-wage job washing dishes in a swank French restaurant at the Harborplace complex, where the rich diners would pay more for a single meal than he'd make in a week, sometimes in a *month*. On his nights off from the restaurant he had driven for a car service, sitting behind the wheel from nine o'clock until three or four in the morning. He had worked hard and saved hard for his grocery. When he had opened it in '92, the rent had been just over five hundred dollars a month, and by staying open long hours he'd been able to make it on time, pay off his utility bills and wholesale suppliers, and still bring home a decent income. But in a city where independent landlords had been largely replaced with quick-kill sharks who bought buildings like crazy, gouged their tenants into default, and resold the vacated properties to the urban redevelopment planners at inflated values, that five-hundred-dollar rent had more than quadrupled over the past few years. Caught between the cutthroat real estate maneuvering and drug trafficking, Hector had begun to feel as if the walls were closing in on him, as if he were being *crushed,* and there didn't seem to be any way out . . . not unless he told the pushers he was ready to accept their offer, and stepped into what he was certain would just be a different sort of trap.

He wished he knew which was worse, wished he knew what his answer would be when they came back tonight . . . but the only thing he *did* know was that he couldn't stand around worrying about it, not if he wanted to get through with his floor.

Taking a last hit on the Newport, Hector pulled himself

from his thoughts and flicked the cigarette butt into the sudsy water in his wash bucket. He sloshed his big rag mop around in the same water, wrung it, and began working his way down the center aisle.

He had gained perhaps ten feet of clean floor when the clutch of tiny chimes above the entrance door jingled briskly.

Still bowed to his task, Hector glanced up at the security mirror angled between the rear wall and the ceiling. Its curved oval surface gave him a fish-eye view of almost the entire shop, and though he was not by disposition a nervous man, he'd been held up more than once in broad daylight and figured you could never be too careful.

The men walking in the door were the same two white men he'd noticed at the phone booth across the street. The big one entered first, looking muddled and glassy-eyed, followed closely by a shorter, wiry guy with hollow cheeks and pale blue eyes that shifted from side to side in a way that put Hector on heightened alert. He rarely saw white dudes in his neighborhood, and certainly would have remembered these particular white dudes if he had seen them before five minutes ago. Putting aside how odd they looked standing together, kind of like Jack and the Giant, a pair like this was not the sort you tended to forget. He trusted his instincts, and right now they were telling him he was facing a couple of dangerous hardcases.

"You fellas want some help?" he asked, leaning his mop on a shelf. His palms felt sweaty and he wiped them on his chinos.

The thin guy's smile was a tight, colorless seam above his chin.

"Thanks for askin', *muchacho*, but my buddy prefers findin' the items he needs on his own," he said. "As for myself, I'm more what you'd call an impulse buyer, can't hardly ever make up my mind. So if it's all right with you, I'll just look around an' see if anythin' strikes my fancy."

Hector didn't say anything, not sure exactly what to make of these two, but thinking he might be in for a bad situation.

The big one was standing absolutely still and looking at him, or rather gazing in his general direction, his eyes unfocused, his features blank and unmoving. Then the left side of his face crinkled with a twitchy contraction and—almost as if some stalled motor inside him had been kick-started—he shuffled deeper into the store, going over to the shelf where Hector stocked the hand soaps and laundry detergents.

At the same moment the thin guy edged over to the sales counter and stood with his back against it, smiling his narrow little smile, his eyes still skipping restlessly back and forth. Without turning away from Hector, he reached back into one of the display boxes of snacks and candy on the countertop, snatched up a chocolate bar, and brought it around so he could examine it.

"Now, this here seems scrumptious," he said, reading the label aloud. "Creamy milk chocolate on the outside, rich caramel fillin' on the inside. Sprinkled with real bits a' toasted *coconut*!"

Hector was perspiring all over now, beads of sweat popping out on his forehead, a greasy dampness spreading under his arms. Over to his right, the big man was loading up a shopping basket with soap bars, going for the ones on the bottom shelf, stooping down to reach them.

"Mmmm-mmm, I do *so* love my sweets," the skinny man said in an excited, weirdly lilting voice that made Hector's scalp crawl. He slipped off the candy bar's outer wrapper, carelessly let it drop to the floor, then peeled back its inner waxed-paper wrapping. "How much one'a these things cost?"

"Take it and get outta here," Hector said, noticing a bulge under the guy's jacket that might be a concealed gun. He kept his own .38 in a drawer beneath his cash register, but he'd have to make it past the skinny man and swing behind the counter to get hold of it—fast action, probably faster than he could manage.

He watched with a mixture of dismay, anger, and confusion as the skinny man crammed the rectangle of chocolate into his mouth and bit off—actually *broke* off—a large chunk by clamping his teeth over it and giving the portion in his hand a sharp downward snap.

"Yeah, I could really get hooked on this shit," he said through a mouthful of chocolate. He gulped noisily, tore what was left of the candy bar out of its wrapper, and wolfed it down. "Especially the toasted coconut."

Hector stared at him. What the hell was this anyway? The last thing he'd needed, the last thing in the *world*, was to have these crazies come floating into his store, playing some kind of sick game with him . . .

"Look, man, I told you to go away," he said, thinking about his pistol, still seriously doubting he could get to it before one of these two guys stopped him in his tracks. "I ain't lookin' for no trouble. You cut it right now, no harm done, all you owe me's seventy-five cents for a candy bar—"

"Let me tell *you*, somethin', *muchacho*," the skinny guy interrupted, licking a crumb of chocolate off his fingertip. "You're a rip-off bastard chargin' that kinda money for what used to cost a quarter, so just to teach you a lesson I'm gonna stuff my pockets with goodies." He nodded his head back at the register and emitted a burst of glassy, high-pitched laughter. "An' before we go, me an' my *amigo* are gonna take some carfare money outta your cash drawer."

Hector swallowed hard. At the border of his vision he saw the big man rise from the soap and detergent shelf, move farther down the aisle, and put a bottle of drain opener into his basket, looking perfectly calm, seemingly oblivious to what was going on around him. If not for the bizarre scene up front, someone entering the shop could have mistaken him for an ordinary shopper stocking up on household supplies.

Hector swallowed again, the walls of his throat feeling

dry as sandpaper, not a drop of spit in his mouth. His back turned to him now, humming to himself, the skinny man was scooping sweets off the counter and cramming them into his jacket pockets by the handful. The pockets bulged with merchandise he had already filched.

Hector inched forward. There was nothing left to say that could defuse the situation, these maniacs were going to rob him blind, he had no choice except to try and get his hands on his gun.

The skinny man was still facing away from him, still humming and loading his pockets.

Hector took another small step on the balls of his feet, then realized he was being baited, and would be kidding himself if he thought he could creep up on this guy. If he expected to have a chance, he would have to *move*.

His heart striking mallet blows to his rib cage, his blood a pounding ocean in his ears, he launched himself up the aisle, almost stumbling as he raced around a knee-high pile of rice sacks on the floor, somehow catching his balance, moving, moving, fast goddamn action. He scrambled toward the edge of the counter, thinking he would make it, really thinking he would, and then the skinny man suddenly rounded on him, his mouth pulled into a vicious grimace, *hissing* between his teeth as he lunged at Hector. His arms rushed out, fingers clawing, grabbing for Hector's arm. Hector tried to swerve out of his reach but the man caught him with one hand. Hector tried to shake him off but he held on, clung to him, got his other hand around Hector's arm. Hector looked down at where the skinny man was gripping him, his bony fingers printing his shirtsleeve with sticky chocolate whorls, his fingers pressing into him, his fingers stronger than Hector would have imagined. He couldn't pull away, the guy was all over him, his crazed, knotted face less than an inch from his own.

"*We're dancin' now, muchacho!*" he screamed, his socketed eyes gleaming. "*Doin' the Boneyard Twist!*"

Hector fought to untangle himself, shoving at the man with both hands, but he couldn't break free of his furious clench; the best he could do was stagger him. Their bodies locked together, they went reeling across the floor, the skinny man's back crashing up against a unit of wall shelves, a violent breath gusting from his mouth. Applesauce and baby food jars rattled overhead. Hector pushed the man back into the shelves again, again, again. Jarred products tumbled down around them and shattered on the floor. Soup cans rocked off the shelves, one striking Hector above the eyebrow and opening a thin cut. A trickle of blood stung his eye. He kept slamming the skinny man backward, using all the strength he could summon, thinking he would never get away from him, thinking the guy's friend was going to grab him from behind at any second . . .

Just then the skinny man aimed a wild kick at Hector's knee, and missed, and when his foot swung back down to the floor it landed in a puddle of green mush that had spilled from a broken baby food jar. He skidded and slipped, his right hand breaking away from Hector's elbow.

Hector immediately knew this would be his one and only opening.

He balled his hand into a fist, hooked it upward, clubbed the skinny man across his face, and brought his fist back for a second hard blow to the cheekbone. Something gave beneath the man's flesh. He made an injured whinnying sound, his head banging against the shelves behind him, knocking more bottles to the floor.

His grip fell away from Hector's other arm.

Hector walloped him again, this time with his open hand, clapping his palm over his throat and pushing him backward until he fell sprawling into the welter of splintered, dribbling jars and bottles.

His whole body shaking, drawing a ragged, exhausted breath, Hector wheeled toward the counter without an instant's pause—

And stopped just short of running into the big man, just short of colliding with his broad, slablike chest.

He saw at once that the guy had some kind of metal

rod in his fist and clumsily backstepped, looking over his shoulder in a desperate panic, caught between the two men.

On the floor behind him the skinny guy sat with his legs spread in a wide V, his hand clasped over his mouth, blood streaming through his fingers.

He'd pulled a gun from under his jacket with his other hand, a jumbo Magnum revolver, and was pointing its menacingly long snout at Hector.

"We're gonna do things to you, *muchacho*," he said, rocking with laughter, trilling laughter through his bloody fingers. "*Terrible* things."

In front of Hector, floorboards were creaking under the big man's weight as he plodded closer. Hector spun his head back around, glancing up into the big man's face, looking into his not-quite-there eyes, and muttering a prayer to God in his native Spanish.

"*Jesus dame mercidad.*"

Jesus have mercy.

The big man raised the rod in his hand and took another step forward. Hector recoiled in horror, caught, caught between them, thinking he had to do something, had to try and get around the big man, make a run for the door, *do something*, but then he heard the explosive crash of the gun behind him, felt a slap of pain below his shoulder blades, heard a second crash, a third, tasted blood, heard more tittery laughter, and, as he poured to the floor, saw the rod in the big man's hand lashing down at him. It struck him on the temple, the side of his face, his neck, his forehead—the blows landing with wet, meaty thuds, hammering his senses until they fused in a great sweeping rush of white heat . . .

On the wall clock above the counter, the hour and minute hands ticked off twelve-thirty, and on the floor Hector Flores took a last gurgling breath, and then ceased to be numbered among the one million survivors in Charm City.

AT EXACTLY 12:30 P.M. Beverly Williams, a salesclerk from the Salvation Army goodwill shop on Hamilton

Avenue, was pricing some recent donations when she heard three explosive bangs from the bodega next door. The noises were so loud they startled her into dropping the porcelain statuette she'd been about to tag, but she hardly noticed it breaking to pieces on the floor. In a neighborhood where twelve-year-old kids thought nothing of getting into firefights over eight-ball jackets and high-top sneakers, and where police protection fell woefully short of what was needed, storekeepers survived by looking after each other. And those bangs had sounded very much like gunshots.

Frightened, Beverly moved to the window just as the door to the bodega was thrown open and two men came rushing out onto the street. She instantly concluded that something terrible had indeed happened and took a mental snapshot of the men. Even in her shock, she realized how important it was that she be able to describe them accurately.

One of them was very tall and built like a house, and the other was all skin and bones. The tall man was carrying a large brown paper bag that appeared to be bulging with items. She noted with horror that both men's clothes were blood-splattered, and that the smaller one's face was a mess, as if he'd been in a fight. A *brutal* fight.

The men went past the goodwill shop to the corner, walking quickly but not running. Then they crossed the intersection and disappeared down a side street.

Overcome with a feeling of helplessness and dread, the sharp, deadly sounding bangs she'd heard reverberating in her mind, Beverly turned away from the window, grabbed the phone off the wall, and dialed 911.

Her hand was shaking so badly it took her two tries to get the number right.

"THOSE ARE THE men," Beverly Williams said.

Kay Howard was standing on the sidewalk outside the bodega and showing her police photographs of Stella and

Campbell, having steered her away from the victim's body after she'd painfully made her identification.

"You're positive of that?" Howard asked. "I know you only got a glimpse of them."

She noticed that Mrs. Williams was sweating profusely, her deep brown skin turning an ashen color, and hoped she wouldn't be sick—although it would certainly be understandable if she were. The corpse had been a gruesome sight and the store had reeked of murder, the sweet smell of blood mixing with acrid traces of cordite to create an odor that was distinct from merely the smell of death. In Baltimore cops got to know the difference soon after they left the Academy, got to know it so well they could walk into a room blindfolded and instantly tell somebody had been blown away in there, even if the body was gone and the walls and floor had been scrubbed with ammonia and all the windows were open and their noses were stuffed from colds. And of course Hector Flores hadn't just been shot to death, he'd had his skull split open and his brains pulverized, which added another subtle aromatic layer to the bouquet.

"I know what they looked like," Beverly said. "Ain't no mistakin' them."

Kay considered asking her to go over what she'd observed again, but could see the intensity of her struggle to remain composed, and decided not to put her through it. She slipped the photos into the handbag on her shoulder, thanked Mrs. Williams, told her she'd be in touch, asked one of the uniforms to escort her past the crowd of onlookers pressing up to the crime scene tape, and went to rejoin Lewis, Kellerman, Munch, and the gaggle of Forensics people inside the bodega.

The body of Hector Flores was slumped against the sales counter in a half-sitting position, drenched in his own blood, his head a ruined mess. The forehead was little more than a seeping, caved-in, jagged-rimmed swamp of blood and brain tissue. The nose and cheekbones had been smashed, and one eye had sprouted from its socket and was hanging loosely from a rootlike

bundle of nerves. Bits of hair and bone clung to everything—the walls, the shelves, the side of the counter—
every damn thing, as if the roof of his skull had
spontaneously erupted.

"Mrs. Williams I.D. the killers?" Lewis asked Howard.

"No question, it was our two loony birds," she said.

Lewis bit his lower lip. Standing over the corpse,
looking down at the biological wreckage of what had
been a living human being, he could feel his stomach
twisting inside out. It wasn't the gore and mutilation;
he'd been a homicide cop too long, and seen too many
victims of violent death for that to upset him.

For him the sickening thing was the candy bar sticking
halfway out of the dead man's mouth, still in its wrapper,
obviously placed there by his murderers.

A candy bar.

Most of the time when someone got killed during a
robbery it was because he'd tried to defend himself, or
because the perpetrator had gotten too jumpy or pumped—
any or all of which may have been factors here, and were
poor enough reasons to take a person's life. But the
candy bar in the groceryman's mouth was evidence of an
added component. The candy bar showed the bottomless
depravity of the individuals responsible for the act,
showed that it had provided them with a monstrous kind
of entertainment. They had shot Hector Flores in the
back, beaten him to a pulp, and then left him to be found
in this ignominious manner.

A candy bar.

The sadistic bastards had stuck a candy bar in his
mouth.

Lewis went over to Scheiner, who was shuffling
around the body, looking peeved at having had his
holiday weekend interrupted by yet another call from
upstairs.

"So what's the official word?" Lewis said. He wondered if the M.E. had been hauled from a family
barbecue, or a picnic in the park, or maybe a stroll on an
Ocean City beach. It was hard to picture Scheiner away

from a crime scene or his lab, but then again Scheiner probably couldn't imagine *him* outside those settings either.

"He was shot and clobbered," Scheiner said. "Or was the precise term I used this morning 'cracked in the head'?"

"Same weapon they used to beat the hospital guard to death?"

"Or very similar," Scheiner said.

Lewis pointed to the gaping, bloody hole in the dead man's abdomen.

"Exit wound's pretty big," he said. "Our boys are gettin' plenty use outta their .357."

Scheiner grunted affirmatively. "I think one of the techs found the slug in the wall."

"Got any idea whether the shooting or the beating came first?"

"That'll have to wait for the autopsy," Scheiner said. "My guess is either one would have finished him, though. This isn't just overkill, it's *double* overkill."

Lewis glanced at the jumble of streaming, broken bottles lying near one of the shelves.

"Poor guy put up a helluva fight," he said.

"Right again," Scheiner said. He pointed to the smudgy, overlapping fingerprints on the victim's shirtsleeve. "See these?"

"Uh-huh," Lewis said, noting that most of the prints were around the elbow area. "One of the wackos have grease on his fingers?"

"They're chocolate, probably left there when he grabbed Mr. Flores *like so.*" Scheiner made a clawing gesture in the air to illustrate.

Lewis looked at him. "You sayin' he stood here snackin' on a chocolate bar before he killed a man?"

"And didn't even have the consideration to toss the wrapper in the garbage," Scheiner said. "Your friend Kellerman found it on the floor a minute ago and put it in an evidence bag."

"The Tragedy of Pudd'nhead Wilson."

This from Munch, who had come wandering over from one of the aisles.

Lewis flared with irritation. "Ain't funny, man."

"Who's trying to be funny?"

"*You* are," Lewis said edgily. Okay, he understood, you were exposed to enough dead bodies, you sometimes had to laugh or go crazy, but Munch didn't know where to draw the line. Or maybe the real problem was that he took these things harder than some of the other guys on the squad and overcompensated. Still, he wasn't the only one under stress, and Lewis wasn't laughing.

Munch gave him a bland look. "I'm telling you, I wasn't—"

"So what the fuck kinda comment is 'Pudd'nhead' when I got a vic with a bashed in skull—"

"What I said was 'Pudd'nhead Wilson,'" Munch said. "You know, as in the book by Mark Twain?"

"No," Lewis said, thinking he really didn't need this shit right now. "I don't."

"Hey, I'm sorry, but for some reason the prints on this guy's shirt reminded me of it," Munch said. "First novel in history to use fingerprinting in the plot. We're talking 1894, mind you, just a few years after police developed the technique." He paused. "Well, Arthur Conan Doyle might've *mentioned* it in a story a few years earlier, but Twain—"

"Skip it," Lewis said.

"Just so you don't get the wrong idea," Munch said, and walked off.

Lewis looked at the body again. He personally didn't care if it had been Mark Twain or Jon Jo'nzz the Martian Manhunter who'd first written about fingerprinting. What he cared about was the dead man on the floor, the man who'd been shot and bludgeoned and then had a candy bar shoved into his mouth by maniacs who'd obviously gotten a rush from killing him. What he cared about was the possibility that this man still might be *alive* had it not been for Barnfather's instructions to keep the breakout at Central Maryland a secret from the public, eliminating any chance that Hector Flores would have been keeping an eye out for the two fugitives, and gotten out of the store, or called the police, or maybe known better than to try putting up a struggle when they made their move to rob him.

As far as Lewis was concerned, the Safeway employee file in his car was certain proof that Lambert was using his connection with Barnfather to run a slick number on the entire Baltimore police department. Lewis resented having become a participant in a cover-up that was recklessly endangering the lives of innocent people . . . and was thinking more and more that he couldn't keep doing it.

"Yo, Mike," he said, looking around for his partner.

Halfway down the center aisle Kellerman was kneeling in front of a shelf full of soap and hair shampoo, looking for any bars of soap that matched the brand name of the one in his hand. He had found it on the sidewalk outside the store and guessed it came from the bag of stuff Campbell had carried away with him, a hunch his quick inspection of the shelf seemed to bear out, since it was fully stocked except in one particular area, where a large bare space indicated a number of items had been removed. It was also conspicuous that the stacks of soap bars on *either side* of the empty space had been toppled, with several bars having spilled onto the floor, while the rest of the merchandise on the shelf was stocked in a neat and orderly manner—which told Kellerman that the goods had been removed in *haste*, leaving him with virtually no doubt they'd been stolen.

He frowned. Had any of the other cops at the scene noticed the missing items, he might naturally have wondered about Stella and Campbell's seemingly absurd theft of *soap bars*, of all things, in the middle of an armed robbery, no less a robbery that had wildly spun out into murder. But none of those cops shared Kellerman's background in the department, or knew what he knew because of it.

There was something else here. Something Kellerman

had remembered the instant he chanced upon the bar that had fallen onto the street and read the list of ingredients on the wrapper. Something that scared the hell out of him . . .

"Yo, Mike!"

"Yeah," he said, the sharp note of urgency in Lewis's voice cutting into his thoughts.

"Come on, we're outta here," Lewis said.

Kellerman rose from the low shelf, slipping the bar of soap he'd found into his pocket.

"Where we going?"

"To talk to Gee," Lewis said.

"About what?"

"A press leak," he said, lowering his voice several notches.

"Huh?" Kellerman said. "You mean the media found out about the case?"

"Not yet, man," Lewis said.

He looked at Kellerman

Kellerman looked back at him. Was he trying to suggest . . . ?

"Okay, we'll do this your way . . . whichever way that happens to be," he said. "Just gimme a chance to check out one more thing before we book."

"I'll be waitin' in the car," Lewis said, and turned toward the door.

Kellerman followed him out less than five minutes later.

EIGHT

LIKE A GHOST who kept popping up to haunt them, Lambert was making his exit from Gee's office when Lewis and Kellerman got there a half hour after leaving the bodega.

"Isn't this an interesting coincidence?" he said, approaching them in the hallway outside the door. "I was just talking about you two."

"I bet," Lewis said.

Lambert pulled his clip-ons from the lapel pocket of his sport coat and attached them to the steel frames of his eyeglasses.

"After bumping into you this morning, I was anxious to put in a good word with your lieutenant," he said. "Tell him how his detectives took the initiative and headed right out to Howard County, even though they weren't supposed to be there. Probably sprang for the gas out of pocket too . . . but there's a price to be paid by the self-motivated."

"Funny," Kellerman said.

Lambert grinned like a crocodile.

"I won't stand around blocking the entrance," he said, brushing past them. "Have a nice meeting."

Kellerman watched him stride over to the elevators. "What the hell did he do, head right over here the second we left him at the hospital?"

"Wouldn't put it past him," Lewis said.

He knocked on the frosted glass door, Giardello blared out a bassoonlike "*Enter!*", and a moment later they were seated opposite him at his desk.

"Well," Giardello said, smiling broadly. "You both look very, shall we say, *invigorated.*"

Lewis tugged at his goatee. Giardello had smiles and Giardello had smiles, and the one he was flashing now was the kind that always made his detectives want to take cover.

"I wonder if the hale and hearty color on your faces has anything to do with taking a ride in the country," Gee said. "Fresh air and sunshine can be very beneficial to one's health."

Neither of them said anything.

"Unfortunately, it can also have a very *negative* effect on police work," Giardello went on. "Assuming that work is supposed to be taking place in this cold and sunless metropolis we call Baltimore."

"Gee, I know what that statie musta told you, but you got to hear us out," Lewis said. "He—"

"Stop." Giardello held up his hand and stared at him. His suit jacket was hung over the back of his chair, his tie was loosened over the open collar of his shirt, and he'd rolled his sleeves up high on his arms. There was a welter of empty paper coffee cups in the trash can beside his desk. "This has nothing to do with Lambert, and everything to do with your having acted in direct contradiction of orders."

The detectives were silent. From the corner of one eye Kellerman saw a pigeon touch down on the narrow ledge outside the office's open window, cock its head investigatively toward the inner windowsill, and then fly off into the wild blue yonder. He couldn't help but envy it.

Giardello had dropped a hand onto his telephone console.

"Gentleman, this device is my sworn enemy," he said. "It has been ringing all morning, assaulting me with a blitzkrieg of calls, so to speak. And every time I've picked up the receiver, I have heard from someone whose voice I would rather *not* hear. Such as the deputy police commissioner. And Stanton from the mayor's office. And Captains Barnfather and Davis, and so on and so forth, I won't bore you with the full roster of departmental and civilian officials who have spoken to me from their rarefied stations." He took a deep breath, exhaled. "What I will tell you is that the message from all of them has been the same: do not fuck up the Stella-Campbell case, because if that happens we will reach our hands down your throat, tear out your intestines, and then hang you by them in front of City Hall."

Kellerman shifted in his seat. He really, really was wishing he could have followed that pigeon out the window. Even *without* being able to fly.

"Let me tell you two something," Giardello said. "*You* have fucked up. And as your commanding officer *I* am in danger of becoming a fuckup by association. And I resent that."

Lewis glanced down at his lap and fingered the large manilla clasp envelope he'd gotten from Ryan at Safeway Security. "Gee—"

"It's Lieutenant Giardello to you. Or preferably just 'sir'."

"Lieutenant, sir, if I could just explain *why* we went to the hospital—"

"Reasons are irrelevant," Giardello rumbled. "All I want to know is that nothing like this will happen again."

"Gee—I mean, Lieutenant Giardello—I promise you it won't," Lewis said.

"Absolutely not," Kellerman said, squirming. "Never again."

"I'm very glad to hear that," Giardello said. "And I take it your promise contains an implicit and sincere apology."

"Right," Lewis said.

"*Very* sincere," Kellerman said.

"Good." Giardello clasped his hands on the desk in front of him. "May I likewise assume neither of you will have a problem offering your *explicit* apologies to our colleague Detective Lambert?"

"That jerk?" Lewis bridled. "If he'd spent the same amounta time lookin for Stella and Campbell as he has doggin' our heels—"

"What the hell is wrong with you?" Giardello boomed, his eyebrows lowering like thunderheads. "Forget about your heels, this is about you stepping on *his* toes, and I want him pacified before Barnfather gets involved! *Understood?*"

Lewis opened his mouth, closed it, and finally nodded.

"I'll phone him," he said.

"Promptly," Giardello said.

"Right," Lewis said.

"Thank you," Giardello said, and leaned back in his chair. "Now, go ahead and tell me why you've come knocking on my door."

Lewis stared at him.

Kellerman squirmed a little.

"Well?" Giardello said, looking from one man to the other. "Dare I say it isn't to report that those escaped psychopaths are in custody?"

"Maybe it better wait," Lewis said.

"Till you ain't mad at us," Kellerman said.

Giardello regarded them suspiciously, a frown creasing his forehead.

"Speak," he said. "*Now.*"

Lewis sighed, edged forward in his seat, sighed again, and said softly, "We want your permission to snitch information about the breakout to the press."

Giardello looked at him.

"Oh," he said. "Is that all?"

"Yeah," Lewis said. "I guess that's it."

Giardello's run-for-cover smile was back on his face. "Before I throw you out of here, I'd like you to satisfy my curiosity and tell me *why* you'd make such a damned idiotic request," he said.

"See," Kellerman said, "it gets back to why we went out to the hospital."

"An' also to what's in here," Lewis said, raising the manilla envelope off his lap and dropping it on Giardello's blotter.

Keeping his eyes on the two detectives, Giardello reached out for the envelope with a sort of slow, guarded hesitancy, as if it might be booby-trapped, or perhaps contain hazardous radioactive material. Then, moving just as slowly, he slid out the papers it contained, read them over, and put them back down on his desk, stacking them neatly atop the envelope.

"So," he said after several long seconds. "According to his employment application, our Mr. Dubick was once a member of the esteemed state police force."

"Till he got the big hammer for stealing cash an' jewelry from the evidence room," Lewis said. "It's all in the follow-up report made by the personnel manager at Safeway. I got it stapled right to the appli—"

"I have eyes," Giardello said. He looked down at his meshed fingers and cracked his knuckles. "How about you act as if I'm not too bright, and explain what Dubick's background has to do with this case."

Lewis nodded, took a moment to collect his thoughts, and spent the next five minutes telling him about the meeting he and Kellerman had with Blair, and the access the hospital administrator had given them to D-ward.

"Inmates didn't make any secret about Dubick runnin' a one-man black market on smokes an' other stuff," he said. "Or about him bein' real cozy with Mutter Campbell."

"Especially once Campbell told him he had a little nest egg on the outside," Kellerman added.

"Just so we're clear on this," Giardello said. "You are telling me Edward Dubick was in complicity with Stella and Campbell all along. That he was never actually their hostage. And that he was probably killed . . . why?"

"Maybe he asked for the bread he was supposed to get for settin' up the break, an' they decided it was better to wax him than cough it up."

"Or *couldn't* cough it up because they never really had it in the first place," Kellerman said.

"Or maybe they had a blowout over somethin' else, it don't matter," Lewis said. "Point is, Dubick was no innocent victim."

Giardello was still pulling at his knuckles. The lines on his forehead had deepened, and there were new ones around his mouth.

"There's no solid evidence," he said. "Only guess-work, and the word of a few crazies who might still bear a grudge toward a dead man who used to be their guard."

"Don't forget the report," Kellerman said.

"An' the lousy feelin' I've had all along that Lambert's got his own secret agenda," Lewis said.

"I'm telling you, Gee, his reason for putting a lid on this case has never been to avoid a panic," Kellerman said. "The staties have kept quiet about one of their boys being dismissed for stealing evidence, and they want things to *stay* that way. Lambert's only lookout is protecting their reputation."

"Even if it means lettin' two killers run free without the people in this city knowin' about it," Lewis said. "Right now they're like wolves prowlin' through a herd of blind sheep."

Giardello rubbed his eyes.

"Jesus Christ," he said.

He stood up suddenly, turned, and looked at the glass case that covered the wall behind his desk. Inside it were the uniform patches of every unit of the Baltimore police department, perhaps two dozen of them in all, carefully displayed in three rows, one above the other. When he had originally gotten the office he'd thought of decorating the wall with something to take his mind off work—a painting of ships at sea, or bare-bottomed nymphs cavorting merrily in the forest, or maybe one of the photographic blowups he had of Baltimore's nineteenth-century shipyards. But in the end he'd decided to surround himself with reminders of the things that mattered most in his life—pictures of his family on the desk in front of him, the insignia of the police force behind him. Between them he had always found his purpose and his bearing.

"This is what I'm going to do," he said, speaking in a low, measured voice. His back was still turned. "I'm going to leave you two in this office while I go into the coffee room and grab something to eat. I'm also going to leave my personal phone book in the top drawer of the desk. In that book, under the listing for the *Baltimore Sun*, are the names and direct phone numbers of three trustworthy reporters. Should you go into my drawer, open that book, call one of them, and confidentially tip him off about the escape, I will never know. *No one* will except you and the reporter that is contacted. The source or sources of the leak will remain anonymous, and this conversation will never be mentioned to anyone. We will not even bring it up among ourselves." He slowly turned to face them. "Am I understood?"

Lewis and Kellerman looked at him for several moments, the room very quiet except for the noise filtering in from the hallway.

"Yeah," Lewis said at last. Beside him Kellerman was nodding. "We got you."

"Good," Giardello said. "Now, if you'll excuse me, I'm taking my break and will be back in ten minutes."

Without another word, he strode around his desk, pulled open the door, and walked out into the hallway.

Lewis waited until the door had closed behind him.

Then he got up, locked it, and sat down behind the desk to make his call.

"YOU ASK ME what I think, we should go out to brunch," Teheran was saying.

She stood in Harry's bedroom doorway, her robe replaced by one of his expensive Armani shirts; obviously she'd been digging around in his closet. From where he sat on the couch he could see her nipples pushing against the thin cotton fabric of the shirt—which Harry had to admit was a very nice picture—but he had other things on his mind right now, and furthermore he didn't really like the idea of her helping herself to his clothes—who the hell had told her she could go into his closet?

"We'll see," he said, wondering if she planned to leave his house with the shirt, claim it just like that. "First I have to make an important phone call."

"I know this cool place, the Blue Plate Luncheonette, that's got *amazing* buttermilk flapjacks," she said. "Or Belgian waffles with strawberries and bananas and tons of whipped cream—"

"Let's talk about it later," Harry said, reaching for the phone on the coffee table. "Meanwhile, why don't you get dressed?"

She made a sulky face, her expression saying he'd hurt her feelings.

"It's those police who put you in this mood, isn't it?" she complained. "I mean, you looked pretty upset when you were talking to them."

"Please, I only need a few minutes of privacy," Harry said. He supposed he could put his foot down, tell her to *take off* the shirt, but it *was* something how it showcased her breasts, and anyway he wanted to avoid an argument at the moment.

She turned into the bedroom, still frowning, her posture stiffening—making a whole production out of her displeasure.

Harry kept his eyes on her ass, watched it sway back and forth under the tail of his shirt. Late Carter-era jailbait she might be, but, ah God, worth every illicit nibble.

He reached for the phone and punched in a number from memory, nervously clicking his teeth as he waited for someone to pick up at the other end of the line. Teheran was right about those cops, but only in a sense. It wasn't their knocking on his door that had set him on pins and needles, but the news they'd brought about Stella . . .

"Yeah?" Vincent LoCicero said groggily through the earpiece, answering on the fourth ring

Reamis checked his watch. It was almost one o'clock in the afternoon, about time the guy dragged himself out of bed.

"Vin, it's Harry. Sorry if I woke you up."

"Reamis? Didn't know you worked on holidays."

"I don't," Reamis said. "Look, I had a couple of homicide detectives ring my doorbell this morning—"

LoCicero hissed air over his front teeth. "What do you mean?" he asked immediately. "Don't tell me the fucking prosecutor's office is cookin' up another bogus indictment—"

"Vin, relax, they didn't come to talk about you specifically," Reamis said.

"Then who *were* they talking about?"

"Frank Stella."

"*Stella?* He telling tales at the bughouse or something?"

"He's out, Vin."

"Huh?"

"You heard me," Reamis said. "He escaped last night."

"It can't be," LoCicero said. "I was watching *television* last night. They'd've had something about it on the news."

"Look, I felt the same way when those cops told me, but why would they make up a story like that?"

"Musta had *some* reason," LoCicero said. "That hospital Stella's in, it's supposed to be maximum lockup."

"I know, Vin. I'm the guy who got him transferred there," Reamis said. "I also know when the cops are trying to run a line of bullshit, and trust me, this isn't one of those times. Stella's out, and they wanted me to point them in the direction he'd go running."

Silence.

"What'd you say?"

"What was I *supposed* to say? I told them I know

141

nothing about his business or social contacts, and that if I *did* know I naturally couldn't tell them because of attorney-client privilege, yadda yadda yadda."

"They accept that?"

"They had no choice," Reamis said.

LoCicero made a sound like an idling diesel engine as he digested everything he'd been told.

"I still don't get why neither of us heard about this on the news," he said after a moment.

"Me neither," Reamis said. "But the fact remains—"

He heard his bedroom door open again and glanced over at it, ready to wave Teheran back inside, then he saw that she was standing there in the hallway with his shirt unbuttoned, its sleeves slipped down below her shoulders. She smiled and came slowly forward into the living room, the open shirt flaps parting back over her breasts to expose the blushy red caps of her nipples, those glorious nipples, ah God, he thought, ah God, there they are. They seemed to wink at him enticingly as she approached.

"You there or we get disconnected?"

"Sorry, Vin," Reamis said. "What I was going to say was that we ought to be ready in case Stella gets in touch with one of us—"

"Ready? For what?"

"Well, I just thought—"

"Listen, Harry," LoCicero said. "Stella wants to talk to me, for old time's sake, I'll do it long as it's on his quarter. But I don't play with him no more. He's trouble, *capice*?"

"Which is exactly why I *called* you," Reamis said. Teheran had sat down beside him on the couch, slid up close to him, her abundant breasts spilling from inside the shirt, her hips and thighs touching his own, pressing softly against his own, her fingers tugging at the sash of his bathrobe . . .

"Goddamn it, Harry, what's wrong with you today? Can't you finish a fucking sentence?"

"Sorry again. I'm a little distracted," Reamis said. "Look, this thing's probably no big deal, okay? I just figured Stella might feel we have some obligations toward him."

"Which we don't," LoCicero said. "Or at least *I* don't."

"Of course not. But if he *thinks* we do, and asks for favors we can't handle, favors we can't *afford*, well, you know, he's got a quick temper."

"Wait a second," LoCicero said. "Are you hintin' I should put a bodyguard on you? Is that it?"

Harry swallowed, thinking he really should send Teheran back into the bedroom until he'd finished his business. But she had undone the sash of his bathrobe and her hand was on his belly, gliding downward over his belly—how the hell was he supposed to stop her?

"No, no, I really didn't mean to suggest anything of the sort," he said, trying to concentrate on what he was saying. "But since you've mentioned it, maybe—"

"No fucking way, Harry."

"But—"

"Look, I hear things through the grapevine, okay?"

"Like what?"

"Like how Stella put you in charge of his money when he got sent up," LoCicero said. "No comment on what I think of *that* financial decision."

"I don't know what you're implying," Reamis said, and gulped as Teheran's hand fell on his crotch. "Besides, even if that was true, and I'm not saying it is, it would be between me and him—"

"Which is exactly why I ain't gettin' in the middle."

"Vin, please, listen to me." Reamis watched Teheran's hand moving between his legs, moving up and down, up and down, kneading him, making him rigid as a board. "We both know Stella's going to come knocking at one of our doors, maybe both, he's got nowhere else to turn—"

"And if he comes to me, I'll be glad to talk about old times over espresso and *granita*," LoCicero said. "I never screwed anybody who's done right with me, and the fact is I got no complaints with Stella. He always did his job and kept his mouth shut."

"Vin—"

"I ain't getting involved," LoCicero said. "Period."

Harry's heart was pounding, his head swimming, and the damned thing was that he couldn't tell whether it was because of what Teheran was doing to him or his agitation over LoCicero's offhand dismissal.

"Okay," he said. "I see it's futile trying to persuade you."

"That's right," LoCicero said. "And Harry?"

"Yeah?"

"Next time you call me, keep your cock in your pants—the heavy breathing gets on my nerves," LoCicero said, and hung up.

Reamis thumbed the disconnect button on his phone and angrily tossed it onto the couch.

"Maybe we should skip brunch, Harry," Teheran said. She flicked her tongue into his ear, her hand clenching him tightly now, working him. "You need to relax."

"I thought you were hungry," he said.

"I can eat in," she said with a coquettish smile, lowering her head to his lap. "You know, Harry, I get seriously turned on by you being gray down here—it makes you look so mature."

"Gray hair is the crown of glory," he said, putting his hand on the back of her neck. "It is earned by virtuous living."

"That Confucious?"

"The Bible."

"*Cool*," she said, and closed her lips over him.

AT AROUND THE same time Harry Reamis was making his phone call to Vincent LoCicero, Stella and Campbell were eating at a booth in a grimy luncheonette perhaps a half mile uptown. They had chosen the place because it was dark and nearly empty, and because it looked like the food would be cheap, and most of all because Stella had

144

wanted to duck into a rest room and wash the blood off his face before it drew the attention of any cops.

"Can't hardly stomach the slop they serve in this joint," Stella complained, taking a last bite of meat loaf and dropping his fork into his dish. "I swear, we were better off with the three squares a day we got at the hospital."

Campbell looked across the chipped Formica table at him and hungrily chewed his food.

"From the way you been diggin' into that tuna sandwich, I'm guessin' you don't mind it, huh?" Stella said.

Campbell chewed his food.

"Mutter, I gotta admit, it's beginnin' to bore me havin' nobody to talk to but you," Stella said. "Bein' you don't hardly ever talk back."

Campbell continued eating ravenously.

Stella turned away from him with a snort of disgust. In the next occupied booth, a couple of old ladies were drinking coffee and circling picks on a racing form they had spread open between them. At the counter a bearded man sat waiting for his lunch while the waitress stood nearby with nothing to do, staring into space and smoking a cigarette. Behind the counter, a cook in a food-stained apron tossed a slab of meat on the grill. The meat sizzled and spat up smoke and grease.

Stella lifted a paper napkin from the table, doubled it, and touched it to his swollen jaw.

"That *muchacho* got in a few lucky hits," he said, wincing as a big spot of blood appeared on the napkin. "Almost knocked out a few of my pearly whites."

Campbell swallowed a piece of his sandwich and washed it down with a gulp of soda.

Stella looked at him, vexed by his unbroken silence.

"You know, Mutter, I ain't one to accuse or judge," he said. "But we wouldn't have to be eatin' in this mud pit right now if you'd've took some food outta that grocery instead'a just soap an' drain cleaner. Lookin' back, you gotta admit it was pretty fucking idiotic—"

Something came alive in Campbell's eyes. "Keep your voice down."

Stella blinked. "Huh? What was that?"

"I told you to be quiet."

"*Shit* on what you told me." Stella was having a hard time believing he'd actually gotten a rise out of Campbell. "We go to the trouble of knockin' over that grocery, I get my head busted up tanglin' with the spic, and what's there to show for it? How far you think that two hundred bucks we grabbed outta his register's gonna go, huh?"

"It's your fault we don't have more."

"I ain't sure I get what you're sayin'," Stella said with a flash of temper. The fog lights had gone on in Campbell's eyes all right, and that in itself had been a surprise. But the attitude was something else. It just wouldn't do.

"You saw the safe in the back room same as I did. If it wasn't for you fighting with that guy, we could've got him to open it."

"I didn't know about no back room till after we put him down," Stella said. "An' neither did *you*—"

"I'm just saying you didn't have to start with him."

Stella's eyes widened with mounting incredulity. One minute Campbell had been sitting across from him without a word, and the next he was making more noise than he had in two or three months . . . which was—not coincidently—when they had upped his dosage of meds at the hospital. Maybe he was finally coming out from under them now that the pharmacy had been closed awhile, so to speak. And maybe that wasn't such a good thing.

"I don't need your lip, Mutt," he said. "I really don't."

"Then keep off my back."

There was a strained silence. Stella kept staring at him with commingled anger and disbelief.

"Okay, forget it, ain't no sense us makin' a scene," he said after a minute, glancing around for the waitress. "Let's get outta here."

Campbell slowly shook his head. "I'm not done eating."

Stella acted as if he hadn't heard him. "Where's our goddamn *check*, missy?" he said in a loud voice, clicking his fingers in the air.

The waitress studied him a moment through a drift of cigarette smoke, then pulled a pen from behind her ear, totaled up the check, tore it from the pad, and brought it over.

"Thank you," she said neutrally, and was about to place the check on the table in front of Stella when he snatched it from her hand.

She frowned and turned back toward the counter.

"*Hold* it," he said. "This ain't right."

The waitress read the check over his shoulder.

"You ordered a tuna sandwich, a meat loaf special, two sodas," she said, running her finger down the menu items they'd ordered. "Comes to thirteen seventy, which is what I wrote down."

"I can see what you *wrote*," Stella said sharply. "But I'm tellin' you the chow in this dump makes me want to puke."

"Mister, I only serve the food, I don't cook it," she said. Her eyes shifted to his plate. "Besides, looks to me like you did a pretty good job putting away that meat lo—"

Stella banged his hand down on the table with such rattling force that ice and soda sloshed over the rim of his glass.

"That the way it looks, huh?" he said, his eyes gleaming. "Well, I ain't payin' a *dime* for your rat feed, let alone almost fifteen bucks."

The waitress stepped back, her face reddening. "Hey, you got a problem, talk to the owner, he's the guy behind the counter—"

"I'll be happy to have a word with him," Stella said. "Just you bring him right on over, tramp."

"Better take it easy," Campbell said.

"Go to *hell*," Stella said. His glittering eyes burned

147

into the waitress's. "I want your boss *over* here so I can set him straight."

"That's all right," the cook said. He had moved away from the grill and cautiously reached beneath the counter. "I can hear you from where I'm standing."

"What you think you're doin' with your hands, you fuckin' soup splash?" Stella shouted. "You wanna take me down, you better be hidin' somethin' with plenty mojo under there."

The cook stared at him, his hand slipping farther under the counter. The bearded guy at the counter also had his eye on Stella and was fidgeting nervously with his fork. Watching from the adjoining booth, one of the old ladies had accidentally swept the racing form over the edge of the table, but neither of them seemed to notice the pages fluttering to the floor.

The waitress's face had gone from red to milky white. Her bottom lip was trembling.

Stella rose off his seat a little.

"Come on," he said to the cook. "Show me what you got—"

Campbell's hand suddenly shot across the table and grabbed Stella by the elbow. "That's enough."

"What the fuck do you think you're doin'?" Stella tried to jerk away, but Campbell's big fingers remained curled around his arm. "Let me go! You hear me you fuckin' lummox, let me—"

"Settle down," Campbell said in a low voice. He reached into his jacket pocket with his free hand, pulled out some folded money, separated a couple of ten-dollar bills with his thumb and forefinger, and let them fall onto the table.

"Come on," he said, and stood up. His hand was still fiercely clenched around Stella's elbow. "We're getting out of here."

Stella started to protest, but Campbell gave his arm a sharp twist, and the only sound to escape his quivering lips was a rasp of pain. He shot Campbell a black, hateful look.

The waitress silently counted the money the big guy had left on the table, and nodded to let the cook know it covered the check. His hand emerged from beneath the counter, leaving whatever he'd been reaching for hidden from sight.

Campbell lifted his bulging paper bag from beside him on the seat, and then hastily pushed Stella through the door and out onto the sidewalk, never letting go of his arm.

Everyone in the coffee shop watched them from the window, and kept watching them until they had moved on up the block and out of sight.

At last the waitress took the money off the table and handed it to the owner, who thought briefly about calling the cops, and then decided he'd already had enough excitement for one day. Those kooks had looked like real bad ones, no question about it, but they had paid their check and then some, good-bye and good riddance.

No harm done, he thought.

Not knowing otherwise.

"MOM, WHAT KIND of fish is *that*?" Vibeca asked, her eyes wide in the pale fluorescent glow coming from the aquarium tank. She had positioned herself in front of her brother and their two friends—being the shortest of the bunch—and was leaning against the visitor rail on her tiptoes, pointing at the glass, her finger drawing an imaginary line in the air as she excitedly tracked the movement of a large spotted ray.

Jolanda checked the visual key below the exhibit.

"It's called an eagle ray," she said.

"But I thought eagles were *birds*," Vibeca said.

Jolanda watched the creature execute a graceful turn, the sleek disc of its body gliding through the blue-green water, its long, whiplike tail whirling out behind it.

"They are," she said, patting her daughter on the shoulder. "But you see how the fins flap like wings? And the way it almost seems to be flying? I guess those things reminded the person that named it of an eagle."

"Dummy," Andrew whispered to his sister. "*Anybody* coulda told you—"

Jolanda caught him from behind in a mock stranglehold.

"Now, now, let's try to be nice to each other," she said, gently wringing his neck.

He giggled playfully. "All I said was—"

"That's enough," she said. "Naturally I don't believe you *meant* to call your sister a name, but I'm warning you not to do it again just in—"

Jamal interrupted her with a tug on her sleeve.

"Yes?" she asked

"Can we see what's upstairs?" he said.

"Yeah, let's *go*!" his sister said.

"Sure," Jolanda said. "If you want."

"But Mom, *I* wanna stay here and watch the *eagle ray*!"

"Vi can stay here by herself," Andrew said. "Or how about me and Jamal go up first and you meet us later with the girls?"

"Yeah!" Jamal said. "How *about* it?"

Jolanda looked down at them. Ah, the joys of parenting, she thought.

"Let's compromise," she said. "Give Vibeca a little while longer, and then we'll all head upstairs together."

The boys frowned but mercifully kept their complaints to themselves.

A few minutes later Vibeca announced she'd had her fill of the ray exhibit, and in keeping with her promise, Jolanda led the kids onto the escalator and up to Level 5 through galleries of captive marine life, where her eye was caught first by a color-changing eel as it phased through the spectrum like a compressed, gaudy rainbow, and then by a chain of sliversides lashing past a mat of aquatic plants, and then by a fish with feathery orange spines that flared and undulated in the cycling water, making it look almost like a tropical flower, the kind she might use in her more lavish arrangements.

Watching the profusion of sea creatures, seeing them

dart, flit, hide, and generally go about their fish business, she wondered if they could sense the difference between the artificial scenery designed for their aquarium habitats, and the natural reefs and rock formations they had been snatched away from . . . wondered whether they had been fooled by the illusion of freedom, or in some dim way perceived that their world was nothing more than a clever deception, its boundaries enclosed by thick walls of glass. It was an odd, gray sort of thought, she knew. And even odder was the fact that it had occurred to her more than once as she and the kids had roamed the ascending walkways of the aquarium.

Looking back on her afternoon, Jolanda supposed her funk could be traced to the series of hang-ups on her answering machine, although she didn't know why they'd spooked her to the extent that they had—there were a lot of winners running around the streets of Baltimore with nothing better to do than harass people, and a prank call was an easy and anonymous way to get on someone's nerves. Besides, it wasn't exactly as if such things were rarities in this city, and at least this morning's round hadn't been of the vulgar or threatening variety— which might have been the case had she been home to pick up the phone. It didn't take any genius to know you couldn't provoke a response from a cassette tape.

When she really thought about it, she guessed what had made the calls so distressful to her was their coincidental timing. She had noticed them on her machine just minutes after she'd been remembering her bad old days in the projects and women's shelters, the ones that bracketed the *worse* old days with Mutter Campbell— a god-awful period she rarely looked back on, and sometimes wished she could entirely strike from her recollection.

Still, there were moments when the memories came rushing into her head of their own accord, and as she'd been getting ready to pick up the kids, she had thought about Mutter for the first time in a very long while. It had been four years since she'd left him, which made it—what?—nearly a *decade* ago that they had met . . . ten years, Dear Lord, ten years gone, yet how clear the images were, once they started coming, and how helpless she was to push them from her mind.

That day, the day they met, she had been working as a clerk in a supermarket, and had been struggling to pull something off a high shelf, and he was there doing some shopping, and noticed the problems she was having, and offered to get it down for her, reaching for it easily, without having to stretch a muscle. He was tall, the largest man she'd ever seen, yet so incredibly shy, even withdrawn—he introduced himself to her as *Matthew*, she remembered, and later, *weeks* later, after they'd gone on several dates and he finally told her his real name, he'd explained that he'd always been embarrassed by it, wondering aloud what kind of mother would stick her son with a name that could be shortened to Mutt.

She had laughed, then, finding it both strange and funny that he'd actually lied about his *name*, thinking about her own mother dumping her off on an aunt's doorstep when she was four and then disappearing forever, remarking that there were worse things a parent could do to a child. And he had become furious with her, and gotten a strange, scary look in his eyes, and told her to stop laughing. And though she'd told him she hadn't meant to hurt his feelings, he had gripped her wrist so hard it bruised, and said not to make excuses, warning her, warning her not to laugh at him. When he finally calmed down, he apologized for hurting her, and said it was an accident, said he was sorry, said it would never happen again, and she had believed him.

If only she had been a little wiser at the time, a little more *knowing*, the ugliness of that scene might have opened her eyes to what she could expect in the years that followed, and she might have avoided the innumerable beatings she would suffer at his hands, perhaps even anticipated his slide into mental illness . . . but she had been an inexperienced girl of seventeen, a girl who had felt lonely and worthless and unwanted all her life, and here was Mutter telling her that he loved her, telling her she was beautiful and special, telling her that he could take her away from the slum, away from her aunt and her crackhead boyfriend and the filthy dangerous halls of the projects, take her away . . .

"Earth to Mom, earth to Mom, do you copy?"

"Hmmm?" She glanced down at Andrew, suddenly aware that she had balled her hands into fists at her sides and was clenching them so hard her fingernails had left little half-moon imprints in her palm.

"I asked if you'd mind if we throw Vi to those sharks." He bobbed his head at the tank they had paused to view and gave her with a mischievous grin. "Since you didn't answer, Jamal said it'd probably be okay."

"I did *not* say that," Jamal said.

"Did so!" Vi shrilled.

"Andrew's *lying*," Beverly added, jumping to her brother's defense.

"You're the one who's—"

"Shhhhh!" Jolanda said. "There are other people here and you're disturbing them."

"But Mom—"

"I don't care who said what, Andrew," she said in the firmest voice she could manage. "Now, quit clowning around before you get yourself in deep trouble."

He frowned at the no-nonsense look on her face and swiftly turned back toward the tank.

Jolanda stood behind the kids, watching the long gray forms of the sharks as they sliced through the water. She saw one of them dive down from where it had been hovering buoyantly near the surface of the tank, glanced at the key to see what type of shark it was, read that it was a sand tiger, then read the descriptive text underneath the species name and discovered that it was both a man-eater and an example of prebirth cannibalism: the pregnant female might typically carry several fertilized embryos, but only one would be spawned, having consumed its developing brood-mates in utero for their nutrients.

She felt a tiny chill that had nothing to do with the temperature inside the gallery. *Prebirth cannibalism.* How nice. Such cuddly animals, these . . .

That very instant, the shark came hurtling toward her like a torpedo, gills pulsing on its large head, its fins leaving a spiraling white wake in the water. Her thoughts cut short, she glimpsed row upon row of cusped, blade-like teeth in its cavernous mouth before it veered off sharply toward the other end of the tank.

Jolanda felt suddenly foolish over the way she'd been startled by the creature—but that did not stop a shudder from running from her arms to her fingertips. For a moment—just a single, doubtlessly irrational moment—she was sure its eyes had been staring at her with a kind of hungry, insensate rage, as if to communicate that it was very well aware of the barrier separating them, and to let her know what would happen if it could break through the glass to her world . . .

Let her know that if it only could, it would make her sorry she had ever come near it.

NINE

IN JOHN MUNCH'S opinion, what made Nicky "the Nose" Blount a first-rate informer was being an abysmal failure at everything else. A longtime flunkie of Vincent LoCicero, the Nose was the perpetual low man on the totem pole, the guy who got handed the crummiest jobs, the penny-ante crap that nobody with standing would touch. This probably would have been the case even had Nicky chosen to lead an honest existence, and become, say, a postal clerk or store cashier—or so Munch maintained, anyway. He hadn't been meant to rise to the top, or even the mid-level, of his occupation. Nicky was a small fish. His place—his natural milieu, to put it in literary terms—was at the bottom, performing the dull, menial, undemanding tasks that nobody much noticed or cared about, but which kept the world spinning on its axis. And having relinquished all hope of ever getting the choice gigs, Nicky had decided his only way of grabbing an extra buck now and then was to fink on his bosses. Which was why Munch believed his negligible status as a crook conversely gave him considerable value as a police informer.

Munch had been working in the Criminal Investigations Division of the BPD when he'd first busted the Nose maybe six, seven years back; at that time his job for the LoCicero family was stocking mob-owned cigarette machines in taverns throughout the city. But Nicky had been too lazy and disorganized to make his deliveries on any kind of regular schedule, and more often than not the machines would remain empty while whole shipments of untaxed cigarettes went stale in the back of his truck.

After being relieved of that task by his boss, Nicky had been given the job of watching the door at one of LoCicero's floating crap games, making sure none of the players brought pieces into the room or got drunk or out of line. That too had fallen by the wayside, when Nicky made a pass at somebody's girlfriend and instigated a rolling, tumbling brawl that spilled out into the street and drew the cops, who promptly drove the combatants away in handcuffs and shut down the action.

Nicky was then given a succession of minor responsibilities that LoCicero hoped would keep him busy and out of trouble: mopping the booths at sex shows, driving Vince's Lincoln to the service station, picking up his weekly order of gorgonzola from his favorite cheese shop in Little Italy, bringing his clothes to the dry cleaners and his shoes to the shoemaker . . . that sort of thing. But, true to form, the Nose had screwed up due to his negligence, unreliability, and penchant for getting on people's nerves. The poor slob couldn't even cut it as an errand boy; it was as if something inside him just wouldn't let him succeed.

Lately Vince had been having him make unlicensed trash pickups at perhaps two-dozen small groceries, delis and bodegas around the city. Though the Nose's worried detractors felt this job left him with as much room for a debacle as he'd had in his cigarette delivery days, Vince reminded them there were significant differences between the two assignments. In his current setup, the Nose did not have to take brand-name inventories. Somebody else collected the payments. Once a week he would cart off the garbage in his van and dump it somewhere in the woods out of town, and that was it. Even the Nose couldn't blow this deal, Vince had said—a statement that reassured no one, but at least his choice of words had been worth some unintentional laughs.

Today Munch had arranged to meet the Nose on the corner of Spencer and Kennett Streets, and watching him pull his panel truck over to the curb, Munch was a little depressed to see Nicky, who was pushing sixty, showing signs of advanced wear and tear. The skin of his face was sagging and doughy. His frame had shrunken. His bargain dentures had yellowed. Whereas the disproportionately large nose for which he'd been nicknamed had once jutted from his face with sharp, hawklike splendor, it had thickened considerably and come to resemble an overripe avocado. He had a bald spot on the back of his head the size of a large yarmulke, and had combed a few greasy straggles of hair across it in a vain attempt at concealment.

Munch frowned as he watched the Nose climb out of his truck. The poor guy was even a loser when it came to how he'd aged.

"Long time no see," the Nose said, extending his hand as he approached. "What's the matter, babe, you look like bad news."

Munch shrugged. No sense explaining it was because Nicky looked like he was getting ready to step off the treadmill of life.

He gripped his palm. "How's the garbage hauling business?"

"It stinks," the Nose said.

"Cute," Munch said.

The Nose winked and rattled laughter.

"So," he said, "how can I be of service to my favorite bull?"

Munch took the mugshots of Stella and Campbell out of his sport jacket and showed them to the Nose.

"Recognize either of these pinup boys?"

The Nose tapped Stella's photo with his finger.

"That mean bastard, sure," he said. "Frank Stella.

Ain't any secret he used to be a hatchet for Vince. The big gorilla don't look familiar, though."

"His name's Mutter Campbell," Munch said.

"Don't ring no bells. Hearda *Glen* Campbell, and Campbell's *soup*, but that's about it."

Munch regarded him a moment and then put away the pictures.

"You know where Stella's been the past few years?"

"Yeah," the Nose said. "That cuckoo cage out in Howard County."

"Up until yesterday you would've been right," Munch said.

The Nose looked at him. "You mean he *flew*?"

"Him and Campbell both," Munch said.

"Wow," the Nose said. "Didn't hear a fucking thing about it."

Munch chose not to mention that nobody else in Baltimore had, either.

"We have reasons for thinking Stella might come around to see Vince," he said. "That happens, I'd like to know about it right away. Or you can call Detective Pembleton—"

"*That* sainted do-gooder?" The Nose blinked. "Guys like him and guys like me don't mix."

"Look, Stella's really his beat, I'm doing this as a favor to him."

The Nose tugged at a loose flap of skin below his Adam's apple. "Listen, never mind Pembleton, you know I'm happy to give you a tip once in a while. But peekin' in Vince's *keyhole*, I ain't sure if I can do that . . ."

Munch reached into his jacket again, and this time slipped a white letter-sized envelope from his pocket.

"Here," he said, handing it to the Nose. "Maybe this will help you decide."

The Nose opened the envelope a little, peeked inside, and then cocked an eye at Munch.

"You pissed at me?" he said. "Or did you think you could put two fifty-dollar bills together and they'd *breed*."

"Nicky—"

"I mean, it was nice of you to look me up after all these months," he said, balking. "But far as what you're askin', Vince would crush me like a *worm* if he ever found out. Plus, I gotta be worried about Stella too."

Munch sighed. "How much you want?"

"Uh, well, lemme think." He gave his scrawny neck another pluck. "How about we make it *two* hundred for starters?"

"For starters?"

'I'm just saying, in case there are any complications—"

"Please, Nicky," Munch said. "Its no fun doing the tough cop routine, but you're leaving me no choice."

"What are you talkin' about?" Nicky spread his hands and shrugged like a Borscht Belt comic. "Business is business, and fair is fair. I don't see where 'tough' comes into the picture."

Munch shook his head with resignation, then quickly stepped off the curb, went around to the rear of the Nose's truck, and grabbed the handle of the cargo door.

"What you *doing*?" Nicky yelled, trotting after him.

"Seeing if you're hauling any garbage back here," Munch said. "There are severe penalties for illegal dumping."

"Aw, come on, you can't be *serious*—"

Munch paused, still gripping the handle. "You'll take the job for a hundred fifty bucks?"

"Let's compromise and make it one *seventy-five*—"

"Sorry," Munch said disappointedly, then hauled up the door and looked inside the truck.

His eyes suddenly widened with surprise. Stacked among the plastic garbage bags he'd expected to find were several dozen shipping crates, each one filled with pint containers of milk.

On the sidewalk, Nicky had gotten a pained expression on his face. "Hey, Munch, I can explain—"

"Milk?" Munch almost reeled from the stink wafting

159

out of the truck. "Are things so bad the LoCicero family's gotten into illegal *milk* deliveries?"

"Don't lay this on Vince, it's my own sideline," the Nose said. "Besides, I just got a few customers, what's the big deal—"

"The big *deal* is that, according to the law, milk has to be transported in refrigerated trucks," Munch said. "Leaving aside the fact that it isn't supposed to share cargo space with trash."

"Munch—"

"*Illegal* trash."

"Munch, listen, I just got a few customers. A deli here, a grocery there—"

"Nicky, do you have any idea who buys these pint containers?"

"Well, no . . ."

"Moms," Munch said.

"Oh."

"Moms who pack lunches for their kids as they go trotting off to school," Munch said.

"Oh." Nicky made a game attempt at looking concerned. "Like I said, I never really thought about it . . ."

"Maybe you should've, Nicky. You know what those kids are getting along with their vitamins when they drink this stuff?"

"Look, there ain't nothin' *wrong* with it—"

"They're getting stomachfuls of botulism, salmonella, and *E. coli* that's what," Munch said. "Every *one* of these milk containers is a Bahamas for bacteria. You're poisoning little children for profit."

"I'm telling you, Munch, I *love* kids, my sister's got three of 'em herself," the Nose said. "Besides, I only do short runs. Twenty minutes from distributor to retailer. Maybe *ten*. Ain't enough time for nothin' to spoil—"

"Then drink some of it," Munch said.

The Nose snuffled nervously. "Huh?"

"You heard me." Munch reached into the truck, pulled a pint container of milk from one of the crates, and held it out to him. "Drink this down right now and I'll believe you."

"Hey, I got no problem with that on principle, but what it is, I already had breakfast——"

"Drink it."

The Nose looked at him with open horror.

"I'm giving you a choice, Nicky," Munch said. "You either take this container of milk from my hand and gulp down what's inside it *right now*, or give back my hundred bucks and keep an eye out for Stella for free. Plus, I want a promise that you'll get rid of this putrefying cow juice and never haul another load."

"Huh? You gotta be kidding, Munch, what kinda deal is that? We're supposed to be pals——"

"Business is business," Munch said. "Decide."

Weighing his choices, Nicky looked at the envelope he'd been handed, looked at the milk container Munch was holding, then slapped the envelope back into Munch's palm with a crestfallen frown.

"I lose," he said gloomily.

As it should be, Munch thought.

EIGHT P.M. ON Saturday, seventy-four degrees outside, a few pale stars sprinkling the clear, dusky sky above the rooftops: it was going to be a mild, unzip-your-jacket-and-bask-in-the-breeze kind of evening.

Alissa Berger walked quickly down the block, wishing she was in the mood to enjoy the weather, wishing her boyfriend hadn't gotten her so mad, wishing more than anything that they hadn't fought on this, her birthday, of all days. She'd left him sitting in his car about ten blocks behind her, and supposed that in the back of her mind she'd thought he would follow, although she had told him not to, and said she would be even more upset with him if he did—*I need time to calm down, need some breathing room, so please, if you want to do something nice for me tonight, being that's what you've been* claiming *you want, just respect my wishes and leave me alone.* How much plainer could she have been?

161

Happy birthday to me, she thought.

She reached the corner and turned right toward home, dressed to kill in a black blouse and miniskirt from which she'd just snipped off the store tags that afternoon, her feet a little cramped in her new high-heeled shoes . . . but what the hell, she hadn't planned on breaking them in with a long hike tonight, hadn't planned on walking *anyplace* besides maybe from Brian's car to the restaurant where they were supposed to have dinner, and afterward from his car to his apartment, where she'd hoped to give Brian an up-close and private look at the other interesting new garments she had bought for today's special occasion, the ones she had on *underneath* her blouse and skirt, figuring she would say good-bye to her twenties, and usher in the big three-oh, with plenty of noise and fireworks in Brian's bedroom.

Well, *c'est la vie*, she wasn't going to spend the rest of the night feeling sorry for herself, or having second thoughts about the way she'd left Brian . . . after all, he was the one who'd done something stupid, and then, instead of admitting it, tried tossing the blame over to her side of the court, acting as if *she* was being stubborn and unreasonable. She would never know what flaw in the male ego made even the nicest guys lash out like bratty schoolboys when they knew they were in the wrong.

Her feet really aching now, Alissa paused at a bus stop, but didn't see anything coming, or even anyone else *waiting*. Then she remembered that the busses would be on a holiday schedule, and decided to keep walking. She was only a short distance from her building, anyway, and was thinking she might stop to pick up some Chinese takeout, maybe rent a video at the place next door to the restaurant. She had left her apartment without much cash—*Your wish is my Amex charge tonight,* Brian had promised—but unless she was mistaken there was a bank with an ATM around the next corner.

She walked on, wondering whether Brian was still sulking in his car where she'd asked him to pull over, thinking their whole ridiculous argument could have

162

been avoided if he just came down from outer space and *listened* to her once in a while. When they had been making plans for her birthday last week, and Brian proposed they go out to dinner at her favorite restaurant, a little Italian place called Amoroso's on Fawn Street, she had advised him to make reservations well in advance, reminding him it was very hard to get a table on an *ordinary* Saturday night, and that the place—which was very small and seated maybe a hundred fifty people, tops—was bound to be even more crowded than usual on Memorial Day weekend. *Sure, you got it, will do,* he'd assured her . . . and then had obviously forgotten their entire conversation, because when they arrived at Amoroso's tonight, and there had been no dinner reservations, he had sworn up and down that he'd never heard her say they would *need* them.

Though disappointed and annoyed with Brian, Alissa had also felt kind of sorry for him—he'd gotten decked out in an expensive suit for their date, and been really sweet when he picked her up, bringing her flowers and an expensive gold bracelet—and she had told him not to worry about dinner, they could still go to a movie or a dance club and have a decent time. But he'd suggested they find a different restaurant, which was about the only thing she absolutely *didn't* want to do after having her heart set on Amoroso's veal parmigiana. And because he knew he'd blown it by not making reservations, and felt guilty about that, Brian soon went from *suggesting* they eat out somewhere else to *insisting*. But she'd remained steady in her refusal, and he'd gotten all wound into a knot, and actually accused her of being spiteful and wanting to punish him for his mistake, making the whole thing about him and *his* hurt feelings . . .

Knowing full well there would be no reasoning with him until his selfish, defensive tantrum subsided, Alissa had told him to park the car and let her out, and then started walking home—which brought her right up to where she was now, heading for the bank so she could pay for her own chicken chow fun and invite Tom Hanks

163

to come home and celebrate her thirtieth, assuming his flicks weren't all checked out at the local video pit.

She reached the bank and peered through the glass entry doors to make sure there were no cash machines in the vestibule, feeling slightly uncomfortable about using the ones outside the bank. True, it wasn't that late, and this was a nice working-class area, but the street was pretty deserted and it was better to be safe.

Unfortunately, though, her recollection proved to be accurate—she didn't see any ATMs inside, and would have to use the outdoor machine around the corner.

Alissa turned the corner, fished around in her purse for her cash card, and then slipped it into the scanner with an automatic glance over her shoulder. She keyed in her password, considered making a fifty-dollar withdrawal from her checking account, then thought about the long and very possibly *lonely* weekend ahead—not to mention the holiday sales she might catch to cheer herself up—and decided to lighten her account by a couple of hundred bucks instead.

She waited as the machine went through the noisy process of dispensing four fifty-dollar bills and a receipt, quickly folded the money, and was about to slip it into her purse when something hard suddenly jabbed her between the shoulder blades.

She jerked with startlement, almost dropping the purse. *What . . . ?*

"Excuse, me, sweetie, but there ain't no need to put away that cash," a man's voice said from behind her. "Just give it here to me."

Her heartbeat accelerating in her chest, she glanced up at the security mirror above the machine and released a sharp, terrified breath.

There were two men behind her. The one hovering farther back in the shadows—the *lookout*, she thought with a surge of panic—was enormous, built like a professional wrestler. And the man who had spoken, standing close enough for her to feel his breath on her neck, was holding a gun, pressing it into her back.

Dear God, a *gun*.

He leaned over her shoulder and made an obscene sucking noise in her ear.

"I told you to give me the money," he said, and jerked the folded bills out of her trembling fingers.

A grin of cruel enjoyment slipped over his lips as their eyes met in the mirror. Alissa could see that his narrow, hollow-cheeked face was covered with cuts and bruises, as if he'd been in a very bad fight.

"Please," she said, her throat tightening around the word so that it came out as a moan. "Don't hurt me—"

"Quiet, l'il missy," he said. Whispering, whispering in her ear, then raising the gun to the back her head, pushing it forward until her chin was almost touching her collarbone. "Ain't nothin' personal, it coulda been you or anybody else."

She heard him cock the gun and swayed dizzily.

"Easy now," he whispered. "I'm gonna make it quick. You might feel some heat for a sec, kinda like a bolt of lightnin' in your brain. But after that there shouldn't be any pain at all."

Alissa had a sudden recollection of Brian standing at her door with his bouquet and gift box less than an hour ago. What was happening to her seemed so irreconcilable with that image, so impossible . . .

"Stella," the big man rasped from the shadows. "Not here—"

Alissa looked in the mirror above her head, saw the man with the gun still looking back at her and smiling, and the last thing she thought before he pulled the trigger was that the eyes above that smile were empty of all compassion.

Then the gun exploded, and she thought nothing ever again.

AT 9:30 ON Saturday night Meldrick Lewis went out to get the Sunday newspaper. He'd been home from work for three hours and the cold wave radiating from Barbara was worse than ever. She had been holed up in the bedroom with some fashion magazines, and he'd been listening to Patti Smith CDs on the living room stereo and wondering if he would have to sleep on the couch. All in all, he was glad he had a reason to leave the apartment for a while.

The *Sun* was on the stand at the nearby 7-Eleven and Lewis saw instantly that the story about Stella and Campbell had made the front page. The banner headline read "MANHUNT" in large block type, and the subhead said "Two Killers Escape From State Mental Hospital." Underneath were the same photographs of the escapees that police had been discreetly showing around for most of the day.

He snatched up a copy and opened it to page two. There were several pieces about the fugitives, and he quickly scanned the lead article's opening paragraphs:

Sunday, May 30
Sun Exclusive By James Thorburn

BALTIMORE—An anonymous source within the Baltimore police department informed this newspaper late yesterday afternoon that two mental patients with a history of violent felonies ranging from arson to homicide have fled a hospital for the criminally insane in Howard County.

Officials at the Central Maryland Psychiatric Center have since confirmed that Frank Stella, 37, and Mutter Campbell, 45, both of Baltimore, forced their way out of a maximum security ward at approximately 6:30 Friday night holding a guard at gunpoint and killing a fellow inmate during the escape.

Taken hostage by the pair and forced to drive them from the facility's grounds in his commandeered car, the guard, Edward Dubick, 36, also of Baltimore, was found shot and beaten to death on Highway 80 early Saturday morning.

The killers remain at large and spokesmen for

state, county, and Baltimore law enforcement agencies have yet to account for their failure to inform the news media of the expanding manhunt. When questioned about the danger to citizens as thousands flock to the parks and beaches for the holiday weekend, Special Investigator Craig Lambert, the commander of the state police search team, said, "While there's no denying the seriousness of their past offenses, we shouldn't assume they're an immediate threat to public safety. Whether or not they stay together, they will probably want to keep a low profile and find somewhere to hide. We've assembled a great team and have our eyes on our goal and are confident we'll apprehend these individuals before too long."

Lambert refused to comment when asked about information obtained from our source indicating the fugitives may have already claimed another victim, a Franklin Avenue bodega owner who was cold-bloodedly slain during a robbery attempt within 12 hours of the breakout.

Between them Stella and Campbell have in the past racked up nearly a dozen criminal convictions. Stella, reputedly a former soldier in the LoCicero crime family, was committed to Central Maryland after serving less than a year of a life sentence for . . .

Lewis closed the paper, paid for it, and left the store, thinking he'd have given his right arm to see that son of a bitch Lambert's expression when the reporter nailed him. The statie would have his ideas about where the information had sprung from, but neither he nor his cronies Barnfather and Stanton could point their fingers at a particular individual, and there was little chance they would do anything to follow up on the matter beyond blowing steam. None of the facts that had been exposed compromised the investigation in any way, and besides making certain parties in the government and law enforcement community look like the self-interested chumps they were, the story's biggest effect would be to force them to place more importance on the lives of human beings than their own reputations—and Lewis figured that only could be a good thing.

Wondering if Deep Throat had ever felt as righteous as he did at that moment, a bounce in his step despite his woes with Barbara, he tucked the paper under his arm and turned toward home.

TEN

ON SUNDAY MORNING, as people across Baltimore were reading about Frank Stella and Mutter Campbell's bloody escape from a psychiatric institution in the *Sun*—as well as hearing about it on early television and radio news broadcasts and even a major on-line service—the two fugitives awoke in a junk- and refuse-strewn lot somewhere between Fell's Point and Inner Harbor, a part of town considered a no-man's-land by all except the winos, dopers, and homeless derelicts stumbling aimlessly down its gutters and alleys.

It had been Stella's idea to spend the night there. After the edge came off his excitement over killing the girl at the cash machine, he had realized they needed a place to lay low, telling Campbell that the city parks would be too obvious, and that the police would probably be watching those areas round the clock. Then he had remembered the desolate slum stretching for miles west of the harbor and decided it would suit him fine. They could disappear there for as long as they wanted. The castoffs who wandered the area would never identify them—most likely they wouldn't be able to recognize their own mothers.

At a certain point while Stella was explaining all this,

Campbell had started acting in a way he found very scary, to say the least . . . They were standing near the dead girl's body, and Stella had just finished telling him where he thought they should hide, when he suddenly got the urge to pick up one of the girl's high-heeled shoes. He hadn't known why it came over him, had just noticed that the shoe had slipped off her foot when she fell, noticed it lying near the spot where her legs were twisted up in a puddle of blood, and had thought how round and terrified her eyes had been in the mirror above the cash machine, and how fine those legs were, how he liked the way her skirt had kind of ridden up her thighs when she'd dropped to the pavement. She'd been a sweet little piece, hadn't she? Probably got it all the time, he'd told himself, staring at the creamy whiteness of her thighs and wondering why he hadn't taken a few minutes to have some fun with the cow before he offed her, just a few damn minutes . . .

An unsettling possibility had occurred to him at that moment—could it be he was so used to making it with Missy Palm that he hadn't seen his chance to do it with a *real* girl when it smacked him in the face? A man was locked up long enough, it could get so he wouldn't know a hole from a pole. Maybe that was the thing, he'd thought . . . and now this urge to pick up the shoe had come upon him, and he went cruising along with it, lifting the shoe off the sidewalk, figuring he might carry the shoe around awhile and get rid of it later, or maybe keep it as a souvenir.

That was when Campbell had suddenly become enraged, growling at him like some goddamn caveman, his face getting all herky-jerky with spasms. Stella hadn't expected him to react that way, didn't know what the hell got him so mad, especially after he'd helped himself to that fucking soap and shit from the spic grocery . . . Who was he to accuse and judge? Who was *he*?

It had for sure been a tricky moment—Stella hadn't known what to do, and had supposed he would have to shoot Campbell if he came at him, let that be the end of it once and for all. But he hadn't really wanted a scene, not right there with the dead whore stretched out on the sidewalk maybe two feet from where they were standing. All he'd wanted was to get *away* from there, and he'd quickly started trying to talk Campbell down, get him to understand they'd *both* be screwed if the cops arrived while they were going at each other. At first Campbell had seemed beyond listening, beyond even connecting with his words—the fucking beast was in his eyes, Stella had thought—but Stella kept repeating that they didn't need to fight, they had to get out of there, repeating the same thing over and over like a parrot in the hope of getting the situation under control. And then by a stroke of luck he'd hit on the line about Campbell's wife, asking him if he wanted to chance getting caught before he had a chance to see her, and Campbell's face had grown calmer, and Stella had kept jabbering on about her, saying anything that came into his head just so he could use her name. *If you want to see Jolanda we'd better get on with things, don't forget you came all the way to Baltimore for Jolanda, you told me you wanted to bring Jolanda a present . . . Jolanda this, Jolanda that— Jolanda, Jolanda, Jolanda . . .*

Finally Campbell's face had stopped twitching, and though Stella saw that the anger was still in him, his eyes were no longer filled with it. It had been pushed behind whatever it was that the woman meant to him, or maybe whatever he had in *mind* for her. Stella didn't particularly care which it was, just as long as he knew Campbell had come down from his rolling boil.

His hand shaking around his gun, his heart slamming, Stella stood there a minute like someone who had come eye to eye with a jungle animal and then watched it turn and stalk off into its den, and wanted to be positive the crisis had really passed.

But everything was okay after that, everything was cool. Campbell had come along when he left the dead girl on the street, keeping silent all the way across town.

They had stuck to the darkest blocks, avoiding the little islands of light cast by the street lamps, and had reached the decaying scab of warehouses, garages, and tenements beyond Fell's Point sometime before midnight. There they had wandered into the lot where they'd slept, a filthy rectangle between two abandoned buildings that reminded Stella of a gap in a mouthful of diseased, rotting teeth. They had entered it through a hole in the chain-link fence that was supposed to prevent access from the street, startled off some junkies who had assembled there amid the darkness and garbage, and then said good night to the world.

Now the morning sun was out, working its way into the lot to intrude upon Stella's gray dreaming. He was curled on his side, his knees drawn up to his chest, his arms wrapped around them, his head propped on a crushed cardboard box that he had scavenged before going to sleep. He had slept with his right hand on the handle of his gun and the dead girl's shoe tightly pressed between his thighs, and all during the night had been disturbed by the gnawing and skittering of rodents, and a kind of uneven tapping sound over to his left. Once he'd even bolted upright in horror after feeling something brush against his cheek.

His eyes pried open by a bar of sunlight, he sat up, yawning and blinking, frowning in disgust as he got a clear daytime view of his surroundings.

The lot was even filthier than he'd thought; he couldn't even *guess* at how many years it must have taken for so much trash to accumulate in one place. There were broken bottles, crack vials, balled-up food wrappers and newspapers, gutted TV sets, rusty twists of metal, piles of concrete rubble mixed with scorched, blackened wood. There was a ragged sofa cushion that he'd tried using as a pillow, but it had turned out to be so deeply saturated with piss he'd had to fling it aside or choke on the stink.

Stella was still taking all this in when he heard the tapping sound again—*tap-TAP, TAP-tap, tap-tap-TAP*—

craned his head to see what was making it, and saw a large rat curled inside the rim of a discarded toilet seat maybe six feet away, its thick, scaly tail whipping from side to side, a litter of pink, hairless young ones wriggling under its belly.

Springing to his feet with a shudder of revulsion, he looked around for Campbell and saw him at the far end of the lot, urinating against a brick wall that was blotched with hardened wads of chewing gum and blaring scrawls of spray-painted graffiti.

"I've fuckin' *had* it!" he hollered. "Sleepin' in garbage an' slime. Sleepin' with a *rat nursery* by my head!"

Campbell stood with his back to Stella and kept doing his business.

"I feel like I been shoved up the asshole a' the world an' just keep slippin' deeper an' deeper inside!" Stella said.

Campbell gave no response.

"We got *problems*, Mutter, serious ones, and ain't nobody but me thinkin' about solutions."

Campbell continued to say nothing.

Stella angrily kicked an overturned bottle near his toe. "I'm tellin' you right now, I can't go on keepin' things together on my lonesome! Like it or not I need some help figurin' out what's next—"

"Enough," Campbell grunted. He turned and came toward Stella, zipping his pants.

Stella studied him as he approached. Not knowing what to expect.

"Look," he said, searching Campbell's eyes for the wild animal he'd glimpsed last night. "We're supposed to be partners, ain't we?"

"No."

Stella wished he had not blown up a second ago. He was hoping to pull another score—maybe a jewelry shop or a check casher, someplace where there would be plenty of money—and was not yet inclined to go it alone.

"I don't guess I'm readin' you too clear," he said with what he hoped was a conciliatory smile.

Campbell lifted a hand, palm upward. "I want my half of the money."

Stella looked at him a moment.

"Sure thing," he said. "Soon as the two of us finish talkin' about—"

"We're finished right *now*," Campbell said, his hand still extended. "Give me the money."

"Like I said, Mutter, I don't understand."

"That girl last night," Campbell said. "I told you not to kill her."

Stella seemed surprised. "*That's* the reason you're so cranky? Feelin' sorry for some—"

"You shouldn't have done it. The cops'll be on us for that."

"Hell, the heat's gotta be so high already, uppin' it a few degrees won't make any difference," Stella said. "Besides, ain't no use bickerin' about it now."

"There's you picking a fight with the groceryman. And that scene at the diner," Campbell said, leaving wide spaces between his words, as if each one had a hurdle to jump before getting from his brain to his mouth. "And Dubick."

"Well, if you're sayin' I get carried away on occasion, I'll admit—"

"Carried away on purpose," Campbell said

Stella gave him a darting glance.

"I don't know what the fuck you mean," he said.

"We could've left Dubick in the woods. But you said to put him in the car. Drive him into the city."

"So?"

"Dumping him on the highway, that was your idea too," Campbell said. "I remember."

"Like I said, so *what*?"

"You want to get noticed," Campbell said. "It's like this is a game."

Stella forced a laugh. It came out much shriller than he'd intended.

"What's *that* supposed to—"

"You're going to get us caught," Campbell said. "Maybe you don't care, but I do. I have to see my wife."

"Mutter, I been listenin' and listenin' and *still* don't get what you're kickin' about," Stella said. "You just better calm down—"

"I told you, we're through." Campbell motioned with his outstretched hand. "Give me my money."

Stella stared, his eyes two slits.

"If that's what you want, go ahead, I got enough troubles," he said finally. "But let's get somethin' straight. That cash from the whore last night, I'm keepin it all. I was the one who worked for it while you just stood there watchin'." A thin smile touched his lips. "I'm sure you won't object, bein' you got such tearful regrets over what happened to the darlin' girl."

The left side of Campbell's face pulled upward, then suddenly drooped, like a rubber band that had been stretched so far it had lost some of its elasticity.

"I want my share of what we got," he said. "From the girl and the groceryman."

Stella shrugged, stalling, thinking Campbell's tone had gotten downright menacing. If the dumb moose wanted to take a walk, let him go and good riddance . . . but he wasn't about to split the pot down the middle.

"Look, I'll let you have fifty, sixty bucks and we can call this thing settled," he said, figuring that ought to pacify Campbell.

He withdrew some folded bills from his pants pocket and peeled three twenties away from the rest.

"Here you go, Mudball," he said, and was about to give the money to Campbell when Campbell's hand suddenly shot out to his throat.

Stella uttered a surprised, strangled groan, Campbell's fingers pressing into him, clamping hard around his windpipe.

"*What*—" he sputtered, gripping Campbell's wrists and trying vainly to tear his hands away from his neck. "*What're you doin'?*"

175

Campbell tightened his choke hold, bending Stella's head backward. His eyes bulged. Air gushed out his nose and mouth. His normally bone-white face reddened as he sucked down a gurgling breath.

"*Stop it*," he rasped, his feet scuffing against the ground, amazement mingling with the fear and pain in his eyes as he felt himself being lifted, lifted off the ground. Air blasted out his nose and mouth. The pressure was crushing, unbearable, he couldn't breathe, couldn't *breathe*. "St—"

"The money," Campbell said.

Wheezing, his feet flailing, the veins in his temples standing out in blue relief, Stella crumpled up the bills he'd taken from his pocket, crumpled up *all* of them, and hurled them at Campbell so they rebounded off his chest.

"*Here! . . . Take it!*"

His face contorted with involuntary spasms, Campbell kept his fingers hooked around Stella's trachea for a very long moment . . . and then at last unlocked his grip.

Stella staggered, swayed on rubbery legs, and then fell crashing to the ground on his back.

"You—you coulda fucking *killed* me," he mumbled, hacking out a cough. He massaged his throat.

As Campbell stooped to pick the wadded bills off the pavement, Stella briefly thought about reaching for his equalizer, just whipping it out from under his jacket and blowing the motherfucker to the far side of the moon . . . but something inside him warned against it. It made no sense, none whatsoever, but it was like a part of him was afraid Campbell would stay on his feet whether he got hit with one, or even a dozen, .357 slugs. Screwy as that thinking might be, he wasn't giving himself any argument about what his prospects would be if Campbell didn't go down.

Still rubbing his throat, he watched Campbell cram the money into his pockets, slowly turn around, retrieve his paper grocery bag from where he'd left it overnight, and walk toward the fence that divided the lot from the street.

Stella stayed on his back for a minute or two longer,

waiting until Campbell had gone through the ragged opening in the fence. Then he sat up, reached for the shoe he'd taken from the whore, and slipped its stiletto heel through his belt loop.

Well, he thought, it looked like their little tag team was kaput. Campbell was so stuck on his wife, fine, let him go to her, and the two of them could rot in hell together. Stella had other things to think about, people of his own to call on. His lawyer. Vince LoCicero. And his mother. In that order. And soon.

Yessiree, it was time to make some serious moves lickety-split, and show everybody that Frank Stella was nobody's fool.

Nobody's.

LEWIS SHOULD HAVE realized making the Stella-Campbell investigation public would also make it go redball, but he didn't begin to suspect that had happened until he got the phone call from Gee Sunday morning beckoning him to headquarters.

If there were any doubts left in his mind by the time he reached the squad room at 8:30, they were dispelled by the sullen, bleary-eyed stares he drew from the other detectives—all of whom had gotten their day off jerked out from under them—as he walked past their desks toward his own. Had any additional proof been needed, he would have had to look no farther than the *tops* of their desks, which were bedecked with copies of the *Sun*, every one of them opened to James Thorburn's exclusive headline story.

"Hi, guys," he said with a self-conscious smile, and tipped the leather hat he always wore with the brim turned up, giving him what he felt was a beat/hip-hop crossbreed kind of look.

"Top of the lousy freaking morning, Lewis," Kay Howard said from where she stood propped against the wall, her frazzled red hair resembling a wildfire in the sylvan forests of Donegal, sipping some caffiene-free Flingy Purple Zapper herbal tea with an expression of profound distaste on her features. "Oh, what a delight it is to see you've joined us."

"A delight," Bayliss muttered from his desk, pulling his head out of the newspaper.

"I'd like to express a very special thank-you on behalf of us *all* to whoever may have leaked this story to the press, thus bringing about this happy gathering," Pembleton said. He was standing behind Bayliss and reading the paper over his shoulder. "Unfortunately, the identity of that party remains a mystery."

"Yeah, well, I don't think we'll ever know it," Lewis said.

"Some of us might do our best to find out," Russert said, looking up from *her* copy of the newspaper. As always she was perfectly put together, her neat blond tresses gleaming like spun gold, her makeup subtly highlighting her sculpted features as if she'd had a cosmetician fluff and powder her the minute she hopped out of bed.

"Good luck," Kellerman said. "There are lots of people who could've let the cat out of the bag."

"Right on, Mikey," Lewis said. He settled into his chair and began riffling through his phone memos. "Lots an' *lots*. Anybody here ever find the sucker, though, I'll help kick his butt."

"What I'd like somebody to tell me is when the feds are gonna pass legislation that'll stop rampant clear-cutting," Munch said.

They all looked at him.

"Huh?" Bayliss said, noticing that although Munch— like everyone else in the room – had an open copy of the *Sun* on his desk, he also had an open paperback book *inside* it.

"Clear-cutting," Munch said. "That's when logging companies chew up whole tracts of ancient forest so we can buy the Sunday papers and bitch about their contents."

"I know what it *is*," Bayliss said. "The thing I *don't*

know is how it has any connection to what we're talking about."

"Not every idea can be summarized in thirty seconds, Timmy-boy," Munch said. "Give me a holler when you've got a few hours."

Bayliss rose from his seat, went over to Munch, and picked up the book.

"*Confessions of An Eco-Warrior*," he said, glancing at its cover and reading the title aloud. "Yesterday it was food, today it's *trees*."

Munch looked up at him and smiled forbearingly. "Tim . . ."

"Will it never *end*?"

"Tim, you're sounding hysterical, not to mention a little dense," Munch said, sighing. "When it comes to the environment, everything has an impact on everything else. Clear-cut a hill and the runoff's gonna be full of silt that flows into streams, rivers, and oceans. Which is where the fish we eat tend to *swim*, assuming they aren't already finless mutants loaded with PCBs, or floating belly-up on the surface from chemical pollutants. We're talking complex interrelationships, macrosystems—"

Listening silently to the conversation, Kellerman studied the bagel and Nova lox he'd brought from the corner deli and decided to exchange them for a muffin.

Bayliss was shaking his head. "You saying you agree with those greenies that go around spiking trees and, uh, what's it called . . . ?"

"Monkey wrenching," Munch said.

"Yeah, right."

"Well *do* you?"

"Right here in this state, they want to flatten the Beltwood Forest, chop down trees that're *five hundred* years old, which makes them contemporaries of Shakespeare," Munch said. "The land rapers have gotta be stopped."

"But not if it means breaking the law . . ."

"Like I tried to explain, it gets complicated," Munch

179

said. He glanced over at Pembleton, smiling. "By the way, Frank, I talked to Nicky the Nose for you."

"Great, thanks a lot," Pembleton said. "How's he doing?"

"Don't ask," Munch said. "I told him LoCicero was your ball of wax . . ."

"And?"

"He said he was thrilled by the chance to assist a cop of your integrity and dedication," Munch said, and grinned.

Pembleton looked at him. "Meaning?"

Munch shrugged.

"You're being *sarcastic*, aren't you?" Pembleton said.

He was still waiting for an answer when the door to Lieutenant Giardello's office suddenly flew open and he burst through it into the squad room, clapping his hands like Thor summoning the power of the storm.

"As of one minute ago we are officially on redball alert," he announced.

"Bowl me over with a feather," Munch said.

"Meaning?" Giardello said.

Munch felt as if he were in an echo chamber.

"Just that we all kind of figured a redball was happening when you called us in this morning," he said. "Being everybody was supposed to have the next two days off except me."

"Not that you seem to feel badly for the rest of us," Russert said to him.

He looked at her.

"Meaning?"

"If our day off gets scotched tomorrow, so does my barbecue," she said.

"Like that's suddenly *my* fault?" Munch said, smiling.

"Look, you haven't been able to wipe that smirk off your face since you walked in the door."

"What smirk?" he said, pointing to his lips. "FYI, this is a sunny *smile*."

"Children," Giardello said. "I share your disappointment at having to be here this morning. But if we can *bring in* Stella and Campbell within the next twenty-four hours, maybe we can *all* still have a well-deserved rest Monday."

"Fat chance," Munch muttered under his breath.

Giardello shot him a look. "What was that?"

"Nothing."

"Good," Giardello said. "Because I'll be walking the coals at a City Hall press conference in about fifteen minutes and am *not* in the mood for any wise comments." He paused to fill his lungs for another resonant vocalization. "Lewis, Kellerman, I want to see both of you in my office right now."

"You got it, Gee."

"On our way."

He turned and cut a line for his door, the two detectives following on his heels.

"Shut the door," he said when they were inside.

Lewis did.

"A woman was shot to death outside an ATM in Brownsville at around eight o'clock last night," he said soberly. "A detective on McCannon's shift caught it."

Lewis was quiet a moment, his brown eyes intense as he looked at him.

"Our birds?" he said at last.

"The gun used by the perp was a .357 Magnum," Giardello said. "I'm waiting for Ballistics to tell us positively whether it was the same weapon used in the other killings. However my gut already tells me it is."

Lewis shook his head.

"Damn it," he said.

"Gentlemen, you both know that this case has been blown wide open as a consequence of an anonymous leak," Giardello said, looking straight at them. "Reporters all across town are joyously doing the Macarena in their newsrooms, and the brass is after my head."

"Woulda gone redball by tomorrow anyway," Lewis said, and took a deep breath. "At least people know what's happenin' now. Ain't gonna be easy victims just so the staties can keep their dirt swept under the rug."

"That may be true," Giardello said. "It's also a fact that the department has been seriously embarrassed."

"There are worse things," Kellerman said.

"Yes," Giardello said. "But we have to do more than panic the taxpayers that pay our salaries. We have to prove we can *safeguard* them. Am I making myself clear?"

"Yeah," Lewis said.

"Excellent," Giardello said, and sat down behind his desk. "Let's get to work."

Lewis reached for the door handle and they started back into the squad room.

"Gentlemen?" Giardello said.

They turned around to face him.

"I want those murdering bastards," he said.

AT TEN A.M. Sunday morning, Longworth's Home Center, a large store on Harris Avenue, opened its doors to a trickle of early-bird customers. Standing unnoticed across the street, Mutter Campbell waited for the small group to enter and then followed them inside. He took a shopping cart from the queue near the register, set his grocery bag on the child seat, and began quickly wending his way up and down the aisles. Having occasionally bought supplies at Longworth's before his incarceration, he knew more or less where to find what he needed.

In the Plumbing department he picked up two two-by-four-inch lengths of threaded vinyl pressure pipe, a two-inch coupling, and a copper flange. In Kitchen Supplies and Appliances he found a couple of rubber drain plugs that would fit inside the pipe ends and a bottle of lamp oil. Several aisles over in Pool and Garden, he finished his shopping by picking up a five-pound bag of crystallized pool cleanser, and then wheeled everything over to the nearest sales counter.

There was nobody on line ahead of Campbell at the register, and the half-asleep cashier barely looked at him as she rang up his purchases. She had been out dancing Saturday night and had neither seen the eleven o'clock television news on which Campbell's picture had been shown, nor read the Sunday edition of the *Sun*. This put her right in step with the statistical norm: weekend news programs drew less than a third of the audience that watched the broadcasts airing Monday through Friday, and readership of even venerable metropolitan dailies like the *Sun* had been declining for years across the country.

The cost of Campbell's purchases totaled sixteen dollars and thirty-nine cents. He payed with a twenty, pocketed his change, stood while the groggy cashier packed his items into a bag, took the bag from her and carried it out of the store along with his other bundle. He had done his shopping without incident.

In the cubbyhole-sized office behind the cashier, the store manager sat at his desk near a two-way mirror installed to give him a wide view of the sales floor and cashier counter, enjoying a Dunkin' Donuts coffee and cinnamon bun special and listening to WBAL, a twenty-four-hour news and weather radio station that could be found in Baltimore at 1090 on the AM dial. The news jock had been repeating the known details of the Stella-Campbell escape every fifteen minutes all morning long, and by now the store manager knew the story by heart. Had he glanced through the two-way mirror as Campbell was making his transaction, he would almost certainly have identified him on the spot.

He did not look out, however, thinking that if there were any exchanges or customer complaints requiring his personal attention, somebody would knock on his door and tell him.

Sunday mornings, he liked to eat his breakfast in peace.

VINCE LOCICERO GENERALLY didn't pick up the telephone when it rang, preferring instead to have one of his *goombahs* answer it for him, or, if nobody else happened to be around, to at least wait until he'd screened the caller through his answering machine.

Unfortunately, LoCicero was alone in the house when he heard the phone Sunday morning, and realized from the unbroken succession of rings that some dope had left the answering machine off.

"Yeah," he said after snatching up the receiver. He was at the wall phone above his kitchen table, where he had been about to pour some orange juice.

"How-do, you ol' vigeroon," a man's voice said in his earpiece. "Been way too long."

LoCicero abruptly put down the juice container, his eyebrows lifting. That goddamned drawl, there was no mistaking who it belonged to.

"Stella," he said. "Jesus, Christ, it's you, ain't it?"

"*Figured* I'd get a rise," Stella said.

"Where the fuck are you?"

"Right here in town, Vince. Bet you thought I was never comin' back."

"Reamis told me you was out, but I wasn't sure he knew what he was talking about. That place they stuck you in, it's supposed to be locked up tight."

"Tighter'n a virgin's thighs," Stella said. "But an ornery stud like me can always find his way through, Vince. Always."

LoCicero clenched his teeth, trying to remember which of his boys had last answered the phone, thinking that whoever it was probably had been the same moron who'd turned off the answering machine. That guy was going to get chewed out but good; he did not need this fucking headache.

"Well . . . ," he said.

"Well," Stella said.

Silence.

"Talk to me, Frank."

"I can't stay where I'm at long enough to do that," Stella said. "The two of us gotta meet somewhere."

Which was exactly what LoCicero had been afraid he'd say. He clamped his molars together more tightly.

"I'm not sure," he said. "Your face is all over the tube.

And the cops are gonna be watching everybody that knows you—"

"I wouldn't worry too much about that, Vince," Stella said. "Tell me the place, an' I can slip in and out like a greased shadow."

"It's too big a chance, Frank—"

"Listen, I'm at a pay phone out on the street, an' there's all kinds a' riffraff walkin' by," Stella said. "Like I said, I can't stick around."

"Sure, I understand, whyn't you call me back when you—"

"Vince, I worked for you a lotta years, an' you were always my kinda people. Figured you felt the same about me."

"Sure, sure . . ."

"We always been friends, ain't we?"

"Course, Frank—"

"Good," Stella said. "Been so many years since we talked, I guess I hadda ask. Find out if things are really the way I thought they'd be."

"Frank, you know I'd bend over backwards to help you," LoCicero said. "Once the situation cools down a little, we can arrange something—"

"Maybe I better make myself clear," Stella said. "The sooner you an' me get together, the quicker I'll be hittin' the trail."

"Frank, you have to try and understand—"

"No, Boss. It's you who gotta do that," Stella said. "I mean what I said. Give me a little slice'a your time, an' off I go. But I'm afraid I'm gonna have to keep hangin' around until then. An' though I know we're pals an' all, I also know you're a busy fella who'd probably rather not have me breathin' down your neck."

LoCicero sighed heavily.

"All right," he said, recognizing when he'd been pushed into a corner. "You remember the club from the old days? Where it is, I mean?"

"I do, Boss," Stella said. "I surely do."

"Be there this afternoon at three o'clock. Not a minute sooner or later."

"Got you," Stella said. "Three on the whisker."

"Another thing," LoCicero said. "You see any cops near the place, get the hell away from it, we'll have to make other arrangements."

"Righty-o," Stella said.

"And Stella?"

"Uh-huh?"

"Don't fuck me on this," LoCicero said.

And slammed the phone onto the hook, promising himself again that he would get whoever turned off his answering machine, and wondering what kind of deep shit he had just stepped into.

HARRY WAS IN the shower when Teheran heard his phone ringing and, after some brief hesitation, decided to answer it. They had spent all of Saturday in his apartment passionately tangled up in each other, doing it here, doing it there, going at it at least twice in every room—Harry was really insatiable, fiftysomething or not—and she'd come no closer to the Blue Plate's weekend specials than pulling some toaster pancakes out of Harry's freezer . . . and even *they* had gotten burned to a crisp while Harry jumped her bones on the kitchen table. Not that she was *complaining* about his enthusiasm, but it was just that she had other needs besides sex, and eating was, like, one of the biggies . . . which was the main reason she'd thought twice before catching the phone. The last time she'd convinced him—*almost*—to pull his boxers up above his ankles, he'd been distracted by those two detectives, Pringleton and Whatsis, and then gotten into a tizzy and called his friend with the Italian name. She didn't want a repeat performance of *that*.

"Hello?" she said into the mouthpiece.

At first the caller said nothing. In fact it didn't seem as if there was anybody at the other end of the line. But then she noticed the hum you got from an open connection, and wondered if whoever was on the phone might have been surprised by a woman answering instead of Harry and figured he—or maybe *she*, hmmm—had reached a wrong number.

"Reamis residence," she said, thinking that came out sounding kind of goofy on account of the double r's.

"Well," the caller said. "Don't tell me Harry's found himself a *missus*."

Teheran laughed a little. "No, I'm just a friend."

"Oh," the guy on the phone said. "I didn't think he'd a' gone and took the plunge . . . no slight intended, l'il missy."

There was another silence on the line. "L'il missy"? Talk about goofy. Teheran thought. Baltimore was a southern city, but it wasn't like it was Montgomery, and you didn't get many people who sounded as deep-fried as this guy except maybe on *Hee-Haw* reruns.

"Is, uh, Harry around?" the caller said.

"Actually, he's in the shower," she said. "I can take a message . . . or he should be out in a second if you want to hold on . . ."

"No, that's all right," the guy said. "I'd just as soon give him a holler some other time."

I'd just as soon you did too, she thought. Like, how about after I've had my waffles?

"Well, we're heading out for a while, but Harry should be back in an hour, an hour and a half . . ."

There was another long silence on the line. This guy really *did* seem kind of odd.

"Thanks much," he said finally. "I hope we get a chance to meet some day."

Click.

Teheran held the receiver to her ear for a moment after he got off the phone, wondering what *that* had been about. Then she hung up too, shaking her head, debating whether to mention the call to Harry. Why bother, really? The guy hadn't even left his name, let alone any kind of message. And besides not wanting him to be sidetracked from brunch again, she was thinking that Harry might be kind of annoyed if he knew she'd answered his phone. He was touchy about some things, as she'd discovered when he hung away his Armani shirt after getting her out of it in his bedroom, and then, afterward, practically scolded her about going into his closet for it without asking him, giving her a ratty old T-shirt to wear around the house instead . . .

No, she decided, she wouldn't tell Harry about the call, at least not until after they were ensconced in a sunny window booth at the Blue Plate. It didn't seem to *her* that the guy had anything important to talk about, and he knew when to reach Harry if he did.

She had, after all, told him when they would be back.

"MELDRICK, WE HAVE to talk."

Lewis glanced over at Kellerman from behind the steering wheel of the Dodge they had requisitioned that morning, a rusty pile of nuts and bolts with four power windows that wouldn't open, a radio that didn't work, a glove compartment that kept popping open whenever they hit a bump, and a transmission that would stick in gear at unpredictable moments, making the car accelerate in a sudden, rapid surge that could only be stopped if Lewis ground his foot down on the brake and held on for dear life, kind of like a rodeo cowboy in the saddle of a bucking bronco.

"If you got some new comments to make about me an' Barbara, do me a favor an' keep 'em to yourself," he said. "I wanna concentrate on gettin' this heap over to Union Street in one piece."

Kellerman pushed the glove box shut for the tenth time in as many minutes. The rowhouse apartment on Union was the last known residence Jolanda Martin had shared with Mutter Campbell before his double-murder conviction, and though their information was that she'd vacated the place years ago, they'd been unsuccessful in tracking her down, and were hoping to find some former neighbors who could point them in her direction.

"It's got nothing to do with you," Kellerman said.

"Look, Meldrick, I'm not fucking around. This is serious."

Lewis was about to ask Kellerman if that was supposed to mean his marital problems *weren't* serious, when he looked at him across the seat again, saw the pensive expression on his face, and instantly determined that he really did have something heavy on his mind.

"I'm listening," Lewis said.

Kellerman reached for the bar of soap he'd been carrying around in his jacket pocket.

"I found this on the sidewalk when we were going into the bodega yesterday," he said, holding it up.

Lewis looked at it out the side of his eye.

"Soap," he said, turning the corner onto a crosstown street.

"*Nondetergent* soap," Kellerman said. "There aren't too many brands on the market."

"Uh-huh," Lewis said. "And?"

"And when we got inside the bodega, I checked the aisle where it would've been stocked," Kellerman said. "There was an empty space on the shelf, and everything around it was kind of scattered, like somebody'd snatched some goods off it in a hurry."

"Our loony birds?"

"Or Campbell, anyway," he said. "He must've dropped one of the bars by accident when they cut out of the place."

"Weird thing to take," Lewis said, thinking about it. "But these guys ain't exactly your typical knockover artists, either. Why's it such a big deal?"

Kellerman stared out the window at nothing in particular, a white stripe of sun across his face. "Nondetergent soap is one of the ingredients you'd use if you wanted to make a simple kitchen incendiary. Break it into little pieces, mix it with heated gasoline or kerosene, and you get a gelatin that isn't so different from napalm."

Lewis said nothing for a minute. He edged carefully past a double-parked station wagon, his foot nursing the brake in case the car decided to surge.

"Shit," he said.

"There's more," Kellerman said.

"Had a feeling. Why didn't you tell me any of this before?"

"I wanted to check my old references at home. Make sure I knew what I was talking about."

Lewis nodded and turned right. The glove box fell open. Kellerman pushed it shut with an annoyed frown and then wedged his knees against it.

"Gimme the rest," Lewis said.

"Reason I hung back before we left the place was to see if they might've taken anything else that can be used to make a firebomb," Kellerman said.

"Uh-huh."

"Hector Flores kept a neat shop, didn't leave too many bare spots on the shelves," Kellerman said. "I figured I'd look for other shelves that were messed up, or seemed like they were missing stuff."

"I'm guessin' you found some."

"One," Kellerman said. "Where the drain cleaners were stocked."

Lewis palmed his horn at a pedestrian who'd sprinted suddenly from between two parallel-parked cars and cut in front of his bumper. The horn let out a kind of frittering whoop and died.

"Another thing wrong with this friggin' rattletrap," he complained, and glanced at Kellerman. "What was it you were sayin' about drain cleaners?"

"There's a brand called Heat," he said. "It's only supposed to be sold to professional plumbers, but you know how that goes. Distributers look this way, retailers look that way, it winds up under the sink in apartments with toddlers crawling around everywhere."

"This ain't soundin' good," Lewis said.

"The stuff is something like ninety-five percent sulfuric acid," Kellerman went on. "A splash on your skin'll cause third-degree burns. A drop in your eye and you better get used to reading braille. Pour it down your sink and smoke starts gushing out."

"Sounds like the brand name's right on," Lewis said with a doomed little smile.

"Flores carried it in his store," Kellerman said. "I found bottles laying on their sides like they were knocked over. Campbell probably glommed at least a couple."

"For his firebomb," Lewis said.

"Sulfuric acid's used as a liquid igniter, especially when you want a time delay . . ." Kellerman shook his head. "Meldrick, that twisted fuck could incinerate a whole city block with enough of what he's been cooking up."

Lewis tilted his chin vaguely up and down. It was as much a gesture of strained, somber thoughtfulness as an affirmative nod.

"Better find him quick," he said.

"Yeah," Kellerman said. "We damn well better."

AS THE TRAIN to Federal Hill pulled into the station, Frank Stella stood at the end of the subway platform, watched it shudder to a halt, and walked through the retracted sliding doors into the last car. Nearly all the seats were vacant and he took the one farthest toward the rear. The subway had hardly changed since he'd been sent away, and he liked that; it brought back memories, made him feel more in step with the world. He'd ridden the trains to plenty of jobs when he was pulling triggers for Vince, and in some ways had preferred that method of getting around to driving. Riding the trains was quick and anonymous. Nobody aboard them noticed anybody or anything.

He stuck out his long legs and crossed them, folded his arms over his ribs, and leaned his head back against the metal wall of the train, making himself comfortable, swaying a little in his seat as the train picked up speed and shot into the dark mouth of a tunnel. He had five stops to go. He remembered. Five, four, three, two, bang. Now that Campbell was gone, he was feeling like himself again, doing what he did best, alone, prowling the city like an alley cat, like a top cat, baby, going wherever he wanted. No doors or windows shut too tight, no locks that could keep him out.

Five, four, three, two, bang, Harry, he thought, trying to imagine the look that shyster would have on his face when he sprang his little surprise.

Five, four, three, two, *bang*.

ELEVEN

"AIN'T NO JOLANDA Madden lived on this block since *I* been here, an' that's goin' on *fifty years*."

"You positive, ma'am?" Lewis said.

"Moved to this neighborhood on February one, nineteen forty-seven. Maybe my eyes ain't what they was once upon a time, but I can add as good as any *poh*-leese."

"Uh, right, I don't doubt it," Kellerman said. "But what we meant was if you were sure about Miss Madden."

A large black woman in her seventies with smooth wide cheeks and a cap of woolly white hair, Annette Warren resided at 245 Carlysle Avenue, several buildings down from the three-family rowhouse that had been Jolanda Madden's address when she lived with Mutter Campbell. None of the *current* tenants of Madden's old building had been renting there long enough to remember her—or so they stated to Lewis and Kellerman, who knew people in this neighborhood were notoriously hesitant to give up information to the cops—but one man had advised the detectives to speak to Mrs. Warren, the block's elder historian by her own declaration *and* popular consensus.

"*Sure* I'm sure." She tapped the side of her head. "Got all the names up here."

The detectives looked at each other. They were sitting in Mrs. Warren's living room, which, in spite of its threadbare sofa and scuffed, slightly sagging furniture, was a tidy oasis providing relief from the depressing shabbiness of every other apartment they'd been inside this morning.

"Maybe it'd help if you see a picture of the man she was living with," Lewis said, and reached into his pocket for Campbell's booking photo. "His name was—"

"That's all right, won't make any difference to me," she said with a shooing gesture. "Boyfriends come an' go, you understand. Folks stick in my head separate from each other, I either remember 'em or I don't . . . an' if I don't, they was never on this block."

"Mrs. Warren, it wouldn't hurt to look—"

"Don't you *insult* me, young man. If I say the pictures in my head are all I need, I mean it!"

Lewis sighed and brought his hand out of his pocket without the mug shot. Mrs. Warren reminded him too much of his own grandmother for him to think he had a chance of pushing through her brickish stubbornness.

Sitting beside him on the sofa, Kellerman edged forward and cleared his throat.

"Would it be okay if we just *described* Mr. Campbell to you?" he said, knowing as well as Lewis that she'd say no, using his question as an excuse to slip Campbell's name over the wall.

Lewis gave him a quick, approving glance. It was a nice try, if nothing else.

Mrs. Warren looked straight at Kellerman, her brow scrunching up in thought. "You sayin' *Mutter* Campbell?"

He nodded, trying to keep the expectancy out of his face.

"*Course* I remember him," she said. "White man. Real big. Had the second-floor apartment over in 293. Did somethin' horrible to a child and her mama . . . four years back, wasn't it?"

"That's right," Kellerman said.

"His woman wasn't named Jolanda Madden," she said.

Lewis scratched his neck. "Mrs. Warren, accordin' to our records—"

"Don't tell *me*, mister! Ain't you got no *respect*?"

"I didn't mean—"

"Ought to be more like your partner with the baby blue eyes," she said, smiling sweetly at Kellerman. "His parents raised him a *gentleman*."

Kellerman smiled back at her.

"It's very kind of you to say that," he said, nudging Lewis with his leg. "But I don't think Detective Lewis meant any harm. He's really okay when you get past his bad manners."

"I *hope* so," she said. "But he's still dead wrong about Jolanda's Christian name."

Kellerman looked at her. "What do you mean by that, Mrs. Warren?"

"It was Jolanda Martin," she said. "M-a-r-t-i-n. Easy to remember, 'cause I had a *brother* Martin once."

Kellerman kept looking at her, wondering if the officers who originally interviewed Campbell's girlfriend could have gotten her name wrong, and almost instantly concluding it was possible. Madden and Martin sounded enough alike, didn't they? And he would not kid himself into thinking cops couldn't be sloppy when they took statements from people . . . God only knew, that happened far too often when the crimes they were investigating occurred in the ghetto. Furthermore, Jolanda had never been charged with anything, or even suspected of a criminal act. There had been no evidence to suggest she had known the depth of Campbell's psychological problems before his arrest, and she hadn't been called to testify against him during his trial. Yes, she'd been in a relationship with a very bad guy—but poor judgment alone was hardly against the law.

"Ma'am, it's very important that we locate Jolanda," Kellerman said. "If you can give us any information about where she might've gone after she moved, it would be really appreciated."

She shook her head with a kind of deep, world-weary sorrow. "When you say a woman *move*, it mean she got somewhere to go. Poor Jolanda, she *run off*."

The detectives were silent.

"Her boyfriend, I remember he'd lay hands on her all'a time," Mrs. Warren said. "You'd see her with a black eye one day, bruises the size'a plums on her arms an' legs the next. She'd make excuses, you know. Tell you she was prone to havin' accidents. But everybody in the neighborhood could tell what was happenin'."

"She stuck with him, though," Kellerman said.

"Sometimes a woman don't know what else to do," she said, shaking her head some more. "There's lotsa talk about *abuse* on TV nowadays, but if it's made things any easier when some poor girl go lookin' for help, well, gotta be someplace beside *this* neighborhood."

Kellerman considered that and nodded.

"I can't imagine how Jolanda felt when she hear what that man done," Mrs. Warren said. "How ashamed she must've been."

"Is that when she left?"

"Think it was a week, two weeks after they come to arrest him." She clasped her hands on her lap. They were bent and wrinkled, with gnarled, arthritic knuckles, and fingertips that were thickened from old calluses . . . the hands of someone who had done hard manual labor all her life. "It wasn't just about her bein' mistreated anymore. It was about protectin' her son, and the child she was carryin' inside her."

"Wait a minute." Kellerman looked at her carefully. "She and Campbell have *children*?"

"Guess that be another thing wasn't in your report," she said, lowering her eyes to study her hands. "The boy was still in diapers at the time, an' Jolanda told me she'd kept the unborn a secret from that evil man."

"He didn't know she was pregnant?"

"She couldn't have been more'n three months along an' wasn't showin' none," Mrs. Warren said. "Knowin' what he'd done to that teenage girl, how could she tell him?"

The room was silent except for the ticking of a wall clock as its second hand circled the dial, Annette Warren sitting there with her head bent and her hands clenched above her knees, the two detectives regarding her somberly from the couch.

"Ma'am, I know I've already asked, but do you have any idea where Jolanda might be nowadays?" Kellerman said finally.

"None at all," she said. "Must be some important reason you interested in findin' her, huh?"

Kellerman raised his eyebrows.

"You mean you haven't seen today's paper? Watched the news on TV?" he said, already knowing what her answer would be. Of course she hadn't. If she'd read about Campbell's escape, she would have probably realized at once why he and Lewis were coming around with questions about Jolanda, never mind the confusion over her second name.

"Didn't know there was some law 'gainst wantin' to get up Sunday mornin' an' read the Good Book, 'steada all them stories 'bout killin' an' robbin'," she said.

"Nothin' the matter with that, Mrs. Warren," Lewis said softly. "It's just that we figured you knew Mutter Campbell's gotten free."

She suddenly lifted her head.

"When it happen'?" she asked.

"Friday night," Kellerman said. "He and another man broke out of a psychiatric institution."

"Sweet Lord," she said. Peering at the detectives from within heavy pouches of flesh, her eyes were filled with a distress that made Kellerman's stomach tighten up. "That sinful man, he goin' after Jolanda?"

"We don't know," Kellerman said. "But he doesn't

have anybody else in this world, and it seems a pretty good bet he'd try to find her. "

"Then you officers better do it first, you hear me?" she said. "Find her *first*, or heaven help that woman and her children."

Kellerman groped for a response, but after a moment gave up and just looked back at her in silence.

There was, quite simply, nothing left to say.

DESPITE WHAT HE'D learned from the cops when they showed up at his door Saturday, despite his own anxious words to Vince LoCicero afterward, despite the irreversible fact that he had cheated Frank Stella out of almost a quarter million dollars in cash, stocks, and property over the years Stella had been locked away, Harry Reamis didn't fully appreciate the gravity of his predicament until he'd passed a newsstand on the way to the Blue Plate Luncheonette and seen Stella's malevolent face glaring off the front page of the *Sun*. It had been as close to seeing a vengeful ghost as he would ever get.

It had also put a very big damper on brunch—until he'd thought things through, that was.

Of course, Teheran had been completely oblivious to his nervous worries, sitting there over her stack of multigrain flapjacks and currants, spewing out a torrent of adolescent prattle about homeopathic remedies and some rock group called the Smashing Pumpkins, as dully annoying outside the sack as she was carnally fulfilling in it. Still, in one sense, her awesome stupidity was a blessing in disguise: it made phasing her out easy. Nod with simulated interest, fling her a counterfeit smile across the table, grunt an occasional, meaningless yes or no, and she would be content, leaving your mind free to disengage and voyage outward to a galaxy far, far away. And after seeing Stella's face—the grainy black-and-white reproduction of his police file photo had somehow printed off-register, unintentionally creating an effect that was not quite a double-image, but more like what might have resulted if the photographer had shuddered while snapping the picture, making Stella look even more like a revenant than he ordinarily did—after seeing Stella's face under the headline, Harry had had a lot to occupy his thoughts.

What he figured he had to do was find a strategy and stick to it, just as he would when preparing for a court case. There was no need for it to be complicated or far-reaching—a simple game plan was always best. Given the vast net the police were throwing up for Stella and his accomplice, and Stella's own violent patterns of behavior, he was bound to be caught before too long. A few days, a week at the outside, and he'd be back in custody. Assuming he could ride it out, Harry was convinced he'd be okay.

He'd pondered this for a few minutes, looking across the table at Teheran's pretty but vapid features, barely hearing the gibberish coming out of her mouth—in his preoccupation it sounded something like *blubba-mubba-frooba-gooba-blug-blug*—and then decided the smartest thing he could do was physically remove himself from the fray, so to speak. He would lay low for a week, maybe a little longer. Book a waterfront suite at the Carousel, or maybe the Lighthouse Club, in Ocean City. Ask for first-class accommodations all the way, make a mini-vacation of it. Sure, he'd be getting his reservations at the last minute, but this was still a month before peak season, and there would be plenty of excellent rooms available. Ocean City, oh yes. Most judges would be extending the holiday weekend and keeping their dockets light anyway. Off the top of his head, he could only remember having two court appearances scheduled for the upcoming week, both pro forma motions that could be argued by one of the firm's junior lawyers as well as himself.

Ocean City, here I come. A four-poster bed, a wet bar, a marble bathroom with a whirlpool Jacuzzi tub, tennis courts, saunas, and sunrooms. Ocean City. He would invite Teheran—why not? Sitting there in the restaurant, watching her tongue swipe a tiny spot of whipped cream off her lip, he had imagined her licking the tip of his cock, his *glans* to use a more delicate term, licking his glans with similar relish while he was sipping a martini on a balcony overlooking the sea. Had imagined fucking her in his luxury suite until the posts collapsed on the bed, fucking her through the mattress and floor and the room below and maybe right down into the lobby.

Sitting with Teheran in the restaurant, Harry had given himself an erection so large it might have been embarrassing if he'd worn tighter pants. He was glad when she finished eating, and had quickly paid the check and hustled her out of the place, hardly even thinking about Stella anymore, wanting to get her through his front door and pull up her skirt and do her right there in the foyer before he messed his boxers. Afterward, he would spring his *other* surprise on her, tell her to go home and pack, they were leaving town for a while. Surely she'd be able to come. Her parents, such as they were, never seemed to know or care where she was. She could even bring her schoolbooks and call in to her teachers for her homework assignments, ha-ha.

Now, after a walk back to his house made rather uncomfortable by his blazing hard-on, Harry followed Teheran up the front steps, ever the gentlemen, and always appreciating the view from the rear. He reached into his pocket for his keys, quickly unlocked the door, and held it open for Teheran, smiling like the spider to the fly as she went through, thinking it might be interesting if she perched on the downstairs bannister post while they made love. But before he could suggest it, she was heading up to the second floor, bounce-bounce-bounce—ah well, his fault, he really should have mentioned something about his little foyer fantasy on the way home. At any rate, the living room was a fair alternative. What it lacked in kinkiness, it made up for in comfort.

Reaching the landing a step or two ahead of him, Teheran pushed open the heavy wood door and preceded Harry into the entry hall.

"Teheran, let's go in the living room, I have something in my pants that you just might want to see," he said to the back of her head, thinking the remark would hardly qualify him as a drawing room wit . . . but you had to consider who your audience was.

"*Coolicious.*" She gave out a bubbly little laugh—confirming that he'd been right to aim low with his humor—and entered a step or two ahead of him. The thick algae-colored draperies were drawn across the windows, giving the shadows in the room a greenish tinge.

Harry almost bumped up against her ass in his eagerness to get inside. He was thinking he'd slip his arms around her waist and kiss her on the neck, right on that spot above the spine that always got her going, and was reaching out to do it when there was an earsplitting crack that sounded like the backfire from a very large truck, a simultaneous flash of light, and then, suddenly, Teheran was dervishing sideways across the room, arms flapping, blood spraying from her chest, buttons and shreds of material flying off the front of her blouse. Somehow she hung on her feet for a second or two afterward, but then there was another flash-crack, and Harry saw her hair whip up around her head as if she'd been caught in a blast of wind, saw a huge glob of blood sprout from her temple and then burst apart in a dark red gush, saw her flop over the coffee table and hit the carpet in a boneless heap.

A low moan of fear and horror ribboned from his mouth.

"Top cat, top hat, *mee-oww* to this world," a voice said from inside the living room.

From over by his wing recliner.

"How-do, Harry?"

Recognition slipping over his features, his heart pierced by the certain, terrible knowledge of who that voice belonged to, Harry turned toward the chair and saw Frank Stella sitting there in the partial shadows, his legs crossed in front of him and his mouth pulled into a

201

mocking jack-o'-lantern grin, smoke trickling from the muzzle of the big revolver in his hand.

"Sorry I broke your baby doll," he said, tilting the gun toward Teheran's inert body. Harry heard a low gurgle in the silence and realized it was the sound of blood pouring from her head and chest wounds, so hideously red soaking into the thick green pile of the living room carpet. He could see spots of the same garish red on the wall nearest where she'd fallen. "She was choice goods, ain't no question about that. But from the looks a' this place, you can afford to buy yourself a replacement."

Harry stared at him numbly. He couldn't move, couldn't wring anything more than a crimped, inarticulate moan from his throat. It was as if some vital connection had been pulled between his brain and body.

"Yeah, I can see you been livin' real posh," Stella said. "An' while I'm probably oversteppin' our relationship offerin' you advice, I really think you oughtta invest in some kinda alarm system, or at least put gates on the basement windows. See, there's lots'a bad people out on the street, and it'd be a shame if they came sneakin' in to take what you have."

Harry stared at him. Stella looked like a distorted reflection of himself. His face was a scrawl of cuts and bruises. His clothes were soiled and bloodstained. And there was something . . . a shoe, Harry realized uncomprehendingly, a woman's high-heeled *shoe*, hanging from his belt loop.

"C'mon, Har, say somethin'. After so many years'a bein' locked up with fuckin' nutjobs, I'm starved for conversation with somebody that's got all his marbles," Stella said. "You truly got no idea how much I need it right now."

Harry kept staring.

Stella thumbed back the hammer of his gun, his vicious slash of a grin spreading across his entire face. "I said *talk to me*."

Harry put the full force of his will into getting his vocal cords to work.

"Why?" He wet his lips. "Why are you . . . doing this?"

Stella produced a high, tattery, inturned chuckle that sounded like an off-key harmonica chord.

"Come on, Har," he said. "One thing you ain't never been is clueless."

"I don't—"

Stella uncrossed his legs and suddenly rose off the chair, looking like an underwater shadow in the membraneous green light sifting through the curtains.

"I trusted you with everythin' I owned. Everythin' I made bein' Vince's dust man," he said, his gun trained on Harry. "Everythin', Har . . . an' you *took it*."

"I . . . I don't know who told you that, but . . . you're wrong . . ."

"Am I?" Stella said. "Then how come I ain't heard from you for over *four years*? If I phoned you once I must'a phoned you a hundred times. Always got your secretary or your answerin' machine, an' always left messages for you to call back. But you never did."

Harry ran his tongue across his lips again, thinking there had to be something he could do to help himself. Some way to hold on to his life.

"Well, maybe I didn't hear from you, but I *did* catch some scuttlebutt from other people I knew," Stella was saying. "Found out how you sold both my homes, includin' the one my mama used to live in. Found out my stocks an' bank accounts had all gone *poof*. Found out about the glossy car you been drivin' . . . a Porsche, am I right? Or is it a Jaguar?" He pushed his gun angrily in the air. "Not bad for a guy who was nothin' but an ambulance chaser in cheap Thom McAns before he met me."

"Stella, please . . . listen to me," Harry said, stalling for time. Trying to think. "It . . . it's true I liquidated your assets . . . turned them over for cash, you know . . . but I swear to God I didn't touch any of it. Every cent's in the bank, waiting for you there, nice and clean—"

"Then why didn't you get back to me, Hardy-har?"

"Look, you know how it is, things come up, fucking Vince and his constant bullshit." Think think *think*. "Maybe I should be more conscientious about returning my calls . . . I'm *admitting* I should've picked up the goddamn telephone, okay? But like I said, it doesn't mean I haven't been working on your behalf. The cash is all sitting in the *bank* . . ."

"Even if I was dumb enough to believe you, the fact is I need my money now," Stella said. "Like that ol' tune says, this town's gettin' hotter'n a matchhead."

Harry glimpsed an opening.

"I can give you at least a thousand right away, maybe closer to two," he said, speaking rapidly. "There's nothing I can do about getting the rest till the day after tomorrow . . . the banks are closed because of the holiday—"

"Two grand down on a *two-hundred-thousand-dollar* balance don't sound like your goin' percentage," Stella said. "Besides, I already told you, I can't wait that long."

"You'll have enough to leave the state, hide out somewhere . . . soon as I hear from you, I'll wire over the rest—"

"Uh-huh." Stella laughed his shrill, ragged laugh again. "I'm sure you'll get right back to me."

"Frank, I'm doing my best—"

"Where's the money stashed?"

"Right here in the living room." Harry nodded toward the glass case on the wall containing his dagger collection. "There's a safe behind the showcase . . . I can open it for you."

Stella came closer, the gun still thrust out in front of him.

"My brains really *would* have to be poached to let you do that, Hardy-har," he said. "What else you got in that safe? A little firin' iron?"

"Frank, I understand your resentment, I'm not trying to play games. There isn't any gun," he said truthfully. If he'd learned anything in the courtroom, it was that lies were most effective when they had a large component of truth, and that a careful omission was superior to *any* lie. No, he didn't have a gun . . . but if he could just get hold of one of those *knives* . . . sure, he'd have to put his hand through the glass, probably cut himself pretty badly . . . and a blade was a poor match for Stella's cannon . . . but what other chance did he have?

Stella took another step forward, holding the gun between them. Harry had a momentary image of himself being sucked into the black hole of its barrel, sucked out of *existence* . . .

"I'll open the safe myself," Stella said.

"Frank, the lock's digital," Harry said. "I'd have to show you how to use the keypad, it'd take—"

Stella suddenly came at him, grabbing the front of his shirt collar with one hand, shoving the gun into his mouth with the other. Harry felt the muscles of his back and buttocks clench with fright, felt a sickening wet warmth in his pants, and realized his bladder had released itself.

"Give me the fucking combination!" Stella said through gritted teeth. He pushed the corner of Harry's mouth up with the tip of the barrel, forcing it into a grotesque lopsided grin. "An' *smile* while you're doin' it."

There were tears in Harry's eyes. "*Shree-shicks-sg-sgevensheen*," he said, the gunmetal in his mouth, his saliva dripping over the gunmetal, his words stretched out of shape by the gunmetal.

"Three-six-seventeen?" Stella repeated. "Did I get it right?"

Harry nodded frantically.

"You *sure* 'bout that, Hardy-har?" Stella twisted Harry's collar in his fist. "'Cause if you ain't, well, I'd hate to see what your smile looks like with your front *teeth* blown down your throat."

"I . . . *shwearr*!" Harry said, tears flowing down his cheeks now. "*Shweaerr!*"

"Good," Stella said, and yanked Harry forward, almost jerking him off his feet, forcing his mouth to slide up over the gun muzzle until its sight was pressing against the back of his throat. Stella took a step backward, a second, a third, dragging Harry with him, pulling him along by the collar, backing past Teheran's splayed, leaking body toward the draperies, toward the *windows*.

By the time Harry realized what was happening it was too late.

"Gonna teach you two, two, two lessons in one, Hardy-har," Stella said. "First is that if you ain't gonna keep in touch with your clients, you better be carryin' either a good excuse or a pistol in your pocket. Second's that you really oughtta have window gates."

A terror beyond anything he had ever known sledged through Harry's brain. He made an incoherent whimpering sound around the gun barrel, wanting to beg, wanting to scream, wanting to *live*—

All within an instant, Stella pulled the gun out of Harry's mouth, brought it up against his chest, pumped the trigger twice, and then tore aside the curtains and boosted Harry headfirst through the window. Harry experienced a jumbled, hellish flood of sensory input: pain ripping through his middle, sound of breaking glass, shards spearing his cheeks and throat, sunlight in his eyes, taste of blood, smell of the street, and then he was plummeting, falling three stories to the alley below, the pavement rushing up at him, sweet God in heaven rushing up *so fast*—

Stella carefully stuck his head through the broken window and stared down at Harry's body for perhaps a minute after it hit the ground. Then, grinning silently, he turned to get the money from the safe.

VINCE LOCICERO WAS out getting some fresh air and walking his two long-haired Chihuahuas, Allen and Rossi, when the detectives came driving down his block at around eleven A.M. on Sunday afternoon.

Vince scoped the bull behind the wheel of the car as Frank Pembleton, big swinging dick of the Homicide unit, even before it had pulled over to the curb opposite his front yard. He didn't recognize Pembleton's baby-faced partner, but what the hell was the difference? Some cops hit you over the head with a stick, some dangled a carrot, but, bottom line, one was just as lousy as another.

Hotshit Pembleton left the car first, wearing a tan suit and matching fedora, head high, back straight, walking fast and pushy, kind of like he expected the world to get out of his way. Babyface did a good job keeping pace, indicating to Vince that he'd been teamed with Pembleton awhile. Vince was no genius, but he considered himself a decent judge of people. Guys like Pembleton never slowed down for anybody; you fell behind, and they'd ditch you without a backward glance.

"Vince, Vince, how splendid it is to see you," Pembleton said, stopping in front of him.

Vince frowned. Allen and Rossi were skittering around his legs and yipping excitedly.

"Look at this crap, you already got my dogs upset," he said, struggling to keep their leashes from getting tangled. "I trip over one of 'em, you pay for my doctor *and* the vet."

"Longhaired Chihuahuas, I see," Pembleton said.

Vince gave him a curious glance. "You know your breeds."

"They're less snappish than the shorthairs." Pembleton glanced down at the shrilling, bouncing dogs. "Usually, I mean."

"Don't insult my babies; they're fine except around cops," Vince said. "Cops make 'em irritable."

"Kinda like the way I get around hoods," Bayliss said.

Vince cocked his thumb at him, still looking at Pembleton. "Pudding cheeks here got a name?"

"Detective Tim Bayliss," Bayliss said, answering for himself. "What was that you just called me?"

"Think it was *handsome*," Vince said. "Now how about you guys tell me why you're here."

"We're looking for Frank Stella," Pembleton said. "You've presumably heard he escaped from—"

"Read all about it." LoCicero shrugged indifferently. "So?"

"*So,*" Pembleton said, "we'd like to know if you've seen him, or have any idea where he might be."

LoCicero scrunched his forehead. "What the hell, you think I got some nutty tea party goin', like that guy in *Alice in Wonderland* with the high hat—"

"The Mad Hatter," Bayliss said.

"Figured you'd know your kiddie stories," LoCicero said.

Bayliss bristled. "What's that supposed to mean?"

"You look *smart,*" LoCicero said.

Pembleton glanced over at LoCicero's house. It was an unobtrusive ranch with a picture window and a neat front yard ornamented with a ceramic greyhound. Very middle-class suburban, not the kind of residence you'd associate right off with one of the most notorious crime bosses south of New York City. Which, of course, made it the *perfect* place from which such a man could discreetly conduct his business.

"Mr. LoCicero, I'm assuming you *would* tell us if Stella turned up," he said.

"Right, absolutely," LoCicero said. One of the dogs pawed at his leg and he bent to lift it off the ground. "Not that I make it a habit to associate with fruitcakes."

Pembleton wondered how much LoCicero knew.

"Listen to me carefully," he said. "Frank Stella's already committed several murders since he got free. It might not distress me much if his victims were mobsters like in the old days, but he's killing innocent people. The man is haywire, and that means trouble for you, for me, for everybody in this city. It's in your best interest to help us bring him down."

LoCicero looked thoughtful. The second Chihuahua was scratching at his pants and he scooped it up and stood there with a dog nestled in the crook of each arm.

"I'll keep in mind what you told me," he said at last. The dogs were swiping his nose with their tongues. "But I can't promise anything."

"Just so you try."

"Sure," LoCicero said. "I'll try."

Pembleton looked at him a moment, then nodded.

"You've got cute dogs," he said.

LoCicero smiled.

"You oughtta see 'em when they're cuddled up together," he said.

IT WAS JUST shy of noon when Lewis and Kellerman arrived back at the squad room for what would turn out to be a very brief interval. Their conversation with Annette Warren had given the search for Jolanda Martin added urgency. Perhaps more than any other group of offenders, physical and sexual abusers tended to fit classic patterns of behavior. The odds were disproportionately high Campbell would seek out Jolanda and victimize her again. He would want to get back at her for running from him and, from his perspective, stealing his son. His reaction to her would be angry and violent. Even more so if he learned about the younger child.

The seconds and minutes piling up on them with steadily increasing weight, they hustled over to Lewis's desk, got the Baltimore white pages out of a drawer, and flipped through the M listings.

Marooney, Marotta, Marovits, Martell . . .

"Here's Mart*en*," Kellerman said, standing behind Lewis and reading over his shoulder. "I know what Mrs. Williams told us, but you think our gal might spell her name like that?"

"Could be," Lewis said. "Would make it sound kinda like Madden anyway."

"Don't see a *Jolanda* Madden."

"Gotta be twenty, twenty-five listings for *J.* Madden, though."

Kellerman leaned forward and ran his finger down the left side of one column. "Here a few J. Mad*dens*, with an S at the end."

Lewis nodded, marked the page with a Post-it, and flipped ahead.

"Shit," he said. Flip, flip, flip. "Check this out, got three, four pages of people name'a Martin in here."

"Lot of Mar*tins* too," Kellerman said. "You see any Jolandas?"

"Uh-uh. But look at all of 'em got the first initial J." Lewis flagged another page.

"Ma Bell's gonna love us," Kellerman said. "We're looking at maybe a hundred phone calls."

"Maybe we'll get lucky and hit right off."

"Or maybe she doesn't have a phone."

"Or does and is unlisted." Kellerman said. "We'd need a phone company supervisor to get those numbers released."

"Won't be easy on a Sunday."

"Especially *this* Sunday," Kellerman said. "Goddamn holiday weekends."

"You're startin' to sound like Munch."

"I know," Kellerman said. "Fucking scary, isn't it?"

"Here's another scary thought, man," Lewis said. "What if Jolanda's name ain't Martin, or Marten, or anythin' like *either* of 'em no more? What if she got *married,* or just changed it?"

"Make it real tough for us to find her," Kellerman said. "Only good thing about it is that it'd be tougher for Campbell too."

"Unless he already *knows* where she lives," Lewis said.

Kellerman looked at him.

"We better get cracking," he said. "I'll Xerox these pages so we can split the job in half."

Lewis was handing him the directory when Giardello's door swung open and he entered the squad room, hurriedly shrugging into his sport jacket.

"Where's Pembleton and Bayliss?" he said, and wheeled to look around the room.

"Out," Munch said from his desk.

"I can *see* that," Gee rumbled. "What about Russert?"

"Out somewhere else," Munch said.

"All right . . . I want Lewis, Kellerman, and Howard to come with me. Munch, you stay here and hold the fort."

"Why me?"

"Why not?" Giardello said. "Now, let's move, people."

"You gonna tell us where we're headin'?" Lewis said. He put the phone book back on his desk and hustled over to the coatrack for his hat.

"Federal Hill," Gee said. "It seems Harry the Reamer's reamed his last."

FOR MELDRICK LEWIS, the redball crime scene—to the police this was no longer a house and its back alley, it had stopped being a *house* the moment two human beings had been murdered here—was like a salad bowl, except instead of broccoli and onions and radishes and lettuce and tomatoes tossed around inside you had an assortment of law enforcement personnel: uniforms from every beat in the city, detectives from five different units, techies, M.E. attendants, and, in this particular case, state troopers and Howard County cops of both the uniformed and plainclothes variety.

For Lewis, who (in spite of his talent for negotiating the bureaucratic minefields of the department) was by basic temperament a loner, being part of this jumbled mix was nothing less than purest misery.

"Where the hell's Scheiner?" he said, and ducked under the yellow tape snaking between the rear of Harry Reamis's house and the slatted wooden backyard fence.

"Still upstairs with the girl," a beefy detective he didn't know shouted out. "You want I should get him?"

Lewis glanced down at Reamis's corpse. When he'd been a kid he'd had a GI Joe doll, not one of the molded, palm-sized action figures little boys had to settle for nowadays, but an original, maybe ten inches tall with articulated joints at the neck, shoulders, hips, wrists, elbows, and ankles, like on those anatomical models they sold in art supply stores. He'd once made the mistake of letting a friend's baby brother play with it, and the kid had gotten so carried away twisting its limbs into odd positions that a leg and an arm had snapped off.

Though Harry Reamis's parts were all attached—just

211

barely in some places—the way they were contorted reminded Lewis of his doll when that gonzo brat had gotten finished with it. Reamis lay staring sightlessly skyward in a puddle of blood and broken glass, his head at an extreme angle to his shoulders, a gaping wound in his throat from a sharp jag of window glass, his right arm bent under his back with the shoulder half out of its socket and a white spear of bone protruding above the elbow.

Lewis knelt and looked at the fist-sized hole in Reamis's stomach. It was a scorched, ragged-edged mire of blood, pulped flesh, and shredded bits of his shirt that could have been made by nothing but a big-caliber gun discharging at close range.

"I asked if you wanted me to—"

"Nah, don't bother," Lewis interrupted the fat detective midsentence. "Reamis musta' died at least five different ways, an' I can see for myself what most of 'em are."

The cop shrugged and shuffled away into the crowd.

"Hey, Meldrake!"

Lewis looked up and saw Kellerman waving his hand out the second-floor window from which Reamis had taken his terminal swan dive.

"Yo, man, I hear you!" he shouted. "Now, pull your arm outta that broken glass before you cut it off!"

"Just thought I'd warn you," Kellerman said.

"Warn me 'bout what?" Lewis asked.

"Me, I'm sure," he heard an unpleasant and unlonged-for voice say from over to his right.

He cranked his head around and looked up at the man that went with it.

"Lambert," he said with a slight nod.

The statie tipped his sunglasses down his curved blade of a nose in acknowledgment.

"I was hoping I'd run into you here," he said. "Find out what you think of that newspaper article."

Lewis shrugged. "Ain't had time to worry about it."

"Well, I've been busy too, but that hasn't made a

difference to the reporters. They've been on me like piranha since that little prick from the *Sun* wrote his story."

Lewis shrugged again and said nothing.

"When Thorburn called me and started poking around for information about Stella and Campbell, I figured right away he'd been tipped by somebody involved in the case," Lambert said. "Somebody in one of our organizations."

Lewis rose and moved aside to allow a tech with an evidence bag to get past him. He could see Barnfather and Giardello talking near the alley opening about a dozen yards behind Lambert.

"Could be," he said.

Lambert waited for more. When nothing came, he took off his sunglasses, carefully folded the stems, slipped the glasses into the breast pocket of his shirt, and stepped very close to Lewis.

"Whoever opened his mouth has made himself a serious fucking enemy in me," he said, his blue eyes narrow. "I don't forget, and I don't let go. He had better watch his ass."

"Tell me about it." Lewis stared at him. "Seems to me you state boys know all about ass coverin'."

"What are you implying?"

"That you could've saved this city a whole lot of trouble if you'd been as concerned with doin' your job as lookin' like none'a you ever put on your Smokey the Bear hats crooked. Now, why don't you just—"

"Back off from each other. This is a crime scene, not a fight ring."

At the sound of Giardello's voice, Lewis broke his gaze away from Lambert and realized that the loot and Barnfather had come walking up the alley to the police line.

"Ain't me who started this. Tell Lambert to quit doggin' my heels, an' there won't be no problems."

"I've every right to be here," Lambert said.

"As an observer, and only at my discretion," Giardello

213

said. "My detectives have work to do and don't need you interfering with it."

Lambert frowned and glanced over at Barnfather. "George, what the hell kind of attitude is this I'm getting from your men. I—"

Barnfather held up his hand to silence him.

"I'm sorry, Craig," he said. "This is Lieutenant Giardello's crime scene. I won't override his authority."

For a moment Lambert seemed too stunned and angry for speech. He stood there staring at Barnfather, his shoulders stiff as fence posts, his upper lip quivering, dragging in long breaths between his gritted teeth.

"Sure," he said finally. "Stand by your men. I understand."

"Apparently you don't," Barnfather said. "Besides giving us another two victims that we believe were slaughtered by Frank Stella and Mutter Campbell, what happened here indicates the killings may be shifting into a new phase. Everything before's been random, but Harry Reamis was Stella's lawyer. Look down at his body and tell me there wasn't a grudge involved, and that those maniacs haven't cast off all restraint."

"If there's a hit list, we obviously have no idea how many people are on it," Giardello added. "But it's a fair guess Stella and Campbell are planning, or even committing, more murders even as we stand here."

Lewis thought about Jolanda Martin and suddenly heard Annette Warren's voice in his mind: *Find her first, or heaven help that woman and her children.*

He would try. He would damn well try his best.

But, sweet Jesus, what if he failed?

AS JOLANDA SAT at her vanity putting on her makeup, zonked although she'd had a good night's sleep, she was thinking it would be the mildest of exaggerations to say that a day and night of playing chaperone to four kids, bless their dear, aggravating hearts, had taken more out of her than a full week at the flower shop. An extra *busy* week.

Well, her tour of duty was almost over, and she had, after all, volunteered for it, without anybody twisting her arm. She also had to admit seeing them have so much fun at their impromptu pajama party had been a kick. Call her a pushover, but when they'd gotten back from the aquarium yesterday and the little connivers had made their pitch for the overnighter—she was convinced Andrew been the mastermind who'd thought of using Robin and Jamal as shuttle envoys, sending them from his room to let her know what a great time they were having, and how none of their other friends had mothers who were so funny and pretty and *young*—she'd found it as hard to turn them down as it had been to listen with a straight face.

Harder, actually, since she'd cracked up even while telling them it would be okay with her if they stayed the night, just as long as they called their parents for permission.

Needless to say Carol and her husband had been anything but reluctant to have their place all to themselves on Saturday night.

Jolanda checked the alarm clock on her nightstand, saw that it was almost noon, and told herself to hurry up and finish putting on her face. She was meeting Carol over at her place in half an hour and didn't want to make her wait. When they had spoken on the phone earlier, they had arranged to take the kids to the park for a while, figuring it was a good way to begin easing them apart. They would ride their bikes, play some ball, and hopefully get too tuckered out to raise a fuss when it was time to return to their respective homes.

Jolanda saw a knowing smile spread across the face in the mirror.

That was how the plan was *supposed* to work, anyway.

"*Ma-aaa!*"

She reached for her eyeliner. "Yes, Andy?"

The boys rushed up the hallway to her bedroom and poked their heads through the open door.

215

"The girls keep saying they're gonna make us ride their bikes," Andrew said.

"Robin's still has training wheels, and it's *pink*!" Jamal said.

"Yuck!" Andy said, holding his nose. "They said you promised they could have *our* bikes!"

"And I suppose both of you are gullible enough to believe them," she said. "Or could it be you just feel like getting your baby sisters in trouble?"

"No way!"

"Uh-uh!" Andrew said. "We just want 'em to quit bothering us."

"Such sensitive boys," Jolanda said, and gave them an enduring smile. "Who'd have known?"

They laughed, conspirators unmasked.

"Now will you two *please* behave so I can finish getting ready?"

"Come on!" Andrew said, and poked Jamal in the ribs. "Let's tell Vi we're selling her Barbies for a quarter!"

They turned and went clomping toward the living room.

"Behave!" Jolanda hollered after them. "If you guys want to make yourselves useful, go fix us all some peanut butter and jelly sandwiches. We'll bring them to the park with us."

"Right!"

"And close my door behind you!"

"*Rii-iight*!"

Andrew doubled back, pushed the bedroom door shut, and hustled away.

Why me? she thought, rolling her eyes.

In the living room, Vi and Robin were sitting on the couch with their shoulders touching and their skinny legs sticking out in front of them, trying to make up their minds whose feet were bigger. Though they had decided that Vi's held a slim edge lengthwise, there was still some disagreement over Robin's claim that she had fatter *toes*.

"Let's take off our sneakers and find out!"

"Take off our socks too!"

"Great!"

"I'll untie your laces and you do mine!"

Vi had removed both her shoes and was tugging down her left stocking when she heard a knock on the front door.

"Who is it?" she said, hopping down off the couch. Robin followed behind her, right sneaker on, left foot bare.

"Super," a voice said from the outer hallway.

She stared at the door for a long moment, her brown face crinkled doubtfully. Randy, the building superintendent, spoke with a pleasant accent her mother had said was Jamaican. The man outside the apartment did not sound like him at all.

"My mom's in the bedroom," she said. "I'll call her."

"The building's on fire," he said. "Open your door."

Vi turned toward Robin and they looked at each other with widened eyes.

"I'd better get my mom," she said, and went running toward the bedroom, passing the kitchen in a flash, too agitated to even think of saying a word to Jamal and her brother about the man in the hallway.

One shoelace trailing behind her foot, Robin pogoed closer to the door as her friend raced off down the hall.

"Is anyone still there?" the man outside the door said.

"Y-yes," she said in a small, frightened voice.

"You have to let me in right now," the man said. "Before you all burn."

She paused, equally balanced between fear and confusion. Her mother had cautioned her never to let strangers through the door. But she had also told her to dial 911 if she was ever alone and smelled smoke in the building, told her to listen carefully to the operator and follow whatever instructions the firemen gave her when they arrived. And though she didn't smell anything unusual right now, and the man outside had said he was the super, not a fireman, maybe *he* had been the one to smell the smoke and was standing out there *with* the firemen.

"Let me in!" he said. "Hurry, or you'll all die!"

Had Robin hesitated a split second longer—long enough for Jolanda to come bolting into the room with her face still only half made up and her compact unconsciously clutched in her hand—the horrors that followed might have been averted. But the man had told her to let him into the apartment or they would all die, told her they would all *burn,* and she found herself more fearful of what would happen if she ignored him than of what would happen if she did what he wanted—listened to him carefully and followed his instructions.

She grasped the doorknob and flipped open the lock.

"Robin, don't—" Jolanda shouted from behind the little girl just as the door flew open with such force it slammed into Robin, hitting her in the face, knocking her backward to the floor with a high bleat of pain and surprise.

Jolanda halted in the arched entryway between the dinette and the living room, her palms flying to her cheeks, her heart seeming to balloon into her throat, her eyes widening, widening, widening at the sight of the man who was standing there, a man she'd been convinced she would never see again, standing there inside her door.

"I'm here, Jolanda," Mutter Campbell said, letting the bags in his arms fall roughly to the carpet. "For you."

TWELVE

JOLANDA DIDN'T MOVE for a long stretch of seconds, the scene in the living room holding her in an inertia of astonishment and terror.

It made no sense.

None.

Mutter. How could Mutter be free? How could he have *found* her?

The door banged shut behind Campbell and he advanced into the apartment, taking one slow step, a second. In many respects he barely resembled the man Jolanda had once known and even loved, but looked more like an imperfect copy of him, a wax museum figure that had been endowed with a clumsy, shambling sort of animation. His eyes were simultaneously dull and wrathful, as if he were hosting some terrible rage without being at all sure how it had attached itself to him. His face had a strange cast, pulling tightly to the left, and his cheek on that side bulged and quivered with horrible spastic contortions.

Campbell came closer, closer, and still she didn't move, just stood in the living room entry, her fingers harrowing her cheeks, her feet nailed to the floor. The compact had fallen from her grasp and split open like a clamshell, spilling powder all over the rug, but she hadn't noticed. No sense, no sense, none whatsoever, she thought. She felt Vi cowering beside her, clutching her blouse, and she automatically dropped a hand from her face, throwing an arm around Vi's shoulders, sweeping her against the curve of her hip. She had only the vaguest impression of what her daughter was saying in a bewildered voice, of the question she was asking over and over—*Mommy, who's that man? Mommy, who's that man?* The wide circles of Jolanda's eyes were locked on Mutter Campbell and they drank in his movements like camera lenses holding a closeup. She saw him reach into the front pocket of his trousers and pull out a cylindrical object that first appeared to be a folding knife, but then his thumb slipped over a catch on the handle and a segmented metal rod telescoped from it in an eyeblink, *snick-snick-snick,* its silvery length catching the sunlight from the living room windows.

It was the baton's cold silver gleam as he crossed the room, combined with the tear-choked cries gusting out of her daughter and Robin, that finally cut through Jolanda's shock—these things, and perhaps most piercingly of all, the hard, questioning look Campbell had shot at Vi as she'd pressed up against her.

The meaning of that look had dawned on Jolanda with a sickening mental slap: Vi had called her Mommy. He'd *heard* Vi call her mommy.

Her mind racing, she flicked a glance into the living room, thought about trying to reach the phone on the coffee table, and realized it would be impossible to avoid running right into him. For an instant she considered going for it anyway, afraid for Robin, thinking she couldn't just leave Robin alone with Campbell, but he had already stalked past the little girl, showing no interest in her, leaving her to pick herself up off the floor. The kitchen phone, then. If she could make it into the kitchen, call the police . . .

She whirled, her arm still slung around Vi's shoulders, almost scooping her off her feet as she hustled her toward the kitchen.

"*Mommy!*" Vi shrieked hysterically, tears running down her cheeks. "*That man hurt Robin, that man hurt Ro—*"

"Not now, baby!" Jolanda plunged down the hall. She saw the two boys coming out of the kitchen to investigate the commotion, saw their mouths pop open with astonishment when they became aware of what was happening. Andy glanced at the man charging after his mother and sister and screamed at the top of his lungs, recognition pouring into his features, old enough to remember his father and the terrible things he had done before he was sent away.

"Hurry into Andy's room!" Jolanda yelled at them, moving swiftly, hearing Campbell's thudding footsteps behind her. "Get in there and lock the door!"

Andy did not budge; he seemed unable to understand her in his terror.

"Mom!" He was still gaping, pointing wildly at his father, his voice cracking. "Mom, he's—"

"Get in there now!" Jolanda cried out. Her free hand swept out, pushing him backward toward his door with such force that he lost his balance and staggered into Jamal. "*Both of you!*"

It was Jamal who grabbed Andy's arm and pulled him the remaining distance to his room. The door was halfway open and Andy hooked his fingers around its edge as he was dragged inside, looking helplessly out at his mother and sister, momentarily trying to resist his friend's frantic tugging—but then Jamal managed to haul him the rest of the way in and slam the door shut behind them.

Jolanda turned into the kitchen, swinging Vi forward the way someone might roll a bowling ball, wanting her in ahead of her, wanting to put herself between Campbell and Vi. She could hear his footsteps pounding on the floor behind her, rattling the glasses in the open cabinet above the sink, could hear him gaining.

Without glancing back over her shoulder, she lunged for the counter, tore the receiver from the phone on top of it, and jabbed at the numbered buttons—nine and one and one—

And Campbell's hand fell heavily on her shoulder, whipping her around. She jerked her eyes up at his twitching, twisted face and started to scream, but before a sound could escape her mouth he flung her against the sink, then moved in and punched her twice in the throat before she could recover. She sank to the floor, somehow managing to hold on to the phone, knives and spoons scattering around her off the dish rack. But then Campbell lumbered over, kicked her in the stomach, and stamped his foot down on the hand in which she was limply clutching the receiver.

She moaned as it skated out of her grasp.

"I love you, Jolanda," he said.

In the living room, Robin had gotten up off the floor and gone to the phone on the coffee table, her body shaking, sobbing violently, tears spilling down her cheeks. She had watched the man she'd let into the apartment chase Jolanda into the kitchen and did not know what he was doing to her, but she'd heard Andy and her brother screaming a minute ago, and could hear Vi screaming now, and was terrified that the man was hurting them, and remembered again what her mother had once told her about calling the police or fire department.

Her arm shaking, she lifted the receiver to her ear, and was surprised to hear a woman's voice already on the line.

". . . operator three-four-seven, where is the emergency?"

She opened her mouth to reply, but then hesitated, confused about how the operator had gotten on the phone, and about something else that was even more basic: Robin's mother had made her memorize her own address, but she did not know Vi's.

"Somebody's hurting my *friends*," she whimpered. "I let him in and—"

"Please, honey, listen to me. You have to give me your name and address."

"Robin. My name is Robin Greene," she said. "I'm at Vi's house—"

"Is Vi your friend or her mommy?"

"My *friend*. Please, please he's hurting them—"

"Do you know the name of Vi's mommy, dear?"

"Yes, it's Jolanda." Something between a sob and a moan escaped her lips. "Jolanda *Martin*, we go to school together, and we live on Union Avenue, but I don't know her address, I don't know her address, I don't—"

"Robin? Robin, are you there? *Robin . . .*"

VINCENT LOCICERO'S SOCIAL club and center of criminal operations—the one cops *knew* about—was a small, no-name storefront on Hester Street with blacked-out windows and a shaded door that was guarded round the clock by a sprinkling of local wiseguys. In the fall and winter the guards would watch the entrance from Lincolns and Caddies parked out front with their polarized windows rolled up and, on the coldest days, their heaters running. In the spring and summer they sat on the hoods of the cars and flipped playing cards, and leaned on the curbside johnny pump opposite the entrance, or, on the nicest days, sat on folding chairs and sipped Coke or iced coffee, keeping an eye out for police surveillance vehicles, people on the street who might be undercover detectives, and members of rival outfits brazen or stupid enough to strike at LoCicero on his home territory. The latter was a remote possibility to be sure, but with some of the young turks being so aggressive these days, you had to keep up your defenses.

Vincent LoCicero's other headquarters—the one the cops had *no idea* existed—was located five blocks away on Thompson Street, in the stockroom of a women's lingerie shop operated by his longtime girlfriend Theresa. At a table surrounded by floor-to-ceiling shelves packed with bras, panties, teddies, stockings, and garters, Vince conducted his most sensitive meetings relatively free of concern over snoopers, spotters, and wiretaps. When cutting a deal with a major mobster, planning a high-stakes score, or ordering a contract on someone's life—to cite but a few examples—Vince would leave his social club through an underground tunnel leading from the basement to an alley that ran behind Hester, and slip over to the cramped but sexy sanctuary of Theresa's feminine undergarment boutique.

Arriving there for his sitdown with Frank Stella in the company of two bodyguards, he had given Theresa a lingering kiss, a playfully intimate squeeze, and a box of pastries from a nearby Italian bakery, and then told her of the visitor he was expecting and gone in back to wait for him. Stella walked through the door ten minutes later at 1:00 P.M. sharp, right on time. He drew a startled glance from Theresa, who remembered him from the old days as a fine dresser, someone who managed to be attractive despite his gaunt and rather sinister features. The man who entered her shop, on the other hand, had a face that was a quilt of cuts and bruises and wore soiled, stained clothes that might have looked right on a homeless derelict . . . or, judging by the reddish color of the stains, a butcher, she thought with a twinge of discomfort. Theresa was hardly a virgin pure, and she knew Vince consorted with some pretty rough types, but this present version of Stella was in a league of his own. Never mind what they were saying on the news, he had changed in the asylum he'd escaped from, changed in ways that made her wonder if it wouldn't be better if he was returned to a padded cell ASAP.

After silently leading Stella into the back room, Theresa had been relieved to close the door behind him so she didn't have to see his battered face and weirdly evasive eyes. No one, but *no one,* could have been a better reminder of why she liked being kept out of Vince's professional dealings.

"Okay, tell me again what you think I can do for you," Vince said now, looking at Stella across a small bridge table. A steaming demitasse and open bottle of anisette were in front of him. Theresa's cat, Juke, was preening on his lap. His bodyguards, Jimmy "Bugeyes" Boccigualupo and Tommy "Fingers" Carbone, sat against the wall to his rear, solid and impassive.

Stella gave him a frozen grin.

"Kinda surprises me to get the brass tacks, get-down-an'-do-it, no-nonsense nitty-gritty hustle from you, Vince," he said. "I thought there'd be at least *some* friendly talk."

Vince added a dash of anisette to his coffee, raised the cup to his mouth, and sipped. Though Theresa had refrained from making any comments to him about Stella's freakish, disheveled appearance, his thinking on the subject was not unlike hers. Something had happened to the guy while he was away, and Vince couldn't wait to be rid of him. All Stella would do was bring him grief.

"Look, I got a visit from a couple of homicide bulls today," he said. "I'm out taking a Sunday morning constitutional and they come and crap on my doorstep. And you know why they were there, Frank?"

"Lookin' for me?"

"Fucking right."

"Guess I'm a pretty important guy these days."

"I suppose," Vince said. "The kind of important I can live without."

He sipped his espresso, stroking the cat on his thighs with his free hand. It was a tiger-striped male he'd found half-starved on the street about a year back, and only pawned off on Theresa because of the fuss his Chihuahuas had raised when he'd brought it home.

"So," he said. "What *do* you want?"

"A way out," Stella said. "That, an' nothin' more."

225

"We talking money?"

Stella's grin tightened up slightly at the corners. "Ain't never asked you or anybody else for a handout. I can pay the price at the door, long as there's somebody who'll sell me a ticket."

Vince regarded him a moment, and then nodded with understanding.

"You need tags," he said.

"A passport, driver's license, an' a new name to go with it," Stella said. "By tonight."

Vince laughed without humor.

"Hold the pickle, hold the lettuce," he said.

"What's that supposed to mean, Vince?"

"Means you only get that kind of service when you order a fast-food burger," Vince said. "Frank, you always done good work for me, kept your lips zipped, and I appreciate that kind of loyalty. I can do the I.D., but these things aren't that simple to arrange. Gonna take a few days, maybe a week."

"A *week*?" Stella said. "I can't wait around, Vince. Like you said yourself, the law's ridin' me down, an' after they get a load'a Harry they're really gonna dig in the spurs. I got to clear this state right away."

"Harry?" Vince said "You mean Reamis? What about him?"

Stella was silent a moment, and Vince was instantly positive he'd caught him in a slipup.

"What *about* Harry?" he persisted.

"Well, I hate to be a wicked messenger, but that buck's seen his last ruttin' season," Stella said. "See, I paid him a surprise visit this morning, an' he got so carried away jumpin' for joy, he accidentally took a spill out his window."

Vince stared at him, incredulous. Harry—he'd killed fucking Harry. The vicious son of a bitch was like a wolf that had tasted blood; out of his cage less than two days and bodies were dropping everywhere. Pembleton had been right, anybody as unpredictable as Stella was

226

trouble, serious trouble, and had to be dealt with in a hurry.

"Okay," he said. "I can call in some favors, try'n get things done by tomorrow."

"Well there you are, boys," Stella said to everyone in the room. He leaned back in his chair, grinned briefly at Vince's watchdogs, and then locked his ice-blue eyes on Vince. "How much am I gonna be payin'?"

"Ten thou," Vince said, adding maybe fifty percent to the actual cost for his own pocket. "Gonna take that much to convince a tag artist to do any fast work, on account this is a holiday weekend."

"Fair enough," Stella said. "I can give you twenty-five hundred now, the rest when I get the goods."

Vince looked at him. "Don't stiff me on the payment, Frank. I depend on people's goodwill."

"Wouldn't think of it," Stella said. "My mama's been sittin' on a chunk a' cash for me while I been locked up, an' I plan to swing by an' see her soon's we're through talkin'. Probably gonna be our last visit together, sad to say, since I ain't plannin' to come back to this burg, an' she's in no condition to travel."

Vince scratched the cat on his lap behind the ears. It narrowed its eyes and purred with pleasure.

"Let's talk about where we're gonna meet," he said.

Stella's eyes darted around the room. "I know your boys're as trustworthy as they come, Vince, but you sure the kitty won't go tellin' tales?"

"I'd rather not sit here all day," Vince said with an impatient sigh.

"All right, Vince, listen up close." Stella leaned forward. "There's this place I kinda like across town, a real quiet spot where the posse ain't never gonna come lookin' for me, an' where I intend to settle in for the next couple days . . ."

THIS IS HOW the summons came down to Giardello and his detectives: seconds after being disconnected, the operator who answered the 911 call from Jolanda Martin's apartment urgently reported it as a possible hostage situation to her shift supervisor, who used a computerized database to trace the address from which the call originated, and then routed the available information to one of sixteen dispatchers in the police communications center at East Fayette Street. The dispatcher then broadcast an all-points bulletin on the radio waveband used by police throughout the city, issuing a special call for help to the Quick Response Team, an elite detail trained and equipped for tactical and emergency rescue operations, and also contacting the Homicide unit downtown, as was routine when the crime in progress held a strong potential for casualties.

Sitting morosely by himself in the Homicide squad room, Munch answered the phone when it trilled, instantly recognized the name of Jolanda Martin as that of the woman Lewis and Kellerman had been seeking in connection with the Campbell manhunt, and called Giardello on his cell phone at the Reamis crime scene.

By that time the general announcement was already crackling from radios in the swarm of marked and unmarked police cars around Reamis's house, and Lewis, who had been giving instructions to a uniform on the sidewalk out front, had no sooner caught his first snatch of it through a cruiser's open window than Gee came running up to him with orders to get hold of Kellerman—who was still in the building overseeing evidence collection—and hurry over to Union Avenue.

His heart pounding, whatever he'd been telling the uniform forgotten in his excitement, Lewis was through the front door and bounding upstairs in two seconds flat, shouting for his partner at the top of his lungs.

HE HAD OPENED the drop leafs on Jolanda's long, rectangular kitchen table, lined up the chairs on one side, made all five of his captives sit in them, and then pushed the table forward so they would be pinned between its edge and the wall. He sat across from them, facing them. The two little girls were at each end, Vibeca to his left, Robin to the right. Next in were the boys, Jamal beside Vi, Andy beside his friend's sister. Jolanda was in the middle, directly opposite Campbell. He had warned them to be silent and they sat there without moving or making a sound, their faces ashen and fearful.

The kitchen smelled of kerosene.

On the table next to Campbell's right elbow were his riot baton and a carving knife he had taken from the silverware drawer under the sink. Below the drawer, the base cabinet's doors were flung wide open. Its contents had been emptied out: plastic buckets, dishrags, boxes of steel wool, and bottles of dishwashing liquid, glass cleaner, and ammonia lay scattered on the kitchen linoleum. From where he sat Campbell could see the plumbing lines running from the basin into the wall in back of the cabinet. He had cleared the space around the pipes so he would have elbow room once he started working under there.

But he did not want to get ahead of himself; better to take things a step at a time. He found it hard enough to concentrate; it was as if a tiny pair of scissors were snipping away at his thoughts, cutting them to pieces even as they sprouted from his brain. His physical discomfort was equally frustrating. There was a bleachy taste in the back of his mouth and every moment was a battle to control his nausea. But the very worst of it was that other thing that had been happening to him. The painful hardness between his legs, and the shame and self-disgust he felt because of it . . . because of the uncontrollable sensations radiating through his body from that central point of heat. He hoped Jolanda had not noticed his swelling, but he believed she must have. The children too.

The girls.

The two girls.

They stared at him with tear-bright eyes, reminding him of frightened birds curled in a nest.

He was sure they had noticed.

Campbell tried to shake off the tormenting thoughts and restrict his attention to the objects he'd set out on the table.

In front of him was a large clay salad bowl he'd taken down from a wall cabinet. A half dozen bars of lavender soap were stacked on his right, near the knife and baton. He held another soap bar in one hand and was scraping it over a cheese grater, holding both over the salad bowl so it would catch the peelings. As he got through shredding each bar, he would reach for one of the others and begin reducing it to chips and flakes as he had done to the previous one, and the one before that, and the one before that. Soon the rising dune of soap peelings would fill the bowl and Campbell would slowly add them to the pot of boiling kerosene on the electric stove, stirring the mixture with a wooden spoon. When this highly flammable solution finished cooking, it would have a sticky, gelatinous consistency similar to Vaseline. Campbell would let it cool, then pour some of it into the plastic buckets he'd removed from the base cabinet. He would apply the rest to the outside of the false drainpipe he was fashioning, molding it to the shape of the pipe like putty.

The pipe incendiary that would be his time-delayed igniter—causing the gelatin to burst into flame—was already assembled. Campbell had constructed it in less than ten minutes using the materials he had bought at Longworth's, the powerful drain cleaning acid that had been on the shelves of the bodega he'd robbed, and sugar from Jolanda's cupboard. He had inserted the copper flange midway into the pipe coupling, where it would act as a delay disk. Then he had screwed the segments of pressure pipe into either end of the coupling, filling one segment with the acid, and the other with a 3-to-1 mixture of pool cleaning crystals—or sodium chlorate—and sugar. Finally he had plugged each end of the pipe assembly with a rubber stopper.

When the pipe was stood on end with the acid placed above the sugar-chlorate mixture, it would gradually eat through the copper disk to the mixture, producing a violently combustive chemical reaction. Given a few minutes to burn through the piping and spread, this intense fire *alone* would be enough to consume the apartment and everyone trapped in it. But Campbell knew the ignited gelatin would ensure none of them would escape. Knew it would cling to walls, flesh, everything, burning whatever it touched, drenching it in fire. In his mind's eye he could see the flame sweeping up and up and up and up, growing like a living thing, like a hungry, unstoppable beast, chewing greedily at the walls, leaping toward the ceiling, reaching its bright, angry fingers through the rooftop to claw at the sky. And in its roaring throat, in its red belly, Campbell would at last find release from his hateful compulsions. Would go from light to dark, light to dark . . .

And Jolanda . . .

His love, his sweet love, his only love . . .

Jolanda would go with him.

NICKY THE NOSE loved Meg Ryan, was crazy about Meg Ryan, had what you would call a real *thing* for Meg Ryan. Married thirty-five, going on thirty-six, years without once stepping out on his wife Dorothy, and proud of it . . . but if there was ever a woman who could turn his head, it would be Meg. Of course, guys like him only met gals like her in their dreams; hell, she'd stared into the eyes of Tom Hanks, Tom fucking Hanks, the biggest star in the universe, and if Meg hadn't left that Quaid guy for *him*, then he highly doubted she would go for a professional gofer, let alone one who couldn't even succeed at carting a truckful of goddamn milk around Charm City without getting his ass burned by the cops.

Well, there was always his VCR. And this afternoon, having gotten the apartment all to himself—Dorothy was out visiting their daughter and grandkids—Nicky was stretched on his living room couch with some brewskies and potato chips, running what you might call a Meg Ryan film festival. He had already watched *Top Gun,* which most people forgot was Meg's first big break, and followed up with *When Harry Met Sally,* and had just gotten past the opening credits of *Joe Versus the Volcano,* a flick he thought was highly underrated, if only because Meg played three different parts to perfection in it, when the telephone started ringing.

He frowned irritably, hit the Pause button on his remote, and reached over to the phone stand without lifting his head off his pillow.

"What is it?" he grumbled into the receiver.

"Nice way to say hello to your cousin," the voice at the other end said. "Whyn't you just tell me to drop dead?"

"Bugeyes? That you?"

"Right."

"Hey, man, sorry, I was just watchin' a movie—"

"What movie?"

"*White Heat,*" Nicky lied.

"That's Cagney, ain't it?" Bugeyes said.

"Right."

"The one where he's in the slammer and somebody tells him his mother's dead and he goes apeshit—"

"Right, right," Nicky said.

"That scene always gets to me," Bugeyes said. "When he finds out about his mother, I mean."

"Look, I put the tape on pause, so if this ain't important, maybe you could call back la—"

"You wanna give me the bum's rush, go ahead," Bugeyes said. "But then you ain't gonna know what I know about Frank Stella an' *his* mother."

Nicky cranked himself to a sitting position.

"What is it?" he said excitely.

"Maybe you don't care, but I'm takin' a big risk by callin' you about him, an' if you're gonna treat me like I'm some kinda jerkoff . . ."

"Come on, man, what you got?"

"Stella met with Vince today."

Nicky was almost speechless. He'd told Bugeyes of his interest in Stella on Saturday, and this was only *Sunday*. The last thing he'd expected was to get any dope about him so soon. "You shittin' me?"

"I was there when it happened, Nicky," Bugeyes said. "My ass was parked not ten feet away from the fuckin' mental case."

"You know where he is? Where he is *now,* I mean?"

"Maybe not right this minute, but I can tell you where he's gonna *be*."

"Jesus Christ, I can't believe it, you are a fucking prince," Nicky said. "So tell me—"

"Not so fast," Bugeyes said. "First you gotta promise you'll have that shipment of chocolate milk at my house tomorrow morning."

"I *already* gave you my word—"

"Yeah, I know, but I want it again," Bugeyes said. "Ain't just Memorial Day, it's my son's *birthday*. There's gonna be maybe fifteen, twenty thirsty kids in my backyard—"

"I swear on my *mother* you'll get your freakin' milk, okay?"

"Okay, okay, don't give yourself a heart attack," Bugeyes said. "Here's what I heard . . ."

STILL ALONE IN the squad room, Munch was startled out of a daydream about Vera Bash by the sound of his ringing phone.

"Homicide, Detective Munch speaking," he said, rubbing his eyes behind his glasses.

"Hey, Munch, it's me. The Nose."

He straightened in his chair. "What's the word?"

"You remember that tip you were after? About Frank Stella?"

"Of *course* I remember—"

"You sound cranky, man. I wake you up or somethin'?"

"No, Nicky, you didn't," Munch said. "Now what have you got for me?"

"I don't know," Nicky said.

"You don't *know*?"

"About you, I mean. Something's the matter. If I'm callin' at a bad time . . ."

"It's fine," Munch said.

"You sure? 'Cause I can always try you la—"

"I said it was *fine*," Munch said.

"Okay, okay, nobody's forcin' you to bare your soul," the Nose said. "It's just that I thought we were friends. Kind of."

"Nicky, I'm going to wait exactly three more seconds," Munch said. "If you haven't told why you're calling by then, I swear I'll—"

"I know where you can find Frank Stella," Nicky said. "That a good reason to call off your countdown, or what?"

Munch slid to the edge of his seat, his hand tightening around the receiver.

"Good enough," he said.

PEMBLETON AND BAYLISS returned to headquarters a little before three-thirty, having spent most of the afternoon on a fruitless stakeout of Vince LoCicero's social club. They had kept their car radio off to prevent its telltale squawk from letting everyone and his mother know they were cops, and were consequently unaware of the emergency that had drawn most of the Homicide squad—and dozens of officers from other units—to the streets surrounding Jolanda Martin's apartment building. Still, the two detectives could not fail to notice the scarcity of vehicles in the reserved parking area outside the station, and were wondering aloud what was going on when Munch came bashing up the sidewalk in their direction.

"Guys! Hey, guys!" Munch shouted, thinking it was a stroke of luck he'd run into them. There hadn't been a single unmarked car available from Requisitions, and he'd figured he would be stuck trying to flag down a lift with a uniformed patrol.

"What is it?" Pembleton said. "And where *is* everybody?"

"There's trouble. I'll fill you in later," Munch said, panting. "Right now we've gotta get to the cemetery. And *quick!*"

THE MAUSOLEUM STANK of black salve.

Stella knew it couldn't be, told himself it couldn't be—the smell had been killed long ago, sure it had, why else would he have gone to the expense of cremating his mother instead of just letting her rot in the ground? The stink was gone, burned away, her body roasted at two thousand degrees Fahrenheit until the flesh was seared off and there wasn't a damn thing left of it but bone fragments . . . great big knobs and handles of blackened bone that were broken into smaller, unrecognizable pieces by a machine, and dumped into an urn, and shoved to the back of a small, dark hole in the wall of the mausoleum. Well, actually, the *calumbarium,* if you happened to be a stickler like the monument dealer who'd explained the fine points of entombment to Stella at no obligation.

"Mama-bitch you're gone, mama-bitch you're ashes, fire's licked your sores an' rashes," he said to himself now. Pleased with that spontaneous little ditty, he repeated it with a hillbilly twang in his voice, snapping his fingers, wiggling his hips, giving it the full-blown Jerry Lee Lewis treatment.

"Mama-bitch you-oo-oo're gooone . . ."

Stella moved deeper into the crypt, his voice echoing flatly off its moist stone walls. Behind him the door had been swung outward on a slant and late afternoon sunlight trickled faintly through the opening. Shadows stretched and wavered in the gloom.

"Mama-bitch you're aa-aa-aa-ashes . . ."

His mother had known a rhyme or expression for every situation, like she'd thought every damn problem you came across could be solved if you were able to sum it up in a nutshell . . . which was pretty funny considering she'd had nothing all her life, *been* nothing but poor, unschooled Southern white trash, lazy as a slug, fat as a summer melon, a woman who would sit outside their trailer morning, noon, and night in neon-pink boy-watcher shades and a shapeless tent of a dress, scratching her thick red arms and filling her face with food, never seeming to enjoy what she ate, just sitting there and scarfing it down with a mean, aggressive look on her face, as if every ounce of weight she gained was some kind of accomplishment, a challenge to the world around her. Sometimes she'd stop eating long enough to holler at the kids monotonously tossing rubber balls back and forth in the next court over, the kids themselves looking pissed off all the time, swearing at each other a lot, stupid and inbred, unable to come up with games that had any kind of sensible rules . . . but mostly she'd just sit at a picnic bench gobbling potato chips, hamburgers, cheese doodles—anything she could lift to her mouth—scratching and eating, scratching and eating, gaining pound after pound after pound, her arms inflamed and scaly from whatever unknown skin condition she'd had all those years, stinking of the black salve she would smear on herself to "draw out the pus," as she'd so daintily liked to put it . . .

Stella took another few steps forward. Shredded cobwebs hung from the low ceiling and caught on his face, making the cuts on his cheeks sting. He brushed them away, wishing he'd brought a flashlight. Even if he hadn't wanted to risk showing himself in a store, there must have been a goddamn flash at Harry's place. Or he could have gotten one from Vince. As it was, he could hardly see in front of him. He hadn't been in this place for years, nobody had, and it was damp and musty and there was loose soil on the cement floor . . .

And goddamn, *goddamn,* it stank of black salve.

"Fire's licked your soooo-ooores an' raa-ashes . . ."

Stella felt something squash underfoot, examined his shoe bottom to find he'd stepped on a fat, curled earthworm, and scraped it off with a snort of disgust . . . although a part of him wanted to chuckle. The dirt and crawling things made this a perfect shrine to his mother, yes indeed, so absolutely right you'd think the filth had been worked into the decor. She had always kept the trailer a mess, stacks of unwashed dishes and silverware in the sink, balled, dusty clothing on the floor and under the beds, streaks of grime on the Salvation Army junk that passed for furniture. It didn't seem to bother her—in fact, she didn't seem to even notice the rust-eaten holes in the walls, not as long as she could plunk down in her La-Z-Boy and watch her staticky black-and-white TV, a nineteen-inch Zenith with a bent metal hanger for an antenna. Whenever there was a bad downpour, water would drip into the trailer, and Stella would lie shivering in bed at night, hearing the music and voices from that television and the tinny sound of the rain beating against the roof as the cold droplets splatted his face, trying to imagine what it would be like having a decent place to sleep, promising himself things would be different if he ever got out of that trailer park, got his hands on some *money* . . .

And he had done it, hadn't he? Done okay for a kid who'd never learned to read, or ride a bike, or even been taught how to tie his fucking shoes, let alone the right way to hold a knife and fork at the table. He had made enough money to buy all the houses, cars, and fine clothes he'd wanted. He had done it by being one mean son of a bitch, a guy who would snuff out anybody— the Pope and his cardinals included—if the price was right.

And he had always kept things neat and clean.

Now Stella reached the back of the mausoleum, his eyes traveling up the wall, seeking the niche that harbored the plain metal urn containing his mother's ashes. For a moment he stood with his hands clenched so tightly their knuckles hurt, afraid the urn would be gone, stolen by some rummy groundskeeper who'd maybe gone snooping around out of curiosity and stumbled upon a jackpot he couldn't have imagined in his wildest dreams. For an endless, excruciating moment he was certain that was what had happened, certain he'd been put out of business . . . but then he saw the recess in the wall, saw the urn half-hidden in a patch of shadows, and felt a rush of excitement.

His breaths coming in sharp little bursts, feeling a desire so intense it was almost suffocating, Stella reached out with both hands, closed them around the urn, and tore it from the niche. There was a film of moisture on its smooth, cold surface and it nearly slipped from his eager grasp, but he held on, hugging it almost tenderly against his chest.

Then, his lips moving in what might have been a silent prayer, he twisted open the lid, turned the receptacle upside down, and watched the dry ashes of his mother spill to the floor of the mausoleum, covering the toes of his shoes, puffing up in powdery gray clouds.

A second passed.

Two.

Pus and salve—Stella was sure he could smell pus and salve.

Beads of sweat on his forehead, still muttering silently to himself, he turned the urn right side up.

Reached his hand inside.

And breathlessly pulled out the sealed Ziplock bag he had stashed inside it nearly a decade before.

An ecstatic whoop tore from his lips as he lifted it to his face. The money was in it, a *stack* of money, fifty thousand dollars, his rainy-day fund, all here, all of it, waiting for him. He let out another cry of elation, kissed the thick packet of bills, kissed the urn before letting it drop to the floor.

Well satisfied with himself, forgetful for a time of the outside world, Frank Stella laughed and laughed with delirious joy among the dusty, discarded remains of his mother.

THIRTEEN

POLICE SIRENS SLICED through the night. From every corner of the city radio cars and QRT vehicles raced toward Hamilton Avenue with their tires screeching and lights pulsing on their roof racks.

Standing within the cordoned-off perimeter around Jolanda Martin's apartment building, Lewis couldn't help but think it looked and sounded as if war had broken out in central Baltimore. Tac teams in Kevlar helmets and flak vests were piling from the crew doors of their boxy armored trucks, carrying ballistic shields, MP5 submachine guns, Ruger Mini-14 assault rifles, and Ithaca 12-gauge shotguns. On adjacent rooftops, snipers crouched with their cheeks pressed against the black synthetic stocks of SSG-PIV rifles, peering at Jolanda Martin's fourth-floor living room window through variable-power scopes. Bell Jet Ranger choppers wheeled overhead like hornets. Officers from the Hostage Negotiating Team bustled around a communications van. There were fire trucks, ambulances nosed up against one another in daisywheel formation, and crowd control personnel with riot batons turning away civilians at the outer margins of the crime scene.

Now Lewis shrugged into one of the light vests a Tac officer had given him, handed the other to Kellerman, and let his gaze rove up the brown brick facade of Jolanda Martin's building. From the moment he had arrived amid the frantic police activity, he'd been experiencing an odd sense of disconnection. Part of it was that he was used to plugging away at a case in the aftermath of violent death, used to wading through the carnage and trying to find out who did it—and used to calling his own shots as he went along. But right now his job was about saving the innocent rather than punishing the guilty, and lives were hanging on every decision, and the very scale of the operation meant that few, if any, of those decisions would be his to make. The other thing was that he wasn't at all sure what he was dealing with here—nobody yet knew if the person who had locked himself up in that apartment had harmed his captives, or planned to harm them, or even if he was, in fact, Mutter Campbell.

It was, Lewis thought, high time those questions started getting answered.

He glanced at the other side of the crime scene tape, seeking out the area where Jolanda Martin's neighbors had been herded after being evacuated from their apartments.

"Let's go, Mikey," he said, tapping Kellerman on the shoulder.

Kellerman nodded and followed him over to the nervous group of tenants. There were about fifteen or twenty people in all—young, old, men, women, a salt-and-pepper mix of middle-class blacks and whites.

"What've you got?" Lewis asked the uniformed patrolman assigned to watch over them.

"What do you mean?"

"Ain't you been takin' statements?"

The cop looked at him.

"Nobody told me—"

"Uh-huh."

Lewis shoved past him to the tenants.

"Folks, I'm Detective Lewis, and this is my partner, Detective Kellerman," he said, his voice raised so they could hear it above the surrounding commotion. "I know you're all upset, but if anyone can tell us somethin' about what happened, we'd appreciate it."

He waited, scanning their faces. On the sidewalk in front of the apartment house, a negotiator was repeating a practiced message into a bullhorn: "Somebody up there, please pick up the phone! We've set up a direct line, you don't have to dial anything. Somebody up there, please . . ."

"I saw the guy," a young lady in a maternity dress said to Lewis, pushing between two of the other tenants.

He took hold of her arm and gently drew her aside.

"May I have your name, ma'am?"

"Lisa," she said. "Lisa Bennett. I live in apartment 4B. My door's just across the hall from Jolanda's."

"Okay, Lisa, tell me what happened."

"Like I said, I got a look at him. That is, I heard him first, then went to the peephole—"

"One second," Lewis said. "Heard him sayin' what?"

"I thought it was something about there being a fire in the building," she said, shaking her head. "I had the stereo on and wasn't sure."

"That when you went to your door?"

"Yes. To see what was going on."

"You hear anything else?"

"He was talking to a little girl. It might have been Vibeca—"

"That Jolanda's daughter?"

Lisa nodded. She was maybe twenty-five years old, cute, with short kinky hair and mocha-colored skin.

"Okay," Lewis said. "So she's talkin' to Vibeca and—"

"I said it might have been her," Lisa said. "I think the kids had friends over, a boy and girl from down the block—"

"Their mother's been in contact with us," Lewis said. "You hear what the girl was sayin'?"

Lisa shook her head again, her brown eyes pained. "My music was pretty loud."

"Okay," Lewis said. "Tell me what you saw when you looked out the peephole."

"The guy had his back to me, so I didn't get a look at his face, but he was big . . . and I don't just mean tall." She spread her hands for emphasis. "Shoulders like this. Built like a football player."

Lewis nodded. Like it or not, the man she was talking about was almost certainly Mutter Campbell.

"You ever see him before?"

"No."

"Was anybody with him?" he asked.

"No."

"You positive?"

"He was alone."

Which meant Stella had gone his separate way.

"How'd he get in the apartment?" he asked

"Somebody opened the door and he walked right in," she said. "What I mean is, he didn't try to push his way through or anything. That was what made me think I was wrong about him saying there was a fire. Maybe about the little girl sounding scared too." Her eyes suddenly became moist. "Detective, if he'd looked like he was going to hurt them, I would've called the police right away—"

"Nobody's pointin' any blame at you, Lisa," Lewis said. "Was that all you saw?"

She nodded.

"Ma'am, if you don't mind, I'd just like to ask you one or two more questions," Kellerman said.

"Of course."

"Did you notice whether the guy was carrying anything?"

She looked at him.

"Well, yes, now that you mention it . . ."

"Go on," Kellerman said.

"I suppose I forgot because it didn't seem important," she said. "He was holding a couple of bags. Shopping bags, I think."

The detectives looked at each other.

"*Is* that important?" Lisa asked.

Neither of them answered.

The last thing they were going to tell her was that they believed those bags had contained the makings of an inferno.

THEY REACHED THE small cemetery behind Saint Francis of Assisi Catholic Church shortly after four o'clock and the groundskeeper told them to park the car in the lot down around by the vestry and walk back.

At this hour most people had paid their respects and gone home and there were only a few other vehicles in the lot. The detectives filed up to the cemetery's main entrance behind three or four small groups of visitors, Pembleton pausing along the way to buy a prayer book from a woman who was selling them out the back of a station wagon, Bayliss picking up some red, white, and blue carnations from a vender near the gate.

"Maybe I oughtta be carrying a prop too," Munch said.

"You don't need one," Bayliss said.

"How's that?"

Bayliss gave him a strained smile. "You already look like an undertaker."

Walking beside them, Pembleton wondered about the sirens bounding up into the rapidly fading sunlight, dozens of them, screaming and howling, reminding him of the air raid drills of his early grade school years. Height of the Cold War, Soviet ICBMs aimed at your town, and you were instructed to crouch under your desks, cover your heads with your hands, and trust that you'd survive nuclear Armageddon.

Jesus, what was going on downtown?

The detectives entered the cemetery and turned along a gravel path to the gatehouse, where they found the groundskeeper staring serenely out at the rows of head-stones.

"Park the car okay?" He was a thin, wiry-haired black man with a face full of concentric lines that looked like a knot on an ancient tree.

"No problem," Pembleton said. "We could use some more directions, if you don't mind."

"What I'm here for," the old man said. He nodded his chin at Bayliss's flowers. "Who's the serviceman you fellas come to see?"

"Well, actually, we're looking for a Mrs. Stella," Bayliss said. "We think she's . . . uh . . ." He glanced over at Munch. "What's the word?"

"Interred."

"Thanks. We think she's *interred* in a mausoleum."

The groundskeeper thoughtfully slid his tongue over his lips.

"She a veteran?"

"No," Bayliss said.

"Why them patriotic colors?" The old man pointed at the carnations again.

"Oh, *these*," Bayliss said, and held them up with sudden understanding. "They're all the guy had left."

"Well, guess it *is* Memorial Day weekend." The groundskeeper lazily scratched the back of his neck, his eyes scanning the grounds. "Wonder if all'a them *si-reeens* I been hearin' got somethin' to do with the holiday. Noise is scarin' the birds. Fine day like today, I can usually hear 'em singin'—"

"Excuse me," Pembleton said, "but we really need to get over to the mausoleum."

"All right, no problem." He gave Pembleton a curious look. "Ah, it ain't my business, course, but which member 'a the family are you?"

Pembleton reached into his jacket pocket for his shield and I.D. card. The thought that Frank Stella might be somewhere on the grounds while they stood there wasting time had made his stomach knot with impatience.

"I'm with Baltimore City Homicide," he said. "Now, please, sir, this is an urgent matter."

"*Ho*-micide." The old man's eyes widened. "Gonna be trouble?"

"We'll be as quick and discreet as possible," Pembleton said, sidestepping the question.

The groundskeeper grunted and pointed down the gravel walk.

"See those maples maybe fifty, sixty yards down?" he said.

Pembleton nodded, his eyes following the old man's finger.

"The path comes out the other side'a them trees an' forks around a statue of the Blessed Virgin. Swing to the left, you'll see the Stella crypt straight ahead. Ain't no other thereabouts, so you can't miss it."

Pembleton slipped his tin back into his pocket, still looking down the path.

"Anyone else visit the mausoleum today?"

"Not that I noticed." The old man shrugged "Course, I been busy, what with folks comin' to pay respects to their soldiers, so it could be. But Mrs. Rose Stella don't get much company."

"Thank you," Pembleton said, and glanced at the other detectives.

The three of them moved down the path without a word, Munch thinking he should have called for backup, would very definitely have preferred having some god-damn backup, except Pembleton had said earlier that he did not want a bunch of uniforms clomping around the cemetery and scaring Stella off. Pembleton had insisted they go alone, and anybody who'd ever worked beside the Great Frank Pembleton knew better than to try and argue with him once he'd made up his mind.

They followed the path through the stand of trees, walking close together, walking faster as they came out of the trees, passed the statue, turned, and all at the same instant saw the mausoleum up ahead, standing alone at the top of a hillock. Munch saw Pembleton slipping a hand under his jacket, saw Bayliss do the same thing, both men reaching for their guns, and a moment later he was wrapping his fingers around the butt of his own service pistol.

Their tension building, feeling it string out between them like a wire humming with current, they approached the gray stone sepulcher, all three of them noticing simultaneously—that was how it worked in dangerous situations when you'd been a cop as long as they had been cops; it was like your senses were keyed to those of the man beside you, and his were plugged into the eyes and ears of the man beside him, so you saw what he saw, heard what he heard, breathed when he *breathed*—that the cast iron door was ajar. Walking slowly to avoid drawing attention to himself, Pembleton stepped off the path to the right, motioning for Bayliss and Munch to move to the left. The air was thick with the smell of grass and budding greenery, and they could hear the sirens in the distance, and the crypt's door was ajar, the goddamn door was ajar, cracked open a good six inches, darkness showing beyond it, the bolt slid back out of the latch— maybe Mrs. Rose Stella didn't get many visitors but *somebody* was in that mausoleum.

Now the detectives fanned out and drew their guns, Pembleton again taking the lead, signaling the others to move up to the hinged side of the door as he positioned himself to the right of the narrow opening, his shoulders against the wall, ready to rush through the door, return fire, or back around the corner of the wall, depending on how things went down—making sure there was some-thing between him and any bullets that might come flying out of the darkness.

"Frank Stella, this is the police!" he shouted into the mausoleum, his weapon cocked, his hand tight around the grip, fingers cold in the warm spring sunlight. "Throw your gun out and put your hands above your head."

Silence from inside.

"Stella, listen to me, we just want to talk. But you have to come on out."

More silence. Stella was either gone or playing hard to get.

Pembleton glanced over at Bayliss, indicating with a toss of his chin that he wanted cover from behind. This was it, he was going in.

Bayliss nodded and started across the door, his gun in his right hand—and then suddenly he realized he was still holding his bouquet with his left. Feeling ridiculous, he let it drop to the ground, his attention momentarily lapsing . . .

And that was when the bullet whammed out of the darkness and plowed through the bouquet, tearing it from his fingers in a red, white, and blue flurry of petals that brought an expression of shock and amazement onto his face.

A split second later, all hell broke loose.

"MUTTER."

Mutter Campbell gave no acknowledgment to the voice from behind him, trying to ignore it, just as he was ignoring the cop with the bullhorn five stories below.

He was crouching at the sink, his thick hands extended into the base cabinet. He had realized earlier that he would not be able to watch his captives while he worked, not as long as they remained at the table, where his back would be turned to them, and he had moved the two girls closer, sliding their chairs over near the sink, keeping them at his side. When he had told them to step out from behind the table, Jolanda had clung to them, and pleaded with him to leave them be, a fierce protectiveness leaping into her eyes. Of course she had not known specifically what he intended to do to them, and her willingness to take their place, perhaps even sacrifice herself, had acutely reminded him of how much he had always loved her.

But still, Campbell had brought up the carving knife he'd taken from the drawer, and looked at her, and warned her bluntly and truthfully that unless she stopped making a fuss about the girls he would kill them. And although the mingled fear and contempt in her expression had been agonizing for him to see, he had thought of the plans and decisions he had made, and had been prepared to slit the girls open before he took a chance of ruining everything.

Somehow Jolanda had known this, looking into his eyes, and, her own gaze unfaltering despite her terror, she had reluctantly let go of the girls and told them it was okay to sit across the room, she was not going to let anybody hurt them.

"Mutter, please, listen to me," she said now, her voice calm and level. "You have to talk to the police."

Campbell kept working. He had gotten lucky; when he'd turned the shut-off valves for the water supply lines, he had found that the building's plumbing system used plastic piping similar to the type he had brought with him. These had gripper ring fittings that allowed him to disassemble the drainpipe and mount his replacement with only a few twists of the wrist. Had he been forced to work with old-fashioned welded metal piping, his job would have been much harder, maybe even impossible under the circumstances. He'd have needed wrenches, drills, tools Jolanda might not have had in the apartment. Campbell didn't understand how he could have made such a stupid oversight; it was like his mind was full of gaping holes.

"Mutter . . ."

He tried to ignore her; there were already too many distractions. Beside him one of the little girls, the one that looked like Jolanda, was crying. Outside on the street, sirens swooped through the darkening sky, the shrill cacophony sawing at his nerves, making his temples throb. Nor had the cop stopped talking through his bullhorn, insisting that somebody up there please pick up the phone, we've set up a direct line, you don't have to dial anything, pick up the phone, pick up the phone, pick up the phone.

"Mutter, just because you talk to them doesn't mean you have to do what they say," Jolanda said in a patient, reasonable tone, almost as if she were speaking to a child. He could feel her eyes pressing into his back. "There's nothing to lose by doing it. It might give you time to think."

A muscle in his cheek quivered. It *was* hard to think. Hard to resist her voice.

He suddenly turned and looked at her.

"I love you, Jolanda," he said.

"Then talk to the police," she said. Her eyes still steady. "Do it for me."

He kept looking at her, drawn to her gaze. Feeling something move deep inside him.

"For you," he said.

And got up to reach for the phone.

WHEN HE HEARD the loud bash of the gun, and saw the flowers fluttering from Bayliss's hand, Munch was wrenched back in time to one of the worst moments of his life.

Three years before, he had been on a call with Kay Howard, his ex-partner Stanley Bolander, and another former member of the squad named Felton, serving an arrest warrant to a suspected pedophile named Glen Holton. They had played everything by the book, wearing Kevlar vests, bringing along several uniforms as backup. Holton had lived in apartment 201, the number on the door written in faded black paint, nearly illegible in the dimness of the hallway. Apartment 201. Munch could remember Howard insisting on going through the door first as the primary on the case, and Felton making a banal little crack about it, *ladies first,* something like that, then stepping aside to let her pass. And then suddenly there had been a rustling noise on the third-floor staircase, and Munch had turned to see a man standing up there in silhouette, a gun in each of his shadow hands, the guns aimed straight at the detectives in front of apartment 201, the guns going off before

Munch or any of the others could react. Bolander was shot in the head, Felton in the neck and thigh, Howard in the heart, the Teflon cop-killer slugs ripping through her protective vest. Of course Munch did not know where they had been hit at the time; he had only seen their mingled blood spray the ceiling, walls, and floor around him, seen their blood splash the painted number on the door, and reached for his gun to return fire. But he'd kept slipping on their blood, falling all over that filthy stinking hallway, helplessly, idiotically slipping on the blood-slicked floor in front of apartment 201 so he couldn't get a bead, blaming himself then and for a long period afterward, maybe blaming himself forever, because he had been unable to take out the shooter, been unable to do anything to stop him or help his friends . . .

Now these images came chugging through Munch's brain in a rush, overlaying the terrible reality unfolding before him—Bayliss standing by the mausoleum's partly open door in an absurd confetti of flower petals, standing in the line of fire, hesitating in the shock of the moment, a moment that would give the shooter more than sufficient opportunity to squeeze the trigger of his gun a second time and blow Bayliss into the next world.

Munch reacted without conscious thought, his feet seeming to move of their own volition, carrying him swiftly over the grassy ground between him and his fellow detective. His hands shot out as he dashed up behind Bayliss, clutching at the sleeves of his jacket, grabbing him above the elbows, yanking him backward—and away from the door opening—with such force that Bayliss went staggering into Munch, bowling him over, throwing him flat onto his back.

Munch had no sooner crashed to the ground than there was another blast of gunfire from the crypt, and another, the bullets whiffling through the air where Bayliss had stood an instant before.

His right arm bringing up his pistol, Bayliss awkwardly fired off a shot at the doorway as he reached down with his left hand, clamped it around Munch's, and started dragging him to his feet. On the other side of the door, Pembleton had sprung into a two-handed shooter's stance and was pumping rounds out of his Glock, the staccato explosions of gunfire blending with the loud, echoey bangs coming from the mausoleum.

"Forget about me!" Munch screamed at Bayliss, pulling his hand free of his grip. He was having trouble getting up; there had been a bolt of pain in his back, some goddamn thing had slipped in his back. "Pembleton needs—"

He bit off the tail of the sentence, focusing his gaze on the door. It had suddenly flung open wider, a man appearing from the darkness beyond, a man Munch recognized as Frank Stella, stepping out of the darkness of the mausoleum, crouching behind the door for cover and continuing to fire away.

Grinning from ear to ear as he fired away.

He fanned the gun toward Munch and Bayliss and a volley of bullets studded the ground around them, tearing up clots of soil and grass. Munch felt another sizzle of pain—this time in his thigh—and registered immediately that he'd been shot. He raised his gun to fire back, shimmying for cover on his rear end, kicking out with his ankles and elbows, a part of him incredulous that he was actually trying to crawl behind a tombstone like a cowboy in some Wild West shoot-out.

Now Stella had straightened and edged out from behind the door, still firing. His gun shuttled back and forth between Bayliss and Pembleton. Both men had held their positions on either side of the mausoleum and were almost fully exposed, but they had realized it would be suicide trying to break for cover while he kept up his assault.

"Drop your gun!" Pembleton shouted, his mouth dry as sand. He'd already fired nine rounds out of a ten-round clip, leaving him with only two shots before he would need to reload—which was admittedly pretty bad, but not as bad as it could have been, since he would have fired his *last* slug if he hadn't started out with an extra in the chamber.

"Listen to him, Stella," Bayliss said "Don't try anything stupid!"

Stella cackled and triggered a burst that went searing past Pembleton's ear. Pembleton took aim and squeezed the trigger of his own gun, heard a thudding report from Bayliss's pistol at the same instant, and then saw Stella jolt nearly off his feet, his shirt puffing out in two spots as their shots slapped into his side and middle, knocking him backward into the mausoleum, inches to the right of the door.

Propping himself against the wall, his legs sagging at the knees, Stella looked himself over, saw the stream of blood flowing from the scorched, tattery hole in his shirt, and put a hand on his stomach. His gun was still in his other hand, but it was pointing straight down at the ground at the end of a limp, strengthless arm.

Half-sitting on the grass less than ten feet away, Munch was astonished to see that the frozen slash of a grin was still on Stella's face—and perhaps even more surprised and confused by the woman's shoe hanging against his upper thigh, its heel hooked through an empty belt loop.

"I told you, Stella, *lose the gun,*" Pembleton said.

Stella stared at him.

Grinning, grinning, tendrils of blood and saliva running from his lower lip to his chin.

"That all I gotta do, boy?"

"That's it," Pembleton said, calmly keeping his pistol steady, braced for a lot worse than some stupid goddamn racist slur.

"Well, *meee-oow* to this world," Stella said.

And started to raise his hands, both of them, the gun still in his right hand, the gun coming up. Pembleton had tightened his finger around his trigger, ready to fire, thinking he would have to take the lunatic out if didn't let go of the gun, when Stella produced a final ripple of laughter—laughter everyone present would remember for as long as he lived—and quickly brought the gun around to his temple and fired, scattering his brains all over the mausoleum wall.

FOURTEEN

"LEWIS, KELLERMAN, COME here!" Giardello waved at the two detectives from behind the Hostage Negotiating Team communications van. "Our man's on the line!"

They hurried over to him from the sidewalk in front of the apartment building, where several of the Tac officers had assembled and were standing by for orders.

"They got a positive I.D.?" Lewis said.

"It's Campbell," Gee said.

"What'd he say?"

Gee shrugged. "Gave us his name, confirmed he's got the Martin woman and four kids up there. That's it."

"No demands?" Kellerman said.

Gee shook his head.

Lewis glanced at the negotiator seated at the console in back of the van, a pretty young woman with freckles and angle-cut brown hair.

". . . we can discuss whatever you want," she was saying into her headset with trained assurance. "Just give me your word you won't harm anybody."

Silence in her earpiece.

Giardello poked his head into the van and wound his

hand impatiently over the negotiator's shoulder. *Come on, get him talking.*

"Mr. Campbell, we have to work together," she said. "You'll have to let me know how I can help you."

She waited.

More silence.

"Mr. Campbell . . ."

"The sirens," he finally said. "They make my head hurt."

"Okay, I understand, they're very loud," she said. Her voice remained calm. "What is it you'd like me to tell the officers in charge here?"

Another pause.

"I don't want to hear any more sirens," he said.

"All right, hold on, let me see what I can do." She cupped her hand over her mouthpiece, looked out at the detectives. "He's saying to cut the sirens."

Giardello inhaled and brushed a hand through his cap of natty black hair.

"Tell him that we want to know why he's holding that woman and kids."

She nodded.

"Mr. Campbell, you still with me?" she said, uncovering the microphone.

"Yeah."

"Good, good. I spoke to a detective, and he wanted me to ask what you plan on doing with the people up there . . ."

"Get rid of the goddamn sirens!" he barked.

"Okay, don't be angry with me, I'm only trying to work things out," the negotiator said, maintaining her poise. "Give me another minute." She put her hand over the mouthpiece again and looked at Giardello. "Lieutenant, I'm afraid we'll lose him unless we stop the cruisers and fire trucks from using their sirens . . ."

Lewis frowned impatiently. "How 'bout tellin' Campbell we'll put him in a nice, quiet cell if he gives himself up?"

"Look, it's hard, I know, but we've got to take it easy

258

with him," she said. "Lower the pressure, get him to cooperate a little at a time—"

"Give me the headset," Kellerman interrupted.

She looked at him. "I'm not sure that's a good idea . . ."

"I know what I'm doing," he said. "Put me onto him."

The negotiator turned to Giardello, pensively awaiting his word.

He looked at Kellerman a moment then nodded.

The negotiator took a deep breath.

"Mr. Campbell, I'm going to let one of the detectives talk to you directly a second, so don't hang up." She pulled off the headset. "You want some quick advice?"

He nodded.

"Whatever you say, don't lie to him. If you break trust, we're through."

"That it?"

"Yeah," she said, and passed the headset to Kellerman. "All yours."

He slipped behind her chair and adjusted the earpiece. "Mutter Campbell?"

Campbell didn't say anything.

"You hear me, Campbell?"

"Uh-huh."

"My name is Detective Mike Kellerman," he said. "I'm going to offer you a deal."

"You in charge?"

"No." Kellerman moistened his lips. The others were all watching him. "No, I'm not, but they'll listen to me."

A beat of silence.

"No deals," Campbell said.

"We've gotta have a give-and-take," Kellerman said. "That way I can convince my bosses to let you have some quiet."

"I'm not coming out," Campbell said.

"Nobody asked you to do that; there's other things we can discuss."

Another pause.

"What do you want?" Campbell said.

Kellerman's heart was knocking.

"Let us have the woman and kids," he said, setting a high price, knowing he'd probably have to bargain down. "Let them go and I'll get the sirens turned off. All of them. Everywhere in the city."

"Jolanda's my wife," Campbell said. "I love her."

"Listen to me—"

"Jolanda stays with me."

"Is that what *she* wants?"

"She stays," Campbell said. There was a shuffling sound, as if he'd moved the receiver to another hand. "My head hurts. I'm sick of talking."

Kellerman tensed.

"Campbell, wait."

"Don't you talk about Jolanda again," Campbell said. "Don't even say her name."

"Okay, okay, I hear you," Kellerman said. "The kids, then. Just give us the kids."

"No."

Kellerman rubbed his forehead. "Campbell, you seem like a solid guy to me. I mean, you said you love your wife, right? I want my bosses to see what kind of person you are, show them you're trustworthy. So they believe we can make some progress here."

He heard Campbell breathing, felt the other detectives still staring at him.

"The boys," Campbell said in a toneless voice. "I'll give you the boys."

Kellerman was thinking furiously. He didn't want Campbell to slip away, but he was sure that would happen if he pressed him for the other two kids.

"All right, what can I say, my boss'll have to be satisfied with that for now," he said rapidly. "What we'll do is this. I'm gonna come upstairs, take the boys, have a quick look around just to make sure the girls are okay. I'll be alone, no guns, no other officers. Soon as—"

Giardello clapped a hand over his shoulder, slicing the edge of his other hand across his throat.

"Soon as you give us the boys, I'll get a dispatch out to all cars. Make them cut their sirens," Kellerman went on, ignoring him. "Okay?"

A second ticked by. Two, three, four . . .

"Okay," Campbell said. "Just don't pull any shit or I'll kill them all."

"No tricks, I guarantee it. Give me five minutes," Kellerman said, then tore off the headset and dropped it onto the console.

Giardello pulled him aside, shaking his head, his eyes large and angry.

"What the *hell* was that supposed to be?" he said.

"Lieutenant, you know my specialty used to be arson. If that psycho's got a firebomb up there, I want to see it. So we can be sure what we're really up against."

Giardello kept shaking his head. "It's too damn risky. I can't let you—"

"Gee, I don't like this any better'n you do. But Matt's doin' the right thing," Lewis said. His face was grim. "No risk, no gain, you dig?"

Giardello took a deep breath, held it, and slowly exhaled.

"I do," he said at last. "Goddamn it, I do."

KELLERMAN STOOD IN the arch of the kitchen, his eyes moving past Mutter Campbell and the boys to the tense, watchful face of the woman at the table, shifting to the frightened little girls near the sink—both looked like they had been crying—then traveling down to the open doors of the base cabinet. The cabinet contained only two plastic buckets, and the rest of what appeared to be its former contents were strewn across the kitchen floor.

All the windows were closed and the odor of kerosene was almost overwhelming in the small, unventilated room.

Outside, the sirens had stopped howling.

"That's enough looking around," Campbell said. He loomed behind Andrew and Jamal, an even bigger hulk than Kellerman had imagined. There was a carving knife in his right hand and a riot baton—the kind his guards had no doubt used at the institution, Kellerman thought—in his left. "Take the kids and get out of here."

Kellerman nodded and motioned the kids over to him, still peering into the base cabinet. They started forward together, but then the taller boy, Andrew, hesitated and looked up at Campbell.

"Daddy," he said, his voice high and quivering. "Daddy, why won't you let everybody go?"

Campbell stared at him. His nostrils were flaring. The left side of his face bulged out, then flattened. Bulged, flattened.

"Jolanda will never leave me again," he said flatly, and then looked away.

"You guys get moving," Kellerman said, putting a hand on an arm of each of the boys. "There'll be an officer waiting for you downstairs; tell them I'll be right along."

Andrew's shoulders stiffened. "I don't want to go without my moth—"

"Do what you've been told," Jolanda said from the table. There was something in her voice that left no room for argument.

The boy looked across the kitchen at her, his eyes moistening.

"Go," she said, and gave him a little smile, her tone gentler, but no less firm. "The rest of us will be okay."

Andrew smiled back sadly as their eyes locked in a moment of intense, nonverbal communication, his features suddenly the spitting image of his mother's. Then he joined his friend, hurrying past Kellerman to the door.

Kellerman watched over his shoulder until they were gone, then shot another glance into the cabinet under the sink. The kerosene smell had to be coming from the buckets. Which meant they were probably filled with the jelly Campbell would have made with the nondetergent soap. But what about the liquid drain cleaner? Why steal that from the bodega unless he'd planned to fabricate a priming device—something with an acid delay? Something . . .

It came to him with such force that he almost slapped his forehead.

The pipes.

The pipes under the sink.

That had to be where Campbell would plant his—

"Why are you sticking around?" Campbell grunted. "You've had your eyeful."

Kellerman was wishing he could get a closer look, wishing he could think of some way to stall for time. But he didn't want to push it. Not with Campbell standing over that woman and kids with a knife and club.

"Okay, I'm leaving," he said, and nodded at the telephone on the wall. "You want to talk, I'm here for you."

Campbell stared at him with an opaque expression.

Kellerman looked over at Jolanda, considered saying something to reassure her, but then decided against it. It was impossible to know whether that would be enough to set Campbell off.

He turned in the archway, and was stepping through into the living room when he heard the heavy pounding of footsteps behind him, saw Campbell's shadow suddenly fall across the front door, saw the shadow of his arm come up and up, and realized he was raising his baton.

Kellerman tried to avoid the downward strike but it was too late.

The baton crashed into the back of his head, and the world exploded into whiteness and then went black.

GIARDELLO AND LEWIS ran up to the door of the apartment building the instant they spotted the uniform bringing out the two boys.

"Where's Detective Kellerman?" Giardello asked.

The uniform shook his head. "I don't know, sir. He—"

Giardello reached out and grabbed his arm so hard he winced. "What do you *mean* you don't know?"

"He told me he'd be coming after us," Andrew interjected, glancing up at the lieutenant. "But he didn't."

"I waited on the third-floor landing for a couple minutes." The cop shook his head helplessly. "Wouldn't have left, but I figured I'd better get the boys safe."

Giardello let go of his arm.

"You figured right, Officer," he said. "I'm sorry I snapped at you."

Lewis was thinking that this nightmare just kept getting worse and worse, thinking he should have never advised Gee to let Kellerman play it solo, thinking that if anything had happened to him in that apartment, if he'd lost Mikey to that fucking lunatic . . .

But he didn't want to go down that thorny path, couldn't *let* himself go down it. Because if he did, he might be tempted to pull down the curtain on Mutter Campbell himself.

"What now?" he asked Giardello.

Giardello gave him a level look. "Get hold of the Tac commander. Tell him to radio his sharpshooters and make sure they're in position. I want them ordered to take out Campbell at the first opening."

Lewis nodded and started toward the curb.

"There's one more thing," Gee said from behind him.

Lewis paused, and turned to look at the lieutenant.

"You need to have faith that Kellerman's going to be okay," Giardello said. "We *both* need to have faith."

KELLERMAN CAME TO his senses with a start on the kitchen floor. Dizziness and nausea were quickly superseded by pain, the back of his head wet and throbbing, hot needles sticking in his eyes. He saw Campbell's face double and triple above him, and he blinked to clear his vision.

Why, he said, or thought he did, but then he realized that his lips hadn't moved.

He tried again.

"Why?"

"You thought . . . were smart. After all . . . work I did . . . hide it . . . you . . . tell them where it is."

It dawned on Kellerman that something was wrong with his hearing, the blow to his head had messed up his goddamn hearing. Campbell's voice kept fading in and out like a radio signal at the outer limit of its range.

"Don't know what you mean," he said, lying through his teeth, thinking he'd been a prizewinning fool to turn his back on the crazy bastard. Campbell had seen him looking into the sink cabinet and suspected he'd known exactly what he was looking *at*. It should have been obvious he'd make some kind of move.

Kellerman wondered how long he'd been out cold, but decided there were one or two other questions about his current status that needed to take precedence. Right now he couldn't even be sure whether he was sitting up or lying down.

He looked himself over and found that the former was the case— Campbell must have dragged him back into the kitchen and all the way across the room, propping him against the wall opposite the doorway. He glanced to the left, and was relieved to see Jolanda Martin and the girls at the table, looking wrung out and ashen but otherwise in good shape.

"I warned you not to pull anything," Campbell growled. His face twisted and jerked through a grotesque series of spasms, the muscles under his features seeming to pull in several directions at once.

Kellerman remembered what Blair, the administrative chief at Central Maryland, had said about withdrawal from antipsychotics. What had he called it? Dyskinesia, something like that.

He willed his lips to move again. "Look . . . I have no idea . . . what you're talking about . . ."

Campbell suddenly came stomping up to him and cut him short with a hard kick to the stomach.

Kellerman slammed back against the wall and then hunched over, gasping for breath, stars firing across his vision. Christ, he thought. Christ. The pain was more extensive than anything he'd ever experienced. He wretched dryly and clutched his middle, struggling to remain conscious.

Campbell stood over him a moment, his eyes staring and excited, his rage expanding until he felt as if it had filled him completely, felt as if he would burst with it. Sweat dripped from his pores. His hands shook. And the humiliating hardness below his waist . . . the pain and *heat* of it . . . was unbearable.

Unbearable.

His mouth parched, the blood roaring in his ears, he turned toward the table.

Stared at the girls.

So small and helpless.

So delicate . . .

With eyes like frightened birds.

He pointed at the one who had let him in the apartment.

"You," he said. Thinking if he could only take her aside and touch her, feel her tiny body against him, press her cool, soft skin to the coil of heat and agony below his waist, he might be mercifully relieved. "Come here."

She looked at Jolanda, clinging to her arm, her eyes wide and terrified.

Campbell swallowed.

"I told you to come here," he said. "Come—"

"No," Jolanda said, her eyes locking with his. "I won't let you touch her. Don't you *dare* even think of it."

Campbell made a rumbling sound in his chest. He felt as if a fissure had opened inside him and released some dark, craving beast.

"I need her," he said, his eyes glazed. "I . . . *need*."

He stepped toward the table, raising his knife.

Jolanda sprang to her feet so abruptly her chair almost toppled over, pulling Robin behind her back.

"Stay away from her," she said fiercely.

His tongue scraped over his lips. "Jolanda—"

"I said leave this child alone, you bastard."

He came closer.

Jolanda stood her ground, looking around frantically for something she could use to defend herself, seeing nothing, nothing at all. In desperation she grabbed the back of her chair and whipped it in front of her, thinking she might be able to hold him off with it—

Just then two things happened simultaneously:

The sulfuric acid in Campbell's pipe bomb finally ate through the copper flange separating it from the first-fire mixture, and Robin bolted from behind Jolanda, running toward the kitchen doorway in a wild panic.

His features so warped they were barely human, Campbell twisted in a half circle and stalked after her, his feet hammering the floor.

"No! Dear God, no!" Jolanda screamed, plunging forward and crashing clumsily into her chair.

She was struggling to catch her balance when she saw the bright flash of light under the sink.

Out in the living room, Robin was running toward the door, her mind focused on one thought, one thought: reaching the outer hallway, making it to the hall, running to where the policemen were waiting out in the hall.

She got to the door and her hand went to the knob, turning it, but the door didn't open, the door was locked. She reached up, crying, not knowing how to open the lock, not knowing, her breath coming in hysterical little gasps, trying to figure out which way to turn the latch, her fingers fumbling with it—

Suddenly the floor shook with heavy footsteps.

His knife thrust out, Campbell had come pounding into the living room behind her.

PERCHED ON THE rooftop across the street from Jolanda Martin's apartment building, Police Officer Stuart Cox—a newbie on the QRT sniper team who, despite glowing scores in marksmanship, had never in his life shot any-thing but a paper target—noticed movement in the living room for the first time since he'd gotten his ready order. He saw the little girl in the apartment dash past the window, and a second or two afterward saw Mutter Campbell follow her into the room.

A prayer flashed through his mind without his even being aware of it.

Realizing that there might be no second chance, he released his breath and centered Campbell in his cross-hairs.

In the controlled pause before his next inhalation he gave the trigger of his rifle a smooth pull, the circuit between forefinger and eye closing without conscious mental effort, a reflex conditioned by months of training on the range.

The .308 Winchester round twinkled from the SSG's muzzle and, a split second later, blew through the living room window and penetrated Mutter Campbell's left ear, killing him neatly and instantly.

JOLANDA MARTIN WAS running to catch up with Campbell when the living room window exploded in-ward from the impact of the slug and Campbell crashed loudly to the floor, a grunt escaping his lips, jags of glass spraying over him, blood ribboning from his head as the sniper's bullet entered it.

She froze in the archway, momentarily too stunned and confused to understand what had happened. Then she looked past Campbell's heaped form, saw Robin cowering against the front door in a shivering, trauma-tized ball, and that snapped her out of it. She needed to get to the little girl.

Jolanda had barely stepped into the living room when a loud, whooshing roar that didn't resemble anything she had ever heard stopped her in her tracks again. It had come from behind her, from the kitchen, from the room where she had left Vibeca, and she would later describe it as what she'd always imagined the breath of a dragon would sound like.

She whirled at once, looked back into the kitchen, and for the first time since that day's ordeal had begun, felt her courage shatter. She screamed.

A bright, red-orange fireball had suddenly burst from under the sink and was swelling out and toward her daughter.

"—*DOWN! I REPEAT, the perp's down!*"

Captain Greg Muldavy, commander of the QRT cops assembled on Hamilton Avenue, came racing up to Giardello and Lewis the instant he heard Stu Cox's voice blurt from his hand radio.

"They've taken out Campbell!" he said excitedly.

"Let's move in, then!" Giardello shouted. "*Now!*"

Muldavy nodded, signaled his men that it was a go, and they quickly formed up into an assault wedge and went storming toward the apartment building's entrance.

Lewis did not wait for Gee's okay before taking off on their heels.

WATCHING THE CONFRONTATION between Campbell and Jolanda Martin play out in the kitchen, angered and frustrated by his own inability to help her, Kellerman had clung desperately to consciousness.

Streaks of red still cutting across his eyes, he began gathering his legs underneath him even as Campbell followed Robin into the living room—dragging himself across the floor, reaching up with both hands to grab the corner of the table, hauling himself to his feet in slow stages. A wave of light-headedness swept over him as he rose, and for a moment he feared he might be sick, or even worse—that he might go spilling back down to the floor. His head hanging limp, he opened his mouth wide, took a deep gulp of air, and somehow managed to remain on his feet.

After a second or two he began moving around the

table toward the archway, gliding his fingers along its edge so he'd be able to catch himself in case of another dizzy spell, moving with shuffling, measured steps . . .

It was then that the base cabinet burst into flame, a gaseous, rapidly expanding *bubble* of flame that swept out from between the cabinet's open doors with the roar of a living thing.

Kellerman felt a rush of superheated air and jerked his head around toward Vibeca, who was still in her chair, staring at the fireball in a blank, dazed rapture of horror even as it swelled outward to envelop her.

Acting on reflex, oblivious to his pain and nausea, he leaped across the room, reaching his hands out for her, knocking over chairs, banging against the table, reaching out, reaching out, and sweeping her into his arms, holding her to him as he dove to the linoleum below the hellish, bulging eruption of fire.

"She's okay!" he shouted to Jolanda, shimmying across the floor toward the living room with the girl held tightly against him. "Hurry up to the door!"

She didn't budge, just stood there frozen in the archway, her hands covering her cheeks, screaming her daughter's name at the top of her lungs.

"*I said get the other girl!*" Kellerman hollered, reaching the arch and springing to his feet, his body moving on pure adrenaline. Behind him the kitchen was burning, being consumed by hungrily lapping tongues of fire.

The mention of Robin was all it took to jolt Jolanda from her shocked paralysis. She turned and ran across the living room ahead of Kellerman, ran past Mutter Campbell's body to where the little girl was huddled on the carpet, reached for her, and snatched her into her arms.

They ran toward the door like that, Kellerman holding one child, Jolanda the other, and had just reached the door when it burst open, its lock and frame giving way before the Tac team's battering ram as they came slamming through from the hallway.

The armored cops flooded around them, enfolding

them, pulling them out of the apartment, sweeping them down the hall toward the stairwell in a solid wave of blue. Kellerman saw two officers hook their arms around Jolanda, and then somebody lifted the little girl from Kellerman's arms and he felt the strength flow out of his legs.

A strong pair of hands steadied him.

"Easy, Mikey," Lewis said, slipping an arm behind his back. "I got you, man. I got you."

EPILOGUE

MEMORIAL DAY.

Rain fell from the slate-gray sky, dripping off awnings and umbrellas, guttering toward sewer grates in serpentine streams, flooding the streets and thoroughfares of Baltimore in a torrential downpour that had caught the forecasters with their pants down, but came as no surprise at all to Meldrick Lewis, who had seen it written in the clouds since Friday.

Munch eyed Lewis and Kellerman from his hospital bed, his bandaged leg raised a little, cruising pleasantly on a raft of painkillers. Though the slug that had plowed into his thigh courtesy of Frank Stella had missed both bone and blood vessels, the doctors had said he'd have to stay on his back a few days. This was something he really didn't mind; the drugs were very effective, and their cost was entirely covered by his health insurance.

No, not a bad way at all to spend the holiday, he thought.

"So, looks like Meg'll have to call off her barbecue," he said. "Unless you're going to be fanning the coals indoors, which I wouldn't recommend."

"Don't have to gloat," Kellerman said.

"Would you rather I entertained myself by making fun of your appearance?"

Kellerman frowned self-consciously, feeling ridiculous in the crushed vinyl rain hat Lewis had given him to keep the bandage on his head from getting soaked in the rain.

"Stoned out of your gourd and you still won't let up," he said.

"You should only know how I treated Bayliss, Pembleton, and Howard."

"No wonder we seen 'em runnin' outta here," Lewis said.

Munch sank back against his pillow, pulled up his blanket, and yawned, feeling snug and relaxed as he listened to the sound of rain pelting against his window. Yes, yes indeed, this was a pretty good deal, his room providing privacy as well as comfort, since the other bed was empty.

"We borin' you?" Lewis asked. "'Cause if we are, we can always split."

"Actually guys, you'll have to leave in a couple of minutes anyway," he said.

"Yeah?" Kellerman said. "Why's that?"

"Well, no offense but—"

There was a soft knock on the door.

"Come on in," Munch said. He winked at the other detectives. "I *do* believe the reason I'm kicking you out of here has arrived."

They both turned toward the entrance as Vera Bash stepped in, water sliding off her shiny red raincoat as she shook droplets from her folded Totes umbrella. Her large, dark eyes were bright, her raven-black hair was pulled back in a ponytail, and her smile was magnificently white.

Kellerman glanced at her appreciatively, wondering how Munch had ever landed a woman who was not only beautiful even in a dripping raincoat, but a *college professor* to boot.

"Hi, fellas," she said, and brushed past Lewis and

Kellerman to the bed, leaning over Munch, putting a hand on his cheek, and kissing him tenderly on the lips.

"The taste of lipstick, the feminine scent of perfume," Munch said. "Mmmmmmm."

Lewis and Kellerman exchanged glances.

"Did I tell you guys my lady fair's come all the way from Washington to stay with me for the next week?" Munch said. "Left there right in the middle of a weekend seminar she was attending."

"Getting shot's a pretty good tool of persuasion," she said, and kissed him again.

"Maybe we better go catch us some lunch, Mikey." Lewis said.

"Yeah," Kellerman said.

They turned to the door.

"Guys?" Munch called from behind them.

They paused and looked over their shoulders. Vera had sat on the edge of the bed and was smoothing Munch's hair.

"Remember to steer clear of the burgers," he said.

PUTNAM *pb* BERKLEY

online

Your Internet gateway to a virtual environment with hundreds of entertaining and enlightening books from The Putnam Berkley Group.

While you're there visit the PB Café and order up the latest buzz on the best authors and books around—Tom Clancy, Patricia Cornwell, W.E.B. Griffin, Nora Roberts, William Gibson, Robin Cook, Brian Jacques, Jan Brett, Catherine Coulter and many more!

Putnam Berkley Online is located at
http://www.putnam.com

• •

PUTNAM BERKLEY NEWS

Every month you'll get an inside look at our upcoming books, and new features on our site. This is an on-going effort on our part to provide you with the most interesting and up-to-date information about our books and authors.

Subscribe to Putnam Berkley News at
http://www.putnam.com/subscribe